THE TROUBLE WITH ROBOTS

To all the kids trying to fit in, make friends, and find where
you belong in the world: You are wonderful and worth it.
This book is for you.

To Mike, my husband. I love you always.

Ω

Published by
PEACHTREE PUBLISHING COMPANY INC.
1700 Chattahoochee Avenue
Atlanta, Georgia 30318-2112
PeachtreeBooks.com

Text © 2022 by Michelle Mohrweis
Cover illustration © 2022 by Kris Mukai

Composition by Lily Steele
Cover design by Maria Fazio
Edited by Jonah Heller

Printed and bound in July 2022 at Lake Book Manufacturing, Melrose
Park, IL, USA.
10 9 8 7 6 5 4 3 2 1
First Edition
ISBN: 978-1-68263-484-4

Cataloging-in-Publication Data is available from the Library of Congress.

THE TROUBLE WITH ROBOTS

MICHELLE MOHRWEIS

PEACHTREE

ATLANTA

CHAPTER ONE
EVELYN

It was my very first robotics tournament, and everything was going wrong.

My robot lay atop the wooden table, new metal gleaming under the gym lights. The bot *looked* perfect. Yet when I pressed forward on the remote control, nothing happened. The robot sat unmoving. Broken.

"No. No. No, no, no," I moaned. "Think, Evelyn. Think. You can fix this." I jiggled the wires on the robot. I pressed the controller's joystick forward again. Nothing.

I checked the plastic wheels, using my fingers to measure the spaces between them. They were exactly three finger widths apart. I pulled on the small metal claw, lifting it up and down. Its gears squeaked as the claw opened and closed.

The gears were perfect. The claw was perfect. Everything was *perfect*. I knew because I had built this robot myself. I'd been working on it since the first day of eighth grade. My school was semi year-round and started in July, so I got to spend the last two months building and perfecting it. Over two hundred pieces were perfectly in place, down to the smallest screws. There was nothing wrong with my robot.

Except, you know, the part where it wasn't rolling.

I pushed on the controller one more time, with my eyes locked on the robot for any movement at all. Nope.

I groaned and flopped forward. My face pressed against the cool plywood of the cafeteria table, and my dark red hair settled around me like a blanket. I breathed in and out, imagining my breath scattering across the grains of wood as I tried to fight back the sick roiling in my stomach. Calm. I had to stay calm.

There was a buzz around me: a hundred other kids, high-school and middle-school teams that had working robots, ready to compete. It would be way too loud if not for the headphones I wore over my ears. They quieted everything just enough that I could still hear conversations but the chaos of the competition wasn't so painfully loud.

I squeezed my eyes shut and listened to the murmur of voices, the clanking of metal, and muffled shouts of excitement. Almost thirty other groups, testing their robots and searching for the alliance teams they would compete alongside. I'd never join them if I couldn't get the robot working.

"This is hopeless," I mumbled into the table. I looked back up at the robot, staring at its boxy form. "Why aren't you working?"

The robot did not respond.

I blinked away tears and swallowed quickly, fighting back the bitter taste rising in my throat. I had to focus. What did Naiely, my best friend, always say? *Take a deep breath and think things through.* I could do that.

Deep breath in.

Okay, I had a problem. I was good at solving problems. Which was funny, because a lot of adults acted like autistic kids weren't good at that. But I liked fixing things and problem-solving. Mrs. Weir, the robotics teacher, had made *me* Team Leader because she knew I could handle tough situations.

Deep breath out.

I poked at the controller again. The robot itself was fine. Which meant the problem was either in the code or the controller's connection. Neither were my fault, though! I couldn't lose because of this. I couldn't—

Deep breath in.

Panicking wouldn't fix the robot. I could fix a problem with the controller, but I would need the others to come back to our table if it was a coding issue. My programming skills were trash.

That was a bigger problem. Alex, Santino, Varsha, and DJ were supposed to be helping me, but they ran off almost ten minutes ago to explore the high school we were competing at and *still* hadn't returned to the gym. Knowing those slackers, they could be anywhere by now.

I wished I could ask Mrs. Weir for help, but she couldn't make it to the tournament and the history teacher who brought us here instead knew nothing about robotics. It was ask my team or do it myself.

I shuddered and stared at the broken robot. With or without them, I could do this. I had to do this.

The easiest thing to check was the controller's connection. I grabbed my phone and pulled up a reference guide. My phone screen was cracked, and I had to use the school's public Wi-Fi since my family didn't have a good data plan. But at least I had a phone. It wasn't as good as the fancy computers some kids brought to the tournament, but it was better than nothing.

The guide loaded slowly. I tapped my foot against the floor, as if I could bounce my nerves out through my foot and scatter them away, across the gym. Finally it was ready. I scrolled down to the directions for resetting the controller. Then I followed the steps, forcing myself to do it carefully.

I pressed the little button beside the controller's screen. Watched it flicker then turn off. Held down the power button until it started back up. Clicked through the screen options to the radio connection and turned it off and back on.

After a long, long moment, the connected symbol flashed on the controller's screen. A matching symbol appeared on the robot brain that was attached to the bottom of our robot.

Controller reset. Done.

With the controller and robot connected again, it should have worked perfectly. Yet when I pushed the joystick forward, the bot still didn't move.

I pushed against the boxy metal frame, forcing the robot to roll. The wheels turned, metal creaked . . . and then one wheel fell off.

The wheel rolled along the table until it fell over with a *plop*.

"Ugh! No!" I dropped the controller onto the table. Everyone else had working robots except me. My school, Barton Junior High, would be a joke. *I* would be a joke.

Cheers rose from the arena. I pressed my headphones harder against my ears, blocking out the noise even as I turned to look. A group of kids grabbed their bot and carried it back to their table. They high-fived the other teams as they passed, laughing and smiling. I wiped away my tears and watched them weave through the mess of tables and robots. They headed back to their own spot, where their team name was printed out on fancy cardstock and stuck in the center of the mess.

Weitzel High School, home of the Tech Tigers.

The rolling nausea in my stomach twisted into want. For a moment, as I watched the Tigers work at repairs, I forgot my own broken bot. They moved so smoothly together. One kid handed another the parts they needed, while another held the robot steady. A third kid ran off to find their next alliance team while a fourth took notes on how they had done.

Their robot was as impressive as the team. They built it big and blocky, but I had seen it move fast in the practice arena earlier today. It stacked four cubes at once in the goal zones, a feat that made my little clawbot seem like a child's toy.

The Tech Tigers were perfect. They were everything.

"Someday," I whispered to myself.

Someday I would be at that table, wearing the yellow-and-black Tech Tiger jacket. I was only in eighth grade now, but next year I was going to Weitzel High School. I'd be one of them. I just had to prove that I was good enough for them to want me.

One of the Tigers pointed to the scoreboard where their team's name rose to first in the rankings, and they all broke out into cheers. I sighed, staring at the scrolling list of team names.

Then I froze.

Beside the scores sat a list of upcoming matches. My team was next.

Oh no. No, no, no-no-no-no! I wasn't ready. My heart stuttered in my chest. My head felt all buzzy. The nauseous feeling returned, and this time I feared I actually would puke. I swallowed hard and looked around. Where was my team?

The two teams we were up against waited by the arena. Our randomly assigned alliance, some school from the east side of Phoenix, was already walking that way. If I didn't hurry, they would have to compete alone, and I . . . well, I wasn't actually sure what happened if a team missed a match. I didn't want to find out.

I stuck a strand of hair in my mouth and looked around again. My neck prickled as I remembered that Mama watched from the stands. I spit out the hair and smoothed it down. My eyes drifted across the school gym, past the round tables that teams built on, past the big arena with its plastic walls and foam mats, and to the stands beyond. There were my moms. Mama smiled when she saw me looking, and Mum waved. They came all this way to watch me compete. Mama even took the day off work.

I couldn't let them down.

Deep breaths. Calm. I had to stay calm.

There was no sign of Alex, DJ, Santino, or Varsha anywhere in the crowded gym. No bright red shirts with "Barton Team B" scrawled across them. They must be out exploring the high school.

Of course Team A didn't have this problem. The other robotics team from my school was three tables away, already done with their first match and chatting with the sleepy-looking history teacher. None of them had gone running off to play, leaving behind a broken robot. None of them struggled with robotics.

Why did I have to be stuck with the hopeless team?

"This is the worst," I whispered, staring around the gym. I didn't even know where to look for the others.

I had never been to this high school before. It sat halfway across Phoenix, on the opposite side of the city from Barton Junior High, in some rich neighborhood that had money for a new gym and fancy water dispensers. It was also big—a massive maze of hallways and rooms with working air conditioning that I'd probably get lost in easily. A new school. New uncertainties. And the others off hiding somewhere unpredictable. I shuddered.

Still, I *had* to find them if I wanted any chance at winning.

I lunged away from the table, praying they wouldn't be far. Sweat broke out on the back of my neck. Then a bell rang in my mind—the water dispensers! When we arrived at the tournament, the other kids were impressed by how they had cold *and* hot water. It would be just like those jerks to wander back over to one and start messing around.

I ran across the gym floor, dodging past other students and skipping around pieces of metal scattered on the floor. When I glanced at the stands, Mama smiled at me again, while Mum lifted up her phone to take a picture. I forced a smile and waved, then kept running.

I scrambled out of the gym, grabbing the doorframe to swing myself around into the hallway. I heard voices from down the hall and around the corner, loud enough to be clear even with my headphones softening the sound. Familiar voices.

"Chug! Chug! Chug! Chug!"

I slid around the corner and stared at the scene before me. There they were. They stood in a semicircle around the water dispenser, holding little cone-shaped cups of water with steam rising from the surface. In the middle of the group stood Alex, my team's programmer. His eyes were red, and tears ran down his brown cheeks as he tried to drink the scalding water. Around him, the team chanted.

"Chug! Chug! Chug! Chug!"

"What are you DOING?" I shrieked, as my nausea evaporated. The others turned to look at me. Alex lowered his cup of water and wiped at the tears. He laughed.

"DJ bet me ten dollars that I wouldn't chug the hot water. I'm proving him wrong."

"What? Why?" I shook my head. "That's dangerous. You could burn your throat."

"Calm down, Evelyn," he said, running a hand along his short, curly hair. "We're having fun. You know what that is, right?"

Oof. That hurt. He didn't know I was autistic—I usually didn't tell people—but still. Ouch.

"I know what fun is. But we have a match. We're next, and you all ditched me." I stuck my hands on my hips and glared at my team.

"We were bored," Santino muttered. He stared at the ground, his shaggy brown hair falling across his eyes.

Varsha nodded. "You weren't letting us help. We had nothing to do." She crossed her arms and glared at me.

"Yeah," said DJ, the team's driver. He yelped and dumped his water into the dispenser drain. "I can't believe this water gets so hot! Ouch!"

The rest of my team giggled and turned away from me. My stomach sank again. Why didn't they care more? This was our first tournament of the year. It was a *big deal.* More than ever, I wished Naiely were there. She would understand, and with her around to help me, we wouldn't need the rest of the team. I rocked on my feet, forcing that thought away.

"Come on!" I cried. "Dump out the water, and let's go. Our robot isn't working. I need the programming fixed."

The other kids bit their lips and looked around at one another.

Alex shrugged. "Fine," he said. He dumped his water and tossed his cup into the trash. He started back toward the gym. DJ held onto his empty paper cup for a minute, then grinned and stuck it on his head like a hat.

"How do I look?" he asked as Santino and Varsha laughed. I groaned and hurried to catch up to Alex.

"I pressed every button, but nothing worked. I think your code is broken."

"Naw." Alex shook his head. "You probably picked the wrong file. I made, like, three, and only one works."

He walked back into the cafeteria and over to our table at an excruciatingly slow pace. I glanced nervously at the stands, where my moms waited. From far away, they probably had no idea how terrible everything was going. My hands trembled as I tugged on my hair. I had to win. If I won this, I could go to the state championship, and if I won State then I could go to Worlds. And if I won Worlds, then the Tech Tigers would 100 percent want me on their team!

When we finally got to our robot, Alex grabbed it and pushed the robot's long metal arm and claw aside so he could reach the robot's brain at the base. He turned on the robot brain's touch screen and pressed a few buttons. The screen lit up, and he navigated to a file folder.

"Yeah. Looks like you had the wrong file. This one should have programming that works."

I grabbed the controller and pressed the joystick. The robot lurched forward a foot, then stopped before lurching forward again.

"This drives terribly," I said.

Alex shrugged. "You were always building and never gave me a chance to test my code. It's the best I can do."

I groaned. There was no time to fix it now. Alex's shoddy programming would have to work. I grabbed the robot and hurried toward the queuing tables, where teams waited right before their matches. I peeked at the stands again. My moms waved and cheered me on. Then I spotted the yellow-and-black jackets in the stands. The Tech Tigers were watching the matches too.

I gulped. My palms felt sweaty against the cool metal of the bot, and I had to grip tighter as the metal slipped in my hands. My stomach was twisting itself apart, like a cloth being wrung out again and again. I had to do well. I had to win.

At the queuing table, a tall lady with curly black hair tied into a bun smiled at me. She wore a green volunteer shirt and carried a clipboard.

"Hello," I said. "I'm here for my match."

The lady smiled wider. Her eyes traced my team's name on my shirt. She looked at her clipboard . . . and her smile fell.

"Oh, sweetie," said the lady. "I'm sorry, but you missed the match. We've already started the next one. Your team got marked as a no-show."

The floor wobbled under me. I stared at the lady, not understanding for two long heartbeats. "Oh," I said. I gripped the robot's frame so tight that the metal bit into my palms.

I missed the match. I missed it.

But wait. Every team got to play at least five matches. They would earn points for each, and the teams with the most points carried on to the semifinals after lunch. I'd be fine. I would just have to win the rest.

"That's okay," I whispered, trying to believe it myself. "Can you tell me when my next match is?"

The woman shook her head. "I'm sorry. The rules on no-shows are clear. You missed your match, so you're disqualified from the entire tournament."

Disqualified.

My world froze, grinding to a halt like misaligned gears. I swallowed, then swallowed again. Reality sharpened painfully around me. The buzzing came back. The lights were too bright. The gym too loud. My headphones painfully tight against my ears. It was all I could do to hold it together.

We'd failed. No. Not just failed. We were *disqualified*, and everyone was witnessing it. My moms. The Tech Tigers. Team A. Even Team B, my own horrible, useless, terrible "team."

There was no chance at taking this tournament by storm. No State. No Worlds.

Just me and a half-broken robot.

Failures.

CHAPTER TWO
ALLIE

I slouched in one of the office chairs, picking at a loose thread on my jeans. Ugh. Here I was, stuck in the Barton Junior High front office. It was barely halfway through first period on Monday morning, and I was in trouble. Again.

Judging stares from around the room bored into me, from the office ladies, the student aides, and even the parents coming to sign out their kids. Their thoughts practically bounced around the brick walls, so loud I could imagine them.

Allie Wells? Again? Hasn't school only been in session for two months? What kind of eighth-grader gets in trouble THIS MUCH?

I slunk lower in the chair and shifted my head to let my hair fall around my eyes, providing a blonde, shoulder-length screen between me and their judging stares. I could still feel them, though, so I clenched my hands into fists and glared out through the gaps in my hair, staring down anyone who dared to look my way.

More than anything, I wanted my sketchbook right then. So I could lose myself in drawing and ignore all the high-and-mighty office staff. But Mrs. Powell, the school secretary, had told me no.

"Just sit there. Don't cause any more trouble. Keep your stuff put away, and wait."

Her annoying orders didn't surprise me. Barton Junior High was a prison, no matter how hard they tried to dress it up. It was a mess of worn brick walls and scratched lino-leum floors in all the rooms.

The front office had half a dozen cubicles, each more decorated than the next. The office ladies papered the walls with cheerful posters full of encouraging sayings that meant nothing. They hung photos of the school in between, as if it were a place to be proud of. Mrs. Powell had flowers on her desk, and their bright blooms seemed at odds with my mood.

I hated this school. I hated that I had to go here, just because it was closer to Oma's house. I hated that Oma couldn't drive every day anymore, since sometimes her knees hurt too much, so she needed me to take the bus. I hated that it started so early, in miserable July, and I hated how all the teachers kept telling Oma that year-round schools were a good thing, as if school was anything but torture. I hated everything about it.

I slouched farther in my seat, glaring at the office.

The door opened then.

"Oh." Mrs. Powell's voice rang across the office. "Mrs. Wells, welcome. I'll let Mr. Gilbert know you're here."

I sat up, staring at the floor as the *click, click, click* of Oma's walker drew closer.

"Hello, Allie," said Oma sadly.

"I'm sorry," I whispered to my grandmother, still staring at the ground. I had promised her I'd do better.

The door beside us clicked open before Oma could say more. Principal Gilbert poked his head out.

"Hello, Mrs. Wells. Thank you so much for being here. Please, come in." He paused a moment as Oma made her way past him, then looked at me. "You too, Allison."

I scowled. *Nobody* called me Allison. I went by Allie, plain and simple. Before I could argue, Principal Gilbert stepped back inside his office.

I slouched as I rose from the chair, trying not to stand at my full height. Even though I was in eighth grade, I was still taller than all the other kids. It was miserable. I grew like a beanstalk. A weed amongst all the flowers springing up higher and higher and . . .

What did it matter? Nobody liked me, and it *wasn't* because of my height.

There were those stares again, following me as I stepped into the office. Before the door swung closed, I heard whispers start up from the office ladies.

I slammed the door hard and turned around to glare into Principal Gilbert's office. Oma gave me a disappointed look and my anger deflated, like the air whimpering out of a balloon.

"I'm sorry, Oma," I whispered again.

My grandmother sat in one of the two plush chairs in front of the principal's desk. She was soft and kind in a room that was all hard angles and strictly organized book-shelves, whitewashed walls, and cold silver picture frames. If I drew Oma, it would be with sweeping lines; gentle strokes to show the wrinkles that deepened whenever she smiled, and the smooth curve of those arms that wrapped you in a hug as warm as any blanket. Oma was pastels and flowing blouses, with a shading of light pink to represent the roses she smelled of after a long day out in her garden, back when she could garden more.

"Oh, Allie," said Oma, shaking her head.

I bit my lip and stared at the ground. Meeting Oma's gaze was like staring at a planet breaking apart. I couldn't do it.

Principal Gilbert crossed the room and sat behind his desk. "Take a seat," he said.

I sat and looked up at him through the blonde screen of my hair.

If I drew Principal Gilbert, it would be with harsh, thick lines. Sharp angles to show his chin and cheekbones, nar-rowed eyes, and broad strokes for the large eyebrows atop them. I'd try my best to capture that heavy gaze he cast upon me, like a giant staring down at a lone ant, as if I were nothing but an annoyance.

Principal Gilbert shuffled a few papers on his desk, then picked one up. The writing on it was a messy scrawl. I recognized it from my own graded projects. I groaned.

Mr. Mathews, my art teacher, had already filled out the referral sheet. Of course he had. He relished any chance to land me in trouble, just because I didn't always like his assignments. I bet he loved filling it out, writing in that ugly, loopy scrawl and giggling over my soon-to-be punishment.

Principal Gilbert spoke, drawing my attention back to him. "Mr. Mathews reports that you insulted both him and his class again."

"I told him his class was garbage. So what?" The words slipped out before I could stop them. Okay, so it wasn't his class that was the problem. It was Mr. Mathews himself, the world's worst teacher. But Oma was shaking her head again, so I clamped my mouth shut.

Principal Gilbert gave me a grim look. "According to this report, 'garbage' is not the only word you used to describe his class." He cast a knowing look at Oma.

Oma closed her eyes and sighed. "Oh my," she muttered. "Again?"

Principal Gilbert nodded. "This is the fifth time in a week that Allison has disrupted Mr. Mathews's class and insulted him. Mr. Mathews has a tough time getting the class back on track after one of her outbursts and often loses significant instructional time."

I clenched my fists. From deep in my heart, a bitter growl

surged up, a hideous beast rearing its head. "His class is worthless! He said anime doesn't count as art, which is the worst thing I have ever heard, and—"

"Allie," said Oma. She laid a trembling hand on my arm. "Be polite!"

Her touch was warm, her skin papery and rough. She squeezed my arm. The anger slunk back like a cat, still there but quiet now. I bit back my next words and blinked away the tears that blurred the room. I couldn't say what I wanted, not with Oma around.

Oma was too kind. Too gentle. She didn't deserve to see my anger.

Principal Gilbert cleared his throat and shuffled the papers in his hands. He had an expression of concern on his face. I knew it well. It was that fake look the teachers all gave when they pretended to care. They acted like they wanted the best for you. They asked you to try harder, told you they worried about you. What they really wanted was for you to shut up and stop causing trouble.

"Allison," said Principal Gilbert.

"It's Allie."

"I understand that this is hard. You've been going through a lot lately. But these behaviors can't continue. You're better than this."

There it was, that fake care and concern. The beast roiled in my head, painting my thoughts red and ugly. I clenched my hands into fists, squeezing so hard that my stubby fingernails dug into my palms. Oma's hand was steady on my arm, her kind touch the only thing keeping me together.

Don't lash out. Don't lash out. Not in front of Oma.

"Mr. Mathews has kicked you out of his class, and I'm afraid we are running out of electives to put you in. You've already been kicked out of drama, photography, and now art." Principal Gilbert shook his head.

"Please," said Oma. She leaned up against the desk, her eyebrows furrowed in concern. "There must be something. Give her one more chance."

I tried not to look at my grandma, at her hunched form and the flowing blouses she always wore. At the walker that sat beside her chair, which she started using in the last few months. The smell of sweet roses drifted around me. The reminder of how gentle and kind Oma was.

The beast in my head whimpered. All the tension holding me together fell away, leaving me deflated, pathetic. I couldn't do anything right, could I? Art should have been perfect. I *liked* drawing. But there I was, kicked out of another class.

I slouched farther in my chair and fiddled with the edge of my shirt, wishing I had a pencil to play with instead.

Principal Gilbert sighed and rubbed at the bridge of his nose. "All right," he said. "We can give Allison one last try. There is a spot open in the robotics classroom. Many spots, actually, and that's a problem we are working on."

Robotics? I didn't even know we had a robotics class. This was the worst possible class for me. I was terrible at math and science, rules and patterns. Even before my parents—before everything that happened . . . I got failing grades on every math test.

I was better off in art. I should have ignored Mr. Mathews. Who cared if he thought anime wasn't art? If I had stayed quiet, he wouldn't have kicked me out. I could always draw my own stuff at home, or in other classes.

Now I would be in stinking *robotics*. It sounded worse than math and science put together all at once.

I felt small in the plush chair. So tiny, like a single spot on a massive canvas that everyone would overlook. My beast faded, leaving me empty. Alone. A failure.

Principal Gilbert continued talking; he didn't see the misery swelling in my head.

"I am trying to be understanding. I know you have a lot going on after, well . . . That is, I know it's been tough. Regardless, you can't keep lashing out. This will be your last chance, Allison. If you get kicked out of robotics, then we will officially begin your transfer to Sunrise Junior High."

Oma gasped. My heart sank even more, though I didn't think it could get lower. Sunrise Junior High was the worst school in the city. Sunrise was where the trouble kids went, the problem kids, the flunk-outs. Sunrise was where they sent kids who were too bad to be in other schools.

If they sent me to Sunrise, that would break Oma's heart. Oma did everything for me. She left me nice notes in my lunch and made sure I had comics and manga to read. When I was a little kid, I used to visit to help her garden in her front yard, and now that I was older and didn't really care about gardening, we still would sit outside together. She made time for me and would listen to me talk about anything but was also always cool with just sitting together in silence. Oma cared about me.

She was all I had left.

All Oma ever asked was that I keep trying. That I try to make the new school work. That I try to do better, to stop exploding at people. That I try to be happy.

But if I went to Sunrise, there was no coming back from that. There would be no trying better. I couldn't let that happen.

For Oma, I had no choice.

CHAPTER THREE
EVELYN

Two days had passed since the disastrous robotics tournament.

Facing my moms after being disqualified was *excruciating*. They hugged me and told me it was okay. Next time would be better. Next time I would win. They made me my favorite spaghetti dinner and didn't mention the tournament all weekend. That alone made me wonder if deep down I had disappointed them.

School on Monday got even worse. I made it through the first part of the day fine. But in fourth period, trouble hit. Trouble was named Jeremy Jacobs.

"Hey, Eeeeeevelyn."

I tried to ignore Jeremy. Our math teacher, Mr. Vincent, had asked us to do homework for the last part of class. Almost everyone was done, so half the kids pulled their desks together and started chatting with one another. The other half had their phones out. I was the only kid doing any type of work.

"Evy-Evy-Evelyn," Jeremy trilled my name again and tugged on a strand of my hair. I turned around in my desk and frowned at him.

"What?"

"I'm surprised you're wearing *that* shirt. I heard you guys failed, bad. If I were on the robotics team, I'd never wear anything that would connect me to them."

"Good one, Jeremy," said D'Angelo, one of Jeremy's friends.

"Yeah!" laughed Mike. Mike was Jeremy's other friend, the third part of their trio, and almost as bad as the king bully himself.

I made a face and turned back around, drawing my hair over my shoulder so Jeremy wouldn't tug on it again. Nobody liked Jeremy except for his two friends. Jeremy picked on *everyone* in the school. He would find something mean to say about anyone, even the most popular and pretty girls.

Still, his words hurt, and I kinda wished I hadn't worn my Barton Team B shirt today. Even if it was one of my best shirts, with soft fabric and a collar that wasn't too tight once I stretched it out.

I slunk down in my chair and stuck a strand of hair in my mouth, trying to focus on my laptop. With my home-work already done for the day, this seemed like the perfect chance to email Naiely.

I wished I could text her, but she didn't have a phone yet. We were stuck with email. She had written to me yesterday morning, gushing about a trip to the Apple headquarters and how she got partnered up with her new crush.

Mum needed the computer all day to job hunt, so I didn't get to reply back. Now, though, I could borrow one of the school laptops and didn't have to worry about waiting for Mum to be done with our crummy old house computer. My fingers flew over the keyboard and as I wrote my email, my nerves calmed.

Hi, Nai! I miss you. You have to call me soon. I need to tell you about the tournament, but it's too terrible to write about. I can't believe you got to visit Apple. You are lucky! Did you see what the next graphics card they are using is? Did you have fun?

My fingers stilled. I took a deep breath.

I missed talking to Naiely, missed those long days sitting in her apartment while we built computers or lay on her bed, giggling over our crushes. She encouraged me to ask out the girl I liked in sixth grade and defended me when that girl turned me down and tried to make fun of me. I pushed her to apply for Space Camp and cheered her on the summer she got a scholarship to go for a week. We were there for each other. Always.

At the start of the year, when we learned that Barton Junior High had an often-forgotten-about robotics class, we decided to join. Together. We got our schedules changed to join and it had been perfect. We were supposed to be running our robotics team side by side. But my best friend was gone now, living in California and leaving me all alone in a school of strangers.

"So, Evel-loser. My older brother went to the tournament," said Jeremy.

I stiffened, my hands pressing down hard on the keyboard and my calm broken.

Did you have fun? Fjasdklj;fksdafjk;dlsa;fjk

I frowned and hit the backspace, trying to ignore Jeremy.

"He told me all about it. He's never seen a team get disqualified before." Jeremy laughed, and his friends laughed with him. "Are you listening, weirdo?" I felt him tug at my headphones, where they rested around my neck.

I slammed the laptop closed and spun around before he could mess with me more.

"It was one tournament," I said. "Next time we won't get disqualified, and we *will* win."

"Sure you will," said Jeremy, leaning back in his chair.

If Naiely were here, she would have something snappy to say that would shut Jeremy up. If she were here, our robotics team wouldn't have failed in the first place.

The bell rang. I jumped out of my desk and ran to put the laptop back in the charging cart, then hurried out of class. Once outside, I stopped to lean against one of the brick walls and pulled my headphones over my ears to quiet the sounds around me. I needed to drive out Jeremy's words. So what if I got disqualified from one tournament?

Deep breath in.

We had another in November.

Deep breath out.

My robot worked. Alex needed to fix the code, and then I could practice with it nonstop for the next six weeks. When the next tournament rolled around, I would be ready. I'd win and make it to State, then eventually Worlds.

My breaths came easier as I imagined it.

Naiely and I made a promise before she left. We would both make it to Worlds. Our teams would make the perfect alliance, and for three glorious days we would hang out and compete together, like before. We'd do so well that the Tech Tigers would beg me to join them next year.

I could see myself now, standing at home in the Tech Tiger's yellow-and-black jacket. My moms would fawn over me and embarrass me. Mum would take a bazillion pictures while Mama would laugh and hug me. They'd forget all about how I had disappointed them this weekend. They used so much time and gas money to go to a tournament I didn't even get to compete in.

I knew things weren't good right now, not since Mum lost her job last year. Mum and Mama had all those hushed conversations in the kitchen at night, when they thought I was asleep. Mama took extra shifts at work all the time, and I'd seen her hidden notes in the kitchen drawer, calculating when she'd next have to fill up the car's gas. So even though they hadn't said so, they *had* to be disappointed. But making it to Worlds would fix everything.

I'd hang out with Naiely, do amazing at Worlds, join the Tech Tigers, get all sorts of college scholarships, and be able to take care of Mum and Mama one day.

Jeremy's words meant nothing. He didn't know what he was talking about.

I squared my shoulders and headed toward class. My feet carried across the school's courtyards, through the cactus garden, and to the 300 Building, in the very back of the school.

There it was. My favorite classroom.

I pushed open the pale blue door and breathed in the wonderful scent of new metal and grease. It mixed with the less desirable odor of too much body spray and burning plastic from the 3D printers. Above it all was a sharp, acidic tang that made me think one of the old robot batteries had exploded again.

They did that sometimes.

Santino, DJ, and Varsha were huddled together, already at work on one of the old metal tables. Alex hadn't arrived yet, but sometimes he came to class late. Team A was also there, halfway across the room and working on a tower of metal and wheels. Our robotics teacher, Mrs. Weir, sat at her desk near the front of the room.

I liked Mrs. Weir. She always wore lab coats painted with gears and loved robots as much as I did. She never treated me differently for being autistic or used the baby voice some adults did when they learned. When my headphones broke at the start of the year, Mrs. Weir found me the pair I wore now. It fit perfectly over my ears, with soft earpads that were only slightly worn out. Mrs. Weir was my favorite teacher. I waved to her, then turned to face Team B.

The disqualified failures.

For a moment, I remembered those first few weeks of school, when my best friend was still here and the world was right. We always raced to find the right parts, giggling like wild when we realized we had double the wheels we needed. Naiely once bet DJ and Santino that she could make a faster race car than they could, and we spent part of the day building mini racers instead of working. In the end, Naiely's and my racer won, leaving the boys' car in the dust. We used that wheel design for our robot afterward. Robotics was fun then. Those days were only a few weeks ago, yet it already felt like a lifetime had passed. A lifetime since my best friend had moved away.

I pushed the memories back. Now I only had this team left. I had to make it work with them, if only because you couldn't enter competitions with a team of one.

I forced a smile onto my face and hurried toward our robotics table. As I got closer, Varsha stepped to the side, and my resolve shattered.

The robot lay in pieces.

For the second time that week, I felt like the floor was falling out from under me. I stared at the broken robot. All six plastic wheels were off, scattered around the table. They had dismantled the claw and set it to the side, broken in half. As I watched, DJ unscrewed a piece from the robot brain, then lifted the blocky box off the robot itself.

"There we go," he said, dropping it onto the table. "Mucho mejor."

I staggered over, my head spinning.

"What did you do?"

"Hi, Evelyn," said Santino. "We're fixing the bot. We got all our work done in social studies, so our teacher called Mrs. Weir, and she said it was okay for us to come to robotics early. We're almost ready for rebuilding."

DJ nodded. "The robot brain was the last piece we had to remove."

He ran a hand through his hair, brushing against the spiral patterns buzzed into his undercut. His blue shirt matched the straps on his leg splint, and he leaned casually against the table. DJ was the sort of kid who radiated cool, even though he was in robotics and never stopped cracking jokes. Today, he looked completely at ease as he tore apart my robot.

"Yeah!" said Santino. He had an enormous smile on his face and didn't seem to notice my growing despair. He motioned to the robot. "We're moving the robot brain so the claw doesn't hit it when it lowers. Oh and we'll change the wheels to those new ones Mrs. Weir bought, and . . ."

With each word he said, my heart sank lower. My robot had been *fine*. It didn't need the brain moved or new wheels put on. All it needed was the code fixed. My breath hitched as I stared at it, remembering the long days spent perfecting the bot.

Back then, this team used to be helpful, united. We were all the castoffs. The kids not good enough for Team A. With Naiely leading and me as the brains, Team B did amazing. Anything had seemed possible. Now, though?

My hopes and dreams were being smashed apart and scattered along that table, mixed in with the metal and screws and broken robot pieces. DJ pulled another piece off the robot and grinned.

"Stop!" I shouted. I lunged forward, snatching an Allen wrench from Varsha's hand and a wheel away from Santino. "Just stop. The robot was great. Why are you taking it apart? DJ, you aren't even a builder, you're a driver!"

"Says who? You never let me drive the robot!" DJ crossed his arms and glared at me.

"Only because you don't pay enough attention to do it well!"

DJ made a face. He looked at Varsha. "I told you Evelyn would be annoying about it."

Varsha shrugged. She offered me a smile, the sort that lit up her heart-shaped face. "Come on, Ev. We want to help. The wheels keep falling off. We want to try the new ones and—"

"No!" I cried. "If you wanted to help, you shouldn't have messed everything up this weekend! Don't any of you care that we got disqualified?"

Santino winced. "We do care. But that wasn't our fault."

"Exactly," added DJ. He sat down on one of the nearby stools and shook his head. "You wouldn't let us do anything.

There was no reason for us to even be there. It was embarrassing, and we got bored."

I scowled. "That's not fair! You all kept messing around when I was trying to get the robot ready for inspection, and then you ditched me before our first match!"

"Yeah, 'cause cracking jokes while waiting for the robot inspection to start is so terrible." DJ rolled his eyes.

"You told us you had it all covered and to leave you alone," said Varsha, her smile long gone. "And now we're a joke around the school because we got disqualified. So why don't you chill? We're just trying to fix the robot before next time, so it doesn't happen again. You know, the *team* robot?"

"No! You're not even supposed to be touching the bot. *You're* supposed to be working on the design notebook, not undoing all my work! Besides, the new wheels are too small. They won't get the same traction."

I started trying to slot the old wheels back onto the robot, shoving them onto the thin metal driveshafts that stuck out from each motor.

Varsha rolled her eyes. "Whatever. I'm high-key bored with this, anyway."

She turned and walked away, flipping her dark brown ponytail over her shoulder. A second later, DJ followed. I scowled and looked at Santino.

His smile had vanished. He bit his lip and looked down at the table. "Sorry," he muttered. He shoved his mop of brown hair out of his eyes and turned to the bot. "They told me you were cool with us making changes. I assumed they ran it by you already, since you're Team Lead and all."

"It's all right," I said. It wasn't all right, but I couldn't be mad at Santino. He *always* went along with whatever people told him. Santino was too nice. "Help me fix it, okay?"

Santino nodded and reached for a wheel.

I took a deep breath and let my thoughts drift for a moment. I imagined the Tech Tigers, the fancy jackets they wore and the way their team worked together. I thought of the college scholarships I would win on that team and my moms crying from joy. I pictured myself sitting on a plane, on the way to Worlds, where I would *finally* see Naiely again.

My goal locked back in. We could do this. *I* could do this.

We set to work, tackling the wheels first. Once all six were on and secured, I started trying to reassemble the claw. We worked for a few more minutes until the classroom door slammed open.

Alex trudged in. His hair was dripping wet. Water ran down his face and beaded up on his glasses. He walked over to the robotics table and dropped his drenched backpack on the ground with a wet *plop*.

"What happened to you?" I asked.

"Jeremy Jacobs," grumbled Alex. He sat down at a computer and pressed the power button.

"Oh," I turned back to the robot, trying to adjust the claw mechanism. "Jeremy's being a jerk today. Ignore him."

"I *was* ignoring him. Then he dumped his water bottle on my head."

I froze. *Oh. Ouch.* Maybe Jeremy saying mean stuff to me hadn't been so bad. It was better than getting water poured over my head.

"That stinks," said Santino, walking over and sitting next to Alex. He slung an arm around Alex's shoulders, sending water splattering onto the computer desk.

"Yeah," I said. "Sorry about that." I bit my lip and glanced back at Alex. "Hey, can you work on the code? It needs to be smoother."

Alex gave me a sullen look. He got up and walked away, crossing to the other corner of the room.

"What?" I asked when Santino frowned at me. "I thought he'd want a distraction."

Santino shook his head and went to follow Alex.

Well. I was all alone at the table then, working on the robot myself. Whatever. I didn't need them.

"Evelyn? Can you come over here?" called Mrs. Weir. Varsha stood by her, giving me a *look*. Then Varsha walked away from Mrs. Weir's desk, joining the others in the corner of the room. My stomach sank as I hurried over.

"What is it?" I asked, staring down at her desk. I liked Mrs. Weir, but I didn't like meeting anyone's eyes, even hers. "Is this about the tournament?"

Mrs. Weir swiveled in her chair and faced me. "I heard about that and I'm so sorry. I wish I had been there to help. Mr. Michaels feels terrible that he wasn't keeping track of your matches. This is not about that, though. Evelyn, we need to talk about your team."

"I know," I said, sending an angry look across the room, to where Alex now played a phone game while the others watched. "I'm working on getting them to do better. Really."

"That's not what I mean." Mrs. Weir sighed and pinched the bridge of her nose. When she spoke, she sounded sad. "I've noticed that you are not letting them help with anything. I was hoping you could work this out on your own. Your team was doing so well at the start of the year, but this is getting out of hand."

My heart sank. Varsha smirked at me from across the room.

"Mrs. Weir." I rocked on my feet, trying to find the words to explain. "I'm trying my best. It's not my fault if they don't want to participate."

"Listen, Evelyn," she said. She crossed her hands in her lap. "You are smart and a natural leader. But sometimes a leader has to step back. You've been taking over everyone else's job, and I've seen you push kids away and not let them help. That's not okay."

She took a deep breath, and I knew what was coming would be bad.

"I want you to succeed in my class, but maybe we have you in the wrong role. I'm considering removing you as Team Lead."

I froze. My brain sputtered and stalled. I couldn't think. Couldn't move. Her words hit me again and again. I squeezed my eyes shut until I found my voice.

"Why? I love robotics. I love being Team Lead."

"I'm sorry, but one person alone can't be a team. Right now, you being Team Lead is causing you stress . . . and because you are pushing away the others, it's causing your team to struggle." She smoothed down her lab coat and offered a small smile. "Maybe you'd do better as Team Builder?"

I shook my head hard. "Please, Mrs. Weir. I can do it. I can be a good Team Lead. Please!"

She took a long breath. "All right. I'll give you one last chance. We have a new student joining our class today. I'm putting her on your team. Help her get involved. Be the fantastic leader you were at the start of the year, and let the others take part again too. If you show me you can lead the team instead of doing everything yourself, I'll let you keep your job."

I nodded. I didn't trust myself to speak, because if I tried to say anything right then, I was going to cry. My head was all buzzy, and the sounds around me felt too loud, even with my headphones. Too distracting. I twisted my hands into the soft fabric of my shirt, trying to stay calm.

I could do this. I had to do this. My life meant nothing if I wasn't Team Lead. Anyone else would mess things up too much. My dreams of winning, of going to Worlds and seeing Naiely again, would shatter. No Worlds. No Tech Tigers begging me to be on their team. No proud Mama and Mum. No future college scholarships.

"Can you do this, Evelyn?"

"Yes, Mrs. Weir," I whispered.

CHAPTER FOUR
ALLIE

If you get kicked out of robotics, then we will officially begin your transfer to Sunrise Junior High.

Principal Gilbert's words echoed through my mind for the rest of the day. They bounced around and around, splattering about in my head. My stomach felt like a bucket of paint being stirred too much, churning and swimming and heaving. Paper crinkled in my hands.

I looked down at the schedule Principal Gilbert had given me this morning. I hated it then, and I hated it even more as I prepared to go to fifth period.

Period 1: Science - Room 507
Period 2: English - Room 808
Period 3: Social Studies - Room 110
Lunch
Period 4: Math - Room 410
Period 5: Robotics - Room 303

He messed up my entire schedule to make robotics fit. I used to have art in first period and science at the end of the day. It was perfect. My science teacher often got too busy yelling at other kids, like Jeremy Jacobs, to notice when I zoned out. Now I had to deal with it at the start of the day *and* with a brand-new teacher.

And math? My old, second-period math class had so many kids in it that I could stay quiet and be forgotten. My new, fourth-period math class was with Mrs. Vern. Already, after one day in that class, I could tell she was strict.

Worse still . . . I was about to end my day with an equally terrible class.

In a few minutes, I'd be stuck with even more strangers, trying to keep up with kids that *liked* math and science. The smart kids. The gifted kids. The kids that weren't me.

I gulped and scuffed my feet in the dirt. I was sitting on a bench in the cactus garden. Across from me was a bright blue door I never cared about before. Room 303. The robotics classroom.

The bell rang. I should have been in class then, but I couldn't make my feet move. Instead, I stared around the cactus garden, letting the shapes calm me. The familiar curves and spines, vivid greens and softer yellows speaking to memories of better days.

Dad liked cacti. No . . . Dad *used* to like cacti. I remembered when he took me to his arboretum, on days when Mom got stuck late at the courthouse. We would sit on the little stone benches while he told me about the many types of cacti.

The cactus garden at Barton wasn't that impressive compared to Dad's arboretum, but it was comforting, anyway. If I drew it, I'd use quick dots of red and brown for the stones that speckled the dirt. Slashes of white for the sidewalk that framed it, and sweeping grays for the shadows cast by the classrooms on each side. The cacti themselves would be in all shades of magnificent green, standing out bright against the plain desert ground.

Prickly pears and mammillarias; squat, round barrel cacti; and reaching cholla. A blue myrtle stretching up countless fingers to the sky in the middle of the garden, and beside it a cluster of tiny pilosocereus. Above them all rose the grandest of the cacti, the great saguaro cactus.

Saguaros were Dad's favorite.

My eyes burned. I wiped at them and sniffled.

What would Dad think of me now? Or Mom? She'd been a judge, smart and perfect. Would she hate me if she knew how much trouble I got in? I didn't mean to mess up this much. I didn't mean to get angry, but when people kept poking at me, I always exploded, my beast of anger surging out. I wanted people to leave me alone, but none of my teachers did. They just kept pushing me to "try harder," to open up, all while giving me that pity-filled look.

I licked my dry lips and looked back at the robotics room, trying to make myself get up and move.

It would thrill Mom and Dad to see me in robotics. They'd never understand why I was dreading it. In the late afternoons as the sun set, we would all sit together and young engineer." She wasn't even looking at me. She didn't actually care.

That angry beast surged forward.

"How would *you* know—" I bit my tongue before I could finish. Principal Gilbert's words echoed in my head.

If you get kicked out of robotics, then we will officially begin your transfer to Sunrise Junior High.

I clenched my fists and stayed silent. I had told Oma I'd do better. I had to do better.

Mrs. Weir smiled. "You'll have fun in robotics. I promise."

What was up with this lady? I didn't get how she could be so calm.

Sunrise, I reminded myself, before my beast could stir again. At Sunrise, there wouldn't be art classes. They wouldn't let me draw or zone out. Rumors claimed every kid had their own guidance counselor at Sunrise, and they followed you around observing you all the time and making sure you didn't get off task. If robotics was a nightmare, Sunrise would be *Hellrise*.

I followed Evelyn.

By the time I caught up to her, she was arguing with the other kids.

"Marsha, pleeeeeeease start the design notebook?" pleaded.

only other girl in the group groaned. "How about no? work on the robot, though." She flipped her long, tail over her shoulder and crossed her arms. You already broke it enough."

watch the colors painted on the cloudy skies. Then Mom and Dad would help me with homework at the old kitchen table. Whenever my terrible report cards arrived, they'd sigh and make me promise to try harder.

They would have loved robotics.

They were both so smart, so perfect. They would often tell me about how they met at a math competition in high school, then giggle and stare into each other's eyes. I'd make fake sick sounds, and they'd tell me I'd understand someday. I never did figure out how to explain that I didn't like anyone like that, didn't have any crushes.

I never got the chance.

I took a deep breath and stared back at Room 303. Part of me wanted to run away, to hide out on the field and ditch class. I wiped at a tear and shook my head. I'd get in trouble and disappoint Oma again.

Oma left this morning after the meeting with Principal Gilbert. Before going, she wrapped me in an enormous hug and made me promise to do well.

"I'm trying, Oma," I whispered to myself right then, as I kicked at the rocks under the bench. "I really am."

I watched as a kid ran by, water dripping from his backpack. He headed straight for 303. Another robotics kid. The door closed behind him, and I took a shaky breath.

If I stayed out there any longer, the hall monitor would spot me, and I'd be in trouble again. He hadn't forgiven me for the time I threw his clipboard in the middle of the prickly pears. It was time to go to class. I got up and walked to Room 303, slouching to hide how freakishly tall I stood.

Stepping through the little blue door was like entering another world.

The first thing that hit me was the smell. It smelled *terrible*. Like, worse than a locker room. Then I took in the room itself. The walls were a plethora of blues, like a color palette at a paint store with those funny names. All Azure and Steel and Teardrop and Seal Butt blues.

The brick walls were painted light blue. The bulletin boards were lined with dark blue. There were blue motivational posters stapled onto the walls saying things like "You can do it!" and "Engineer Your Future!" I stood stunned in the doorway, blinking at the clashing colors.

Then I noticed the other students. Ten kids gathered around the room. Four sat in one corner, huddled by a kid playing some phone game. Five leaned on an enormous table, putting together what looked like a monster of gleaming metal and wheels.

The teacher sat at a desk all the way across the room, talking to a girl with wavy red hair and large blue headphones. I felt the others stare at me as I trudged to the teacher's desk and dropped my schedule onto the clutter of paper and tools. I was sweating so badly that I probably added to the stink in the air.

"Hey," I muttered. "I'm new."

The teacher reached for my schedule. "Allison Wells, right?"

Just like that, my nerves twisted and swirled, mixed into a hue of anger instead. I liked the beast. It was better than being nervous. I scowled and glared at her.

"It's Allie. A-L-L-I-E."

The teacher laughed lightly, as if she didn't feel the frustration rolling off me in waves.

"I'm sorry, Allie. I'll make note of that on the attendance chart. I'm Mrs. Weir, your robotics teacher. This here is Evelyn. You'll be on her team."

The girl standing beside the desk, Evelyn, didn't seem happy about that. She looked at the floor, avoiding my gaze. I wondered what stories she had heard. Half of them were exaggerated, really. Except for the one about Mrs. Frost's wig. And the broken window in Room 702. But the rest were mostly made up.

Mrs. Weir cleared her throat. Evelyn forced a smile was 100 percent fake, though she was still barel at me. I bristled, instantly on edge.

"Come on," said Evelyn, in a falsely cheerf she even hear me with the headphones? didn't care. "I'll introduce you to ever job for you." She spun on her heel kids in the corner.

I froze. No way. I was not the room for an escape.

"It's all right," said Mr stared at her computer, clickin attendance chart. "You'll do fine he

"I'm sorry," said Varsha, giving Evelyn the stink eye. "We weren't breaking it. We were *fixing* it. The twelve to twenty-four gear combo you are using is trash. It needs at least a twelve to sixty-four if you want the claw to be strong enough to hold the cubes."

"Okay, fine. If we change the gear ratio, will you start the notebook?" Evelyn stuck her hands on her hips. She sounded irritated.

Varsha seemed to think about it for a minute, twirling her hair around her fingers. "Why can't DJ do it?" she finally asked.

A boy with brown hair so dark it was almost black and a pattern of gears shaved into his buzzed sides, DJ presumably, laughed. "I suck at technical diagrams. I'd make it so bad, we would fail. I have cerebral palsy, remember? My drawing skills are trash." He waved a hand around and grinned. He looked familiar. I was pretty sure I had seen him around school before. He wore shorts and a fake football jersey with a Nintendo controller on it instead of a sports team, and he had a plastic cast–looking thing around his ankle, the bottom tucked into his shoe.

Varsha made a face at DJ. "You're still better at diagrams than any of the rest of us."

"Why twelve to sixty-four?" asked a second boy with golden brown hair so long it fell into his eyes and a sheepish grin on his face. He sat near the back of the group, watching as a third boy played some phone game. "Wouldn't the sixty-four-tooth gear be too bulky?"

"Good point, Santino. What if we swap out the motor cartridge instead?" asked the boy playing the phone game. He had loose black curls and brown skin with warm undertones. He wore basketball shorts and a T-shirt with a sci-fi looking robot on it. He looked back down as his phone chimed, his fingers flying over the screen.

"To what?" asked Evelyn. Her voice was rising in pitch, colored with frustration. Apparently, she really could hear with the headphones on. "Alex, we're already using the two hundred rpm motor. Do we even have any other ones?"

"Calm down, Ev. I'm just throwing out ideas. You're draining all the fun from robotics, you know." Alex shook his head.

"I think we have a 100 cartridge in the supply pack Mrs. Weir ordered," offered Varsha. "Let's try it. Then I'll start the notebook."

"Oh yeah! And I'll sort out the parts bin, like you were asking me yesterday," said Santino, brushing his long hair out of his eyes. "Please, can we try the stronger cartridge?"

My stomach sank as they talked. I tried to cling to my beast, to have it burn away the nausea rising in my throat. They were practically speaking a foreign language. I didn't understand any of it, and every word they said made me feel more out of place. I took a step away from the group. Any minute now they would notice me. They would talk to me and realize I didn't belong. I wasn't smart like them.

But they didn't notice me edging away. One more step, then another.

All this talk of motors and gears and smart stuff made me itch for my sketchbook. With how small and disorganized this class was, maybe I could find a spot to hide away and draw. There was only one other team in the room, and they seemed too focused on their own robot to notice me.

I glanced at my "team" one more time. They were still arguing, with Evelyn shaking her head and DJ spouting off something about cartridges again. Varsha was waving her hands in the air, while Santino and Alex nodded. I let out a breath and walked away, pulling my backpack off my shoulder.

Evelyn followed me, breaking away from her team's debate. "Where are you going?" she snapped.

"Ummm . . . somewhere out of your way?"

"Oh no." Evelyn ran in front of me and planted her feet on the ground, crossing her arms. "You're on my team now, which means you *have* to help us. Look, I'll make you the . . . supply manager."

"Supply manager?"

"Yeah. I'll tell you what parts I need while I build, and you'll get them for me."

"Yeah, no. That sounds boring." I turned around and walked the other way, toward the boxy 3D printers in the corner.

"Mrs. Weir won't let you stay in robotics if you don't help out."

Evelyn's words stabbed into me, a sharp scratch against my canvas. I spun around. What was wrong with this girl?

Why couldn't she leave me alone? My beast growled and rolled, burning in my bones. It made my head buzz and my blood boil.

"Just so you know," I snapped, walking toward her. "I don't care about robotics. I'm only here because Principal Gilbert put me in this class."

Evelyn crossed her arms. "Huh. Well, I guess he won't mind putting you somewhere else."

I opened my mouth to let her know what I thought of her.

Sunrise Junior High.

I snapped my mouth shut.

Mrs. Weir stood across the room now, talking to the other group of kids. The other team, probably. She looked nice enough, but so had a lot of my other teachers. Was Evelyn right? Would she kick me out for not participating? I couldn't risk it.

I thought about Oma, waiting at home to ask me how my day went. Oma, who would be heartbroken if I got transferred to Sunrise, forever labeled as a problem kid. Oma, who was the only person I had left.

"Fine," I growled. "Show me what to do."

CHAPTER FIVE
EVELYN

I loved robotics. Building robots made the world feel right. It gave me a goal to work toward, something I could understand. Everything made sense when I broke it down to gears and simple ratios, motherboards and wiring.

When I did robotics, it didn't matter that I wore the same shirt twice in a week because my other shirts were too worn out and it was hard to find new clothes with loose collars and comfy sleeves. It didn't matter that my shoes were scuffed, and my right sock had a hole by my pinkie toe, or that sometimes I got so nervous it was hard to breathe. Or that when I tried to make friends, half the time other kids gave me funny looks and walked away. Robotics, I could understand. Robotics was just gears and wheels, Keps nuts and bolts, all lined up in perfect order. It was the one thing I could control.

Robotics centered me and relaxed me.

Usually.

Today it was frustrating.

"Okay, where is Allie?" I looked up from the robot, adjusting my headphones. I wasn't listening to music—I never used them for that—but on days when the 3D printers were running and the sound of metal clanging on tables was just a lot, I liked how they made everything a little softer. "Did she disappear again?"

It was Friday afternoon, and Allie was nowhere in sight. Not at our table, not across the room by the 3D printers, not even over by Team A. Somehow, I had lost Allie again, and fifth period had barely started.

"Uhhhh . . . I think she went to get an Allen wrench?" said DJ. He leaned against the table with his head in his hands, observing the robot. Atop his head was a crown made of tank treads and random gears, built from the parts we were *supposed* to be using on my robot.

"I sent her to get that ten minutes ago," I said.

DJ shrugged and reached up to adjust his crown. DJ was cute, in a goofy way. He had that prankster streak that used to be fun but was lately more annoying than anything.

I cast a quick glance toward the corner, where Mrs. Weir sat at her desk, talking to the office. Her voice drifted across the room, tinged with frustration. "I'm telling you, I took attendance. I submitted it just now. It must be a problem on your end because everything looks fine on my side. Please, can I just—"

She was completely distracted.

Right. Allie only disappeared when Mrs. Weir wasn't paying attention, and she always showed back up with an excuse when Mrs. Weir came to check on our team. I couldn't call her out on it, though. If I did, Mrs. Weir might think *I* was driving Allie away. Then I'd lose my job as Team Lead.

The idea made my palms break out into a sweat and my head spin.

I set down the wrench I had been using and glanced around. "All right," I said. "I'll go find her."

"What should I do?" DJ asked. He looked at me with a mischievous grin. "How about I help build?"

I gulped, remembering the broken robot on Monday.

"Tighten the screws more. Don't mess with anything else." The thought of DJ messing with the robot scared me, but I had to give him something to do. Mrs. Weir wanted me to get everyone more involved. I had no choice.

DJ waved me away with a "ya ya."

Now, more than ever, I wished Naiely were here to help me. Naiely was good with people. *She* would have stopped them from taking the bot apart in the first place.

It had taken all week to fix the bot. An entire week wasted. But now, on Friday afternoon, we were finally done. The claw was back on, the robot brain in place, and the wheels secured. Mrs. Weir spoke to the rest of my team after talking to me on Monday. Whatever she said, they were helping again. Kind of.

Alex sat at a computer with the programming software loaded, but he was also playing a game on his phone.

Santino announced at the start of class that he would help Alex. His "help" looked more like hanging out with Alex and talking about the game, but that wasn't surprising. Everyone knew that Santino and Alex were dating.

Varsha, meanwhile, messed with a long piece of metal. She tied a rubber band to it and stuck a pencil up against the rubber band. Her brows furrowed as she pulled the pencil back. The rubber band stretched out, growing thin. Varsha grinned and looked at us. I shook my head.

Don't do it!

DJ flashed her a thumbs-up.

Varsha's grin grew wider. She released the pencil, and the rubber band snapped with a loud *thwang*. The pencil shot across the room and whizzed past Mrs. Weir's ear. It slammed into the wall, inches away from one of the bright blue posters.

Varsha howled with laughter. I groaned and took a step away from her.

"Varsha, please don't make rubber-band crossbows in class," called out Mrs. Weir, before turning back to her computer and resuming her phone call.

"Sorry!" Varsha stuck the contraption behind her back.

My spirits fell further. Who was I kidding? They might be hanging around the robot, but nobody had any intention of helping one bit. They were so off course that they were sailing toward the Bermuda Triangle.

Only I could steer them back onto the right path.

That was my job, after all. Mrs. Weir had given me one more chance, and I *had* to get my team to shape up. Besides, the rules for the robotics tournaments clearly stated that you needed at least two people on a team to attend, and I didn't think Mrs. Weir would let me kick any of them off.

I grabbed the notebook, lying ignored on the table, and dropped it in front of Varsha.

"Come on," I said. "Can you start the notebook already? You promised!"

I had met my part of the deal on Tuesday, swapping the weaker motor cartridge for a more powerful one. Now it was Varsha's turn.

She huffed and pulled the notebook toward her, clicking open a pen.

I took a deep breath. One problem solved. Now I had a hundred others to handle. I scanned the room again, searching for Allie. She'd sneaked away every day this week, and it was getting on my nerves.

On Tuesday she hid behind the desk with the broken 3D printer.

On Wednesday she crept outside to the cactus garden.

On Thursday she somehow climbed up into the ceiling rafters.

But every time I thought about complaining, I couldn't do it. What if Mrs. Weir blamed me for not being a good enough Team Lead? Besides, Allie always showed back up the moment Mrs. Weir came to check on our group, usually claiming she had been fetching parts or getting paper. It was like she had a sixth sense for when the teacher was paying attention. It was so annoying!

The room was spinning again. My head felt all buzzy, like the stress and noise and too-bright lights were bees bouncing between my ears. I pursed my lips together and closed my eyes.

Deep breaths. Be calm.

Even the best engineers faced problems. I remembered that from a book Mama bought me years ago. This was another problem to solve. Another way to prove I could handle the world of STEM. I could think of Allie as training for getting along with all the tough coworkers I might have someday. Except those coworkers would love robotics and *wouldn't* run away and hide all the time.

Focus. Deep breath in.

Deep breath out.

Alex's phone game chimed, and my eyes flew open. He was *still* hunched over his phone, ignoring the computer in front of him. We weren't even supposed to have our phones out in class, but Mrs. Weir had given Alex permission to use it for programming research, since the school computers blocked YouTube. Video games were *not* research, though. I clenched my fists and stormed over.

"Alex, can you *please* finish the programming?"

Alex shrugged. His fingers flew over his phone screen, and it lit up with a burst of bright colors.

"Alex," I repeated.

"Okay, okay." He sighed and lowered his phone, glancing over to where Mrs. Weir was as if to check that she wasn't coming over. "I need to test what I have on the robot, though."

"Maybe if you all hadn't taken it apart on Monday, there would be more time for that."

Alex groaned. "I wasn't part of that! I was busy getting water dumped on me by Jeremy, remember?"

I scowled and crossed my arms. "Whatever. DJ needs to finish tightening everything before you can haul it around and test the code. Do what you can without it for now. Throw in some loops or something to smooth out the code."

"Fine. In that case, let me finish this level." He made a shooing motion with his hand and went back to his game.

I harrumphed and glanced around. "I'm looking for Allie. You better be programming by the time I find her."

Alex nodded, and I continued my search. I checked back by the 3D printers first. No sign of her. I peeked out the window to the cactus garden. No Allie. I paused in the middle of the room, trying to ignore the feeling of my pinkie toe poking through my sock. I didn't have time for this!

Team A let out a loud cheer, drawing everyone's attention. Their robot was a reverse stacker. It had a long tray to hold the cubes, and tank treads that would suck them up and stack them against the tray. As I watched, the tank treads spun, and the bot sucked up four cubes. Then their driver nudged the controller joystick. The tray shifted from an angle until it was totally vertical, putting the cubes one on top of the other. The robot backed up . . . and the cubes tumbled off. The team groaned. One kid tried to catch the cubes, and the others laughed.

Something twisted inside me. How long had it been since my team had fun like that? Even though Team A had failed—they made it to the semifinals but lost in the first round—they could still laugh.

I wished my team cared about robotics, like at the start of the year. I wished I knew how to make them care again, how to hold the team together. We had so much fun back then. Yet it only took a few weeks for us to fall apart. Now we were just a remnant of a team, broken like my robot last week.

Mrs. Weir set down the phone and walked over to Team A, clapping her hands together. "That was so close!" she said. "Let's talk about this. What plans do you have to stabilize the tray?"

I let out a breath. With Mrs. Weir focused on Team A, she wouldn't yet realize Allie was missing. I had a few minutes before she turned her attention to our team. A few more minutes to find my missing classmate. I scanned the room again, trying to think where Allie could be hiding.

I imagined Naiely beside me, helping me search.

Maybe check the obvious spots first, hmm? She'd giggle, before flicking my forehead with a finger, then running away laughing.

Right. Check the obvious.

My eyes locked on to the door to the supply closet. Allie went there for the Allen wrenches. Maybe she decided to not come back out. I scowled and strode over, yanking open the door.

Sure enough, Allie sat inside, wedged between a box of solar panels and a crate full of gears. She had her sketchbook out and hummed softly as she dragged her pencil across the page. I cleared my throat.

Allie glanced up. "What?"

"You're supposed to be helping get supplies, not drawing," I snapped. I stuck my hands on my hips and stared at her. Well, at the spot just above her eyes. Eye contact was the *worst*.

Allie sighed and rolled her eyes.

"I was getting the supplies. Slowly. Give me a minute," she said, turning back to her drawing. She dragged the pencil across the page again, then flipped it over and erased a bit.

"We don't have a minute. Time is ticking, and we have work to do. Let's go."

"Whatever," snapped Allie. She closed her sketchbook and trudged out of the supply closet. I followed her back to our table.

"Did you get the smaller Allen wrench?" I asked.

"Yeah, yeah." She slapped it down on the table, the metal hitting metal with a sharp *clang*.

I bit back the remarks that swelled to my tongue. I took a deep breath, then another. Calm. I would be calm. A good team leader didn't get mad at her team, even when she couldn't understand why somebody was in her class.

I looked around for anything to distract me. Varsha was hunched over the table, quickly writing on a piece of paper.

"Varsha, how goes the notebook?" I asked.

I walked over and looked down at our design notebook. It was one of the most critical parts of the tournament. In the notebook, we needed to document our journey, drawing diagrams and writing descriptions to show how the robot had changed through the year. There were several awards that we could win thanks to the notebook, from the Design Award to the coveted Excellence Award that brought with it a chance to go on to State, even if we didn't win the tournament itself.

Our notebook was empty. Every page blank.

I blinked, my gut twisting. "Varsha, why is it empty?"

"Hmm?" said Varsha. "Oh, because I'm working on my fanfics instead." She held up a piece of paper already half full of writing.

"But . . . the notebook?"

"Calm down," said Varsha with a sigh. She flipped her dark brown hair over her shoulder and stared back down at the paper, chewing on the end of her pencil. "I'll get it started later. You know I hate technical drawings, so I need to work up the motivation first. Let me finish this fic so I can show it to my friends tomorrow. Then I'll start the notebook. Hey, do you think I should ship this character with the hot villain guy or with my OC?"

DJ dropped the screws he held and leaned over to look. "Oh! Pair him with the villain. They have *chemistry*."

I groaned and opened my mouth to argue, but Alex's game chimed and caught my attention instead.

Alex was sitting next to Santino, the light from his phone casting flashes of blue and green against his face.

Santino leaned close to him, and they were whispering back and forth while Alex played his game. He was very much *not* working on the programming yet. This was not the time to play games, or flirt with Santino!

I scowled, stormed over, and snatched the phone right out of Alex's hand.

"Hey!" he shouted.

"No!" I said. "I don't want to hear it. You need to stop playing pointless games and start programming already." We weren't even supposed to have phones out, except at lunch. Alex only got to use his phone because he was the programmer and had to do research, but how would he like it if he got that taken away? "I'm gonna tell Mrs. Weir that you keep playing games!"

I slammed his phone down on the table, next to the computer. My team went silent. I rocked on my feet, aware of them staring.

"Are you serious?" Alex asked, throwing his arms in the air. "You're gonna snitch like we're in elementary school? I can't finish programming because you never let me test the code on the bot!"

"If you were good enough, you wouldn't need to test it that much!" The words slipped out before I could stop them. It was mean, I knew, but also true. I crossed my arms and glared at his phone.

He frowned, then got up and grabbed his phone. "I get bullied enough outside of class. I don't need this from you too," he said. "I quit."

Alex spun on his heel and marched toward the door. He pushed his way outside. The door slammed closed behind him. For a moment, silence echoed through the room. Santino glared at me, and I felt Varsha's and DJ's judging stares digging into my back as well.

Mrs. Weir spoke first. "Oh dear. I'll go talk to him," she said, looking up from where she had been working with Team A. She hurried after Alex, her lab coat fluttering behind her.

"Nice one. Driving your friends away."

That voice was biting, cold, and sarcastic. I spun on Allie, my eyes wide. When she saw me look at her, she pretended to applaud.

"Shut up!" I cried.

Allie raised an eyebrow. "I'm impressed, is all. I thought *I* was bad." She smirked, then grabbed her backpack and turned away.

"Where are you going?"

"To draw and wait for you to give me more stuff to fetch. Clearly I'm not needed right now."

Allie walked back toward the supply closet. I clenched my fists, watching her go. This was too much. All of it. The empty notebook, Alex quitting, Allie being . . . Allie. My head was buzzing worse. The lights were too bright and the room too loud and—

"You're going to let us down, huh?" I cried.

Allie hesitated. "Sure."

"You can't just walk away!"

"Teacher's not here right now, so yes I can. This class is for losers, anyway."

"Your mom's a loser!" It was silly. Really silly. "Your mom" insults were so elementary school. But the words slipped out before I could stop them, mixing with the too-loud noise of the room.

Allie froze. She turned around. I took a step back as her eyes locked onto me. There was something in her gaze, in the rigid way she stood. Her fists clenched, then unclenched. Then she clenched them again and gave me the coldest glare I had ever seen.

"You think you're so great," she hissed through gritted teeth, taking a step toward me. "You bully everyone and push them around because you are so smart and so perfect. You think all I'm good for is fetching parts for you, because you're so much better than me."

Allie took a step closer to me. Then she stopped and strode back toward the robotics table instead. She dropped her backpack onto the ground and glared at the robot.

"Well, here's what I think about you and this worthless class." Allie reached out and shoved the robot off the table.

It landed on the ground with a tremendous crash. Loose screws and wheels flew everywhere. The claw broke halfway off, then lay swinging inches above the ground. Metal scraped against the linoleum floor. My robot was, for the second time that week, broken.

Santino gasped. Varsha whistled.

"Oops," whispered DJ. "That's going to be tough to fix."

My breath hitched.

Forget calm breathing. Forget making Allie do her work. I wanted to make Allie pay for this!

I clenched my fists and ran at Allie, even as the others shouted for me to stop. Her eyes widened a second before I punched her. She staggered back, holding her shoulder where I had hit. When she looked at me again, her eyes burned as hot as mine.

Allie lunged forward, crashing into me. I gasped as she knocked me down. I hit the floor *hard*. My headphones fell off, bouncing across the ground.

I screamed and reached for her hair, twisting my fingers into her blonde strands. I pulled as hard as I could, even as I squirmed, pushed, and tried to get her off me. She slammed her free fist into my cheek, and a stinging pain shot across my face.

My head ached, but I refused to let go of her hair. She broke my robot. She broke my only hope of winning. My future was scattered there along the floor, amidst the robot parts we rolled though. No Worlds. No college. No way to end my moms' worried conversations at home. It was all ruined.

Then Allie froze.

She was staring at the door. I gulped and looked up.

Mrs. Weir stood there, hands over her mouth.

The room came back into focus. Team A was staring, all five members with their eyes wide and their jaws dropped open. My own team looked just as shocked. Santino had backed away behind the computers. DJ was leaning on the robotics table for support, and Varsha was clutching his arm, gaping at us.

Even Alex, a step behind Mrs. Weir in the doorway, looked stunned. For once, he didn't have his phone out.

Mrs. Weir took a step inside. When she spoke, her voice trembled. "Both of you. Follow me. We are going to the office."

CHAPTER SIX
ALLIE

Somebody really needed to redecorate the front office at Barton Junior High. Sure, the crumbling brick walls gave it kind of a retro vibe. But the motivational posters everywhere were tacky, and the colors clashed. Bad. It looked like a preschool threw up in the office, all pretty posters and flower pens and bright colors at everyone's desk.

I had a lot of time to study it as I sat there for the second time that week.

I held one of the flower pens in my hand, twisting it through my fingers as I glared around the office. I had snagged it off Mrs. Powell's desk when she wasn't looking.

The office ladies did *not* look back at me. They wanted to, though. I could tell from the way they kept almost glancing over before turning away. The minute I left, they would start whispering about me, gossiping all about how I was here again.

I messed up. I knew it. The office ladies knew it. Evelyn and her "team" knew it.

Why did I always do that? Robotics wasn't so bad. Sure, Evelyn was always nagging me to get this and grab that, but as long as I got back to the table when Mrs. Weir was checking in with Team B, I could hide away and draw way more than in any other class. And I *was* participating, like I promised Oma.

Kind of.

I was grabbing the supplies when Evelyn told me to, anyway. I only sneaked away when she was being *really* annoying or when there was nothing for me to do.

But now I had gotten in a fight, and it was all over for me. I messed up big-time.

I scowled and started tugging at the fake flower on the pen, working it loose from the hot glue glopped around it.

My blood burned, remembering what Evelyn said. I closed my eyes, and the faces of my parents swam in the darkness, lined with disappointment. I growled and tugged the flower loose. It fell to the floor, the bright pink cloth petals standing out against the dirty white linoleum.

Principal Gilbert's door opened. Evelyn trudged out, her shoulders slumped. She didn't look at me as she walked past.

"Allison?" Principal Gilbert stuck his head out the door.

My beast reared and roiled.

"It's. Allie," I snarled, glaring at him. He kept his face bland as he motioned for me to come inside.

I walked into his office slowly, dragging my feet and slamming the door behind me. It was just me and him today. No Oma. I slunk into a chair and crossed my arms.

Principal Gilbert looked at me and sighed.

I glared back at him.

We waited like a Western standoff, staring each other down. The principal versus his problem. Deep down, I knew this was it.

I shouldn't have done it. I should have ignored what Evelyn had said. But after even a few days in the class, I was sick of being pushed around. Treated like I was nothing better than her personal supply gopher. Too useless for real robotics work, not that I *wanted* to do robotics stuff.

My beast got the better of me.

It hadn't even taken a week to get in trouble again. Maybe I did belong at Sunrise. The thought made me madder.

"I'm disappointed," said Principal Gilbert, finally looking away.

"She came at me. She punched me and wouldn't let go of my hair! I was defending myself!"

"I believe you." Principal Gilbert picked up a stack of papers on his desk and began shuffling them. "Evelyn admitted that she egged you on and started the fight."

"Oh, so you only believe me because a *good* kid told the truth?" I clenched my fists and wished with every fiber of my being that I had hit Evelyn harder.

"I believe that you both made poor choices. Evelyn also mentioned the robot you broke," said Principal Gilbert.

"That is expensive equipment. It's already hard to get new robotics parts with our funding, much less when students are breaking parts on purpose."

He paper-clipped his stack of papers and set it to the side. Then he turned back to me, steepling his hands together.

"Allison, the last time you were in this office, I told you that you would get transferred if you were removed from another class."

I shuddered, my beast cringing back. "Are you sending me to Sunrise?" I asked. I hated how small my voice sounded.

I knew the answer. I had gotten in a fight. Even if Mrs. Weir forgave me, there was no way Principal Gilbert would let me stay.

"I want you to tell me what happened," he said instead, leaning forward. "What is your side of the story?"

I squirmed in my seat. How much had Evelyn told him? Did it even matter? I messed up. I shoved the robot off the table. I reacted without thinking.

This was it. It was all over. *Sunrise Junior High, here comes your next problem kid.* "She . . ." The words stuck in my throat. I swallowed, then forced them out. "She insulted my mom."

Principal Gilbert let out a long sigh. His gaze softened. He leaned back in his chair.

"No, Allison," he said. "I'm not sending you to Sunrise yet. Mrs. Weir hasn't kicked you out of class and . . . I understand how difficult this is for you. Your parents are a sore spot and reasonably so. I—"

He sighed again and glanced down at his desk. My eyes followed his, locking onto a paper next to his stack. It was covered in a messy scrawl of notes, with numbers and class periods written on it. I spotted the word *robotics* twice and *low enrollment* was circled in the corner. I frowned.

"What's that?" I asked, leaning forward, trying to shift the conversation away from my parents.

Principal Gilbert's cheeks flushed, like drops of watercolor paint spreading across a wet paper. The color rose to the top of his balding head.

He cleared his throat and shoved the memo under several other papers. "Don't worry about that. Listen, I want you to succeed. I know you are going through a lot, and I want to help you—"

"I don't need help," I snapped, cutting right through his speech. My beast was back again, uncurling as Principal Gilbert's words poked and prodded at all the spots that *hurt*. My eyes locked onto his desk, where the memo had been. "Do you not like the robotics class? Why did you put me in with a bunch of losers if you don't like it?"

I was pushing too far, messing up all over again. It was like an avalanche, and I didn't know how to stop it.

Sure enough, his eyes narrowed. But then he took a deep breath and steepled his hands together again. "Ms. Wells, we are talking about you. Mrs. Weir is letting you stay in her class, but you will first serve one week of in-school suspension for breaking the robot parts."

He was just sending me to ISS? I could do that. I spent more time in the ISS room than class some weeks. That room, with its small windows and the wobbly desks, didn't intimidate me. I was used to ISS. I liked it, even. The teacher, Miss Hawk, didn't care if I sat and drew pictures all day. She wanted us to be quiet and not pick fights, and she actually cared about how we felt.

ISS was better than Sunrise.

"Fine," I said, clenching my hands together in my lap.

He looked down at his desk, shuffling his papers again. "Like I said, I want you to succeed. You don't believe me, I can tell. But we all want you to do better here. Along with one week of suspension, you will need to start meeting with Mrs. Macquarie, the school counselor. She's out of town right now, but as soon as she returns, we'll have her schedule a session with you. Will you agree to that?"

"Sure," I said, as if I had a choice. I'd meet with the counselor, fine. But no way would I talk about my feelings with her.

"I will, of course, have to call your grandmother to inform her of today's events," added Principal Gilbert.

Oh. Oh, that wasn't good. My heart plummeted. My beast ran whimpering away, into the dark corners of my mind.

"Do you have to?" I asked. I imagined Oma making her way to the phone, her papery hands reaching out. She moved slowly with her walker, so slow she often missed calls. But she would listen to the voicemail, and her face would fall. Any good cheer or happiness she felt would vanish.

"You know the rules," said Principal Gilbert. "I hate having to deliver such news to your grandmother. Remember, though, I wouldn't have to do this if *you* hadn't pushed the robot. I want you to think about your choices and think twice before acting next time."

I barely heard him. My mind stuck on Oma, on how heartbroken she would be.

The bell rang, and I jumped. It rang again, a sharp, chiming sound signaling the end of the day. Mrs. Powell poked her head in the door.

"Jeremy Jacobs's parents are here for their after-school conference," she said.

Principal Gilbert nodded. He grabbed a hall pass and scrawled on it, then handed it to me.

"This is for Monday. You will report to the in-school suspension room first thing in the morning. *Don't* make the security guards have to search for you again."

That happened once. Once! I clenched my hands into fists and stared at the grains of wood on his desk, imagining the swirls as eyeballs floating in a vast mess of nothing.

"Fine," I muttered.

"You may go now."

I stood up and trudged out of Principal Gilbert's office. Mrs. Weir stood nearby, at the copy machine. She sighed and shook her head when she saw me. I blushed and looked away. I didn't care what some teacher thought.

Outside the office, the air was sunny and hot, the sort of hot that hits you like an oven. I trudged through the crowds of students leaving and walked toward the cactus garden. I wanted to be mad, to let my beast run wild. Anger was easy to handle, easy to hide behind. When I was angry, I didn't have to feel guilty or sad. Instead, I kept thinking of Oma and what she would say.

I had promised her that I wouldn't get in trouble again. Oma wanted me to do better, to make her proud like Dad always did when he was a kid, and I was failing so hard at that.

The saguaro's shadow fell across me as I crossed through the cactus garden. When I looked at it, I imagined Dad standing beside me.

Well, Allie, the memory whispered. *This is disappointing, isn't it?*

Tears welled up in my eyes, and I dashed them away before anyone saw. I never got in trouble back then, before Mom and Dad died. I wasn't angry all the time, either. I wished I could stop it. Could go back to the Allie I used to be. The quiet kid that watched anime, drew cool pictures, and may not have had many friends but wasn't hated, either. The kid who didn't have a beast she couldn't control living in her heart and making her explode again and again.

Now there was too much sadness, hate, and frustration piled up in my bones. My beast held me together, kept the misery at bay. If I lost the anger, would I deflate? Drift away on the wind like an old paper bag, forgotten and unloved?

No, I needed it. Without it, there would just be the sadness.

I shuddered and pushed open the blue door of Room 303. It was time to grab my backpack and go home. Time to see how disappointed Oma was.

I expected the classroom to be empty. Mrs. Weir was in the office and the bell had rung for the day. Yet when I stepped inside, I heard sniffling. Evelyn sat by the robotics table, her head in her hands. She looked up as the door closed. Tears filled her light green eyes and spilled down her cheeks.

Evelyn Cole, the most annoying kid at Barton Junior High, was crying.

CHAPTER SEVEN
EVELYN

Nobody was in the robotics room when I got back. Mrs. Weir had sent the others to end the day with the photography teacher while she took me and Allie to the office.

I was glad.

My head was buzzing, buzzing, buzzing. I ran to the robotics table, standing beside my backpack, and rocked back and forth on my feet. It was too much. Too bright. Too loud. Too many mistakes. I couldn't breathe. All the emotions were building up in my body, and I just wanted them out!

My eyes ached, and my nose was stuffy. The fluorescent lights whined loudly in my ears, and I couldn't take it anymore! I grabbed my backpack and threw it, as if that could toss away all the emotions spinning through my head. But the emotions were still there, buzzing around and bouncing from my fingers to my toes. A jumble of too much. Too much everything.

I didn't feel myself in that moment, not as snot ran down my face and my head buzzed and buzzed. I hated this. I hated this-I hated this-I hated this—

I slid down against the robotics table, then rocked back and forth again and again as I tried to block it all out and make it all go away. The lights were painful. The clanking of the printers and whining electricity grated against my head.

"I hate this. I hate it!" I kicked at a robotic part lying on the ground, then started crying more when that just made me feel even worse.

I sobbed and rocked, and rocked and sobbed, until finally the buzzing faded, and the too-loud sounds of the classroom came back in.

Heat raced through my cheeks as I sat there, rocking back and forth, trying to get back to me.

The bell rang. Sharp. Painfully loud. I pressed my hands against my ears and took a deep, shuddering breath. I felt so empty now. All the emotions were gone, the bees having buzzed away. I was tired and empty, and my butt hurt from the hard linoleum floor.

I wiped at my eyes and looked around again. My headphones lay on the floor, amidst the broken robot. I grabbed them and shoved them on, the cushioned fabric comforting as it pressed around my ears. Then I got up and sat at the robotics table. The cool metal felt good, so I pressed my head against it, waiting for the last of the buzzing to go away. I was so tired.

I sniffled and wiped at my eyes, then blinked as the room brightened.

Allie Wells stood in the classroom doorway, staring at me.

Had she seen? I didn't have meltdowns often. Mum and Mama were working with me on recognizing when buzzing was too bad, when I was stressed and overwhelmed and spiraling and needed to get away to somewhere quiet, like the counselor's office. So I didn't have them often, and almost never at school. I tried hard to make sure nobody ever saw.

I tensed up. Did Allie notice? Would she start the fight again or say something mean? Would she tell people about it?

Instead, her eyes snapped to the piece of paper on the table. The hall pass Principal Gilbert had written, condemning me to a week of in-school suspension for fighting. Her brows furrowed.

"Why are you crying?" she asked. "It's only a week."

She hadn't seen my meltdown. I wiped at my eyes again, my breath thundering back into me. "I'm not crying," I muttered, even as my eyes were drawn to the hall pass.

A week of ISS. *A week.* I couldn't believe it. Maybe a week meant nothing to her, but I never got in trouble. My family would be disappointed. Worse still, if I spent a week in ISS, I'd lose time that I needed to prepare for the next tournament.

My heart was locking up. My head felt heavy; that buzzing was creeping right back in. I wiped at my nose and took a deep breath, trying to get control. Trying not to think about it. If I thought about my meltdown, it would be too easy to fall into another, to lose myself again.

Allie raised an eyebrow and crossed her arms. I hiccuped. My mind kept jumping back to earlier, when I had started the fight. When I provoked Allie. It was all my fault. If I had kept my calm and been a good Team Lead, this never would have happened.

"I shouldn't have kept bugging you," I whispered. Something about the way she stared at me made the thoughts well up and spill out, the words coming easier now that all my emotions weren't locked up inside and fighting to get out. I still felt strained and tired, battered by the too-bright lights and the constant noise of the robotics room, but I was also scared of spiraling back into that place. Instead, I let the words pour out. "I shouldn't have picked a fight. All you wanted to do was draw, and now we're both in trouble."

I looked at the table as I spoke, tracing my fingers along the scrapes in the old metal.

"Why'd you take the blame? You could have told Principal Gilbert anything, and he'd probably believe you," said Allie.

I stared up at her. "I can't lie to the principal! Besides, you were right to get mad, I think. I just . . . Mrs. Weir told me I couldn't be Team Lead if I didn't get you involved. Robotics is everything to me, and I got scared. Everyone on the team keeps getting distracted, and the tournament is coming up soon, and—"

"So what?" asked Allie. "It's one tournament." There was something odd in her voice. Anger, pain, maybe even hurt? She crossed the room to the robotics table and leaned down to grab her backpack. It lay on the floor, amid the broken robot. My gut twisted as I stared at the robot. Over two hundred pieces, now scattered across the floor.

I loved robotics. At least, I usually did. I had loved it every day since I was a kid.

When I turned seven years old, Mum bought me my first robotics kit. She found it in the clearance section of a craft store while buying beads for her jewelry side business. It was a simple robotics kit, nothing fancy. Nothing more than a little toy bot with a single wheel that rolled in a straight line across a table.

But Mum came carrying it into the house, held high above her head like a trophy. It wasn't used, but rather new and just for me. That alone caught my attention. Mum plopped it down in front of me and smiled until I agreed to try building it.

I remember being surprised. Like, robotics? Really? Wasn't robotics for boys? I never heard of *girls* doing robotics. Still, Mum acted so excited that I gave the kit a try.

It made sense in a way I never knew. The way the pieces clicked together, the way the little bot rolled once I turned it on. I created something amazing in that tiny little bot. From that day forward, building robots became my obsession.

I scoured yard sales for every robotics kit I could find. I watched BattleBots on YouTube and spent way too much time reading about the rovers that NASA drove on Mars. I met Naiely when she was trying to drive a remote-controlled robot outside our apartment complex and found my best friend thanks to our shared love of tech.

By the time I had turned ten, I started building my own bots with parts taken from old toys. It didn't always go well. There was the time Mama's hair dryer exploded after I borrowed the fan from it. Not to mention the time I fried the family computer while trying to upgrade it. Naiely found it hilarious when something went wrong. She would double over with laughter at the situation. Afterward, she would help me figure out what to fix and why my project had failed.

I hated whenever I messed up, especially when I broke stuff at home. It wasn't like we could replace things easily. Mum and Mama always said it was okay, but I could see the worry in their eyes. It was like NASA used to say: Failure is not an option. For years, that was my motto. I was determined to figure out how to do things and to do them right.

Yet the broken robot on the floor was 100 percent a failure, and this time there was no Naiely to help make it better. I was all alone in the world now.

"It's not just a tournament," I said to Allie. She raised an eyebrow, and I sniffled. "It's my only chance to see my friend. We joined robotics together. I thought it was per-fect. I'd be with my best friend. We'd win a tournament, go to State, and eventually Worlds. We'd do amazing, and the Tech Tigers would beg us to join them next year. They're the best high-school robotics team, and they make it to Worlds every year. If I'm on that team, I'll get college scholarships and a good job one day and all that important stuff."

"Are you serious?" asked Allie. She tucked a strand of her pale hair behind her ears and made a face. "Why are you worried about *college* already?"

"I have to!" I cried. "My moms can't afford college. It's expensive, you know?"

"No, not really. We're in middle school. Who even thinks about college? There are bigger things to obsess over." Allie shrugged. Then she slung her backpack over her shoulder and straightened up.

"I'm not obsessed." I blushed and stared at the tabletop, tracing the scratches in the metal with my gaze. I *wasn't* obsessed. But this stuff was important.

I didn't talk about money at school. It was embarrassing. But I saw how nice other kids' clothing was. I knew it was hard for Mum when half the clothing she could afford had too-tight collars and sleeves that I didn't want to wear. I noticed when everyone had cool new tech, while my phone screen was still cracked, my phone five years old, and my headphones were so used, the padding was wearing thin.

Mum had gotten fired last year from her main job, and she didn't make a ton of money from crafting jewelry. Mama and Mum had so many whispered conversations in the kitchen, and I knew it was bad. What if things got worse? What if we had to leave our apartment? What if we couldn't keep the power on, like that one time when I was in elementary school and Mama's car broke down, and everything was really bad for a couple of months?

At the start of the school year, my science teacher had talked about scholarships. He told us about how scholarships were basically free money for college, if we could just prove we deserved it. Naiely and I knew that was our answer. We'd rock robotics, get on to a good high-school team, and win all sorts of scholarships. Then we would be the best college roomies ever.

I wanted to see Naiely again. But more than that, I wanted to go to college and become an engineer. Engineers were rich. Engineers could take care of their families and never have to worry that they didn't fit in.

I couldn't—*wouldn't*—tell Allie that.

Instead, I sniffled, still staring at the table. "I'm not obsessed, but it matters, you know?"

Allie shrugged. She didn't say anything, didn't even look at me. She wasn't leaving either, though. This was kind of helping, even though Allie was the last person I had wanted to see. Talking about this all took me a little further away from my meltdown, away from spiraling back into that place. So I dropped my head back into my arms and spoke again.

"All I wanted was to see my friend again," I mumbled into the table. "And robotics was my answer. It was my way to see my friend and to go to college and to make life better. But it doesn't matter anymore. You broke the robot. Our programmer quit. Our design notebook is empty. By the time we're out of ISS, there will only be a month left until the tournament, and this is our last one for the year unless we win and make it to State. There won't be time to fix things. We'll never make it to State or Worlds. I'll never get to see Naiely again. I'll never have friends who understand. I'm an enormous failure who let my entire family down."

Funny how I accused Allie of letting us down earlier. Instead, it was me proving to be a disappointment. I was crying again, that buzzing creeping right back into my head. The sobs shuddered through me, stronger than ever. My hands shook, and my head throbbed. I was a failure. I couldn't do anything right. Even my team hated me.

"Well," said Allie from across the room. "That sucks."

A moment later, the door closed. When I looked up, I sat in an empty room with only the too-bright lights and my misery keeping my company. Allison Wells didn't care about my pity party.

CHAPTER EIGHT
ALLIE

Oma's house looked ordinary on the outside, another adobe-style home in a neighborhood full of them. Inside, it was a time capsule. When I was little, I tried to draw all the things in Oma's house. The grandfather clock in the entryway, given to Oma by her own grandfather. The giant wooden fork and spoon hanging on the wall in the kitchen. The shadow box full of the dried roses she had preserved, from the first rosebush she had ever planted in the backyard, when Dad was a kid.

Oma had no pictures out. She gathered those up and put them in a box almost a year ago. But the items around the house told as much of a story as pictures. Sometimes I would stop and stare at them. Sometimes I'd ask Oma to tell me the story behind something, and we'd sit on the couch for hours while Oma regaled me with stories about our distant ancestors.

Today, I barely looked at anything as I let myself into

the house. My heart was twisted into one enormous ball of stress. My eyes ached, from trying not to cry.

I wondered if Principal Gilbert already had called Oma.

When I stepped into the living room, I saw that Oma knew. She sat on the couch, her walker off to the side. She was hunched over, and a tear ran down her cheek, drifting along the canyons of her wrinkles.

"Oma, I'm sorry." I squeezed my eyes shut.

"Oh, Allie," said Oma softly. "I didn't realize the time." She wiped at her eyes and patted the couch beside her, an invitation. I sat, twisting my shirt between my hands.

"I'm sorry I let you down. I'm trying to do better. Really." My eyes blurred, but I fought to stay strong. I never cried in front of Oma.

Oma squeezed my arm lightly. "I'm not crying because you got in trouble," she said. "Though we need to talk about that." She took a large, shaky breath. Her gaze drifted around the house, her eyes finally settling on the giant fork and spoon barely visible over in the kitchen. "I used to get in trouble too, you know."

"Really?" I asked. Her hand rested on my arm. Her other held a picture frame, one I never expected to see again. Suddenly, I knew why she was crying. I didn't know what to say, so instead I said nothing.

"All the time. And Beatrice, my sister, constantly cleaned up my messes. It runs in the family, I think." She snorted, still looking at the giant wooden spoon and fork, as if facing them were easier than the picture she held.

"Can you tell me the spoon story?" I asked. When I was little, I used to think it was normal. Didn't everyone's grandparents have a giant wooden spoon and fork on their wall? Learning that it was unique to Oma made me love her even more.

Oma hesitated. "Are you sure you want to hear that one?" Another tear slid down her cheek, and she wiped it away. I fought with the lump in my own throat.

"I like that story."

"All right," said Oma. I leaned into her side, blinking my vision clear as she settled into her story. It was an old story, one she hadn't told me in a long time. "When I was much younger, with joints that didn't creak, my son used to be terrible about the dishes. He'd leave them in his bedroom, beside the couch, and all over the house. Every time I knew we had company coming, I'd have to search the house for old dishes to clean, just to make sure we had enough plates and forks for everyone."

It was nice to listen to Oma talk, to lose myself in the story. To forget about getting in trouble and how I disappointed her. Even if I knew the story would hurt, it was still nice to hear Oma tell it.

"One day I got so fed up that I started yelling at him. I yelled about the silverware and how the forks and spoons always got lost. And do you know what your father did?" She smiled fondly as another tear escaped from her eyes.

"What did he do?" I asked, even though I had heard the story before.

"He turned around and bought me those darn ugly decorations. Then he gave them to me like it was the best gift in the world and told me he found a fork and spoon I could never lose." She chuckled and shook her head.

I laughed with her. Dad was always playing pranks. Always being silly and fun. He used to tell me he got in trouble all the time, but trouble for pranks was different from getting in trouble because you couldn't do anything right.

"Oma, I'm sorry about the fight." I finally felt ready to say it. "I let you down and made you sad all over again."

"I already told you, sweetheart. I'm not sad because of you." She sighed. "But, Allie, why did you do it?"

I stared at the couch, my eyes following the old flower patterns. The memory of the day tasted bitter in my throat. Oma waited, and I knew she would not let me go without explaining myself.

"Evelyn, the girl I fought, insulted Mom," I said. "And I got mad again."

I felt Oma's shoulders slump. "Oh, Allie," she said, her words a sigh. "I'm so sorry."

I sniffled and kept talking, the words spilling out like a waterfall. "I didn't mean to get mad, but it just happened. I'm sorry. I need to be better. For you. For them."

I forced myself to study the picture Oma held. To really see it. Oma took it last year, a few weeks before the car crash. Mom and Dad stood behind me, squinting into the sun and smiling. Dad wrapped his arms around me, and I held onto them, my smile equally big. Mom stood beside us, one hand on my shoulder and her other arm around Dad's waist. My face was happy, sunburned and scattered with freckles, but happy.

Oma never brought out the pictures. We tiptoed around Mom and Dad being gone. We smiled for each other and tried to be strong. We talked about normal things and avoided the emptiness that echoed through the house and through our hearts. It was a silent, unspoken rule. If we both pretended to be okay, then we wouldn't shatter.

Only, I wasn't okay. In that empty hole, my beast kept growing, again and again. Every time it exploded out, I got in trouble.

"They'd be disappointed in me," I whispered now.

"No, Allie." Oma lifted her hand off my arm and traced the picture's glass, her fingers brushing across Dad's face. "Never. They might be sad, yes. But not disappointed."

I bit my lip and looked away. "That's not true," I said. My voice broke around the words. "I bummed them out even before the car crash. All my terrible report cards for math and science. I was never smart enough. Not like Mom and Dad. They were geniuses, and I'm their pathetic daughter who can't even multiply without counting on my hands."

"Allie Wells." Oma's voice was sharp. She set the picture to the side and took my hands, wrapping them in her own. "You know that isn't true. Your parents were smart, yes. But you're gifted too. Your father *loved* the pictures you drew. Your mother always bragged about how talented you were, how you view the world in such color."

"Really?"

"Yes. Allie, when they cleaned out your dad's office at the arboretum, they gave me an entire box full of pictures you drew him. You are smart in a different way, in the way of art and colors and seeing beauty and shapes where nobody else does."

"Art doesn't matter in the actual world." I hung my head in shame. Besides, it didn't matter if I was good at art when everyone could see how bad I was at everything else.

Oma's eyes flashed with fire. In that moment, the gentle strokes I imagined her with turned strong and sharp. "Oh yes, it does. Who do you think designs the advertisements for companies? Who makes technology look *good*? There is art in everything, Allie. In the buildings outside, in the shape of every item we buy and use. Even in those robots you hate so much."

"Art's not in robotics," I muttered.

"Nonsense. Somebody must design the robots and make them look good. Otherwise, they will be all function and no style. Art matters in so many ways. Those comics you enjoy wouldn't be possible without art, nor would those cartoons. Imagine how plain books would look without their beautiful covers or if movies were never animated. Art matters, Allie, and it's everywhere."

"I guess," I whispered.

Oma sighed and sagged, reaching a hand out to brush my cheek. "Your parents loved you and were proud of you. You are talented in more ways than you realize."

I pulled my legs up on the couch and leaned into Oma. Then I let go, letting myself cry, truly cry, for the first time in a year. Oma sobbed with me. I felt it in her shaking shoulders and trembling arms. In the quick breaths she took. For a while, we sat together, crying, and for once my beast stayed in its cave, as if our tears were the rain keeping it burrowed away.

I didn't believe Oma, not truly. But it felt good to hear her say that. To know she believed in me, even if I messed up so many times. To know she thought my parents might believe in me too.

"I miss them," I said finally, pulling away and wiping at my eyes.

"So do I," said Oma. "I'm sorry, Allie. It's been hard to talk about them. I thought if I did, it would make you hurt more, but now I see that not talking about it was worse."

"No, Oma." I looked up at her eyes, those soft blues. "Oma, *I* was avoiding talking about them because I didn't want *you* to be sad. You've had all the doctor appointments, and the walker, and I was afraid that . . ." I couldn't bring myself to finish the sentence.

Oma laughed. I blinked at her and sat up, wiping at my eyes.

"Why are you laughing?" I asked.

"Oh, Allie," said Oma. She wiped at her own tears and smiled at me. "I will not die of a broken heart. I'm not *that* old. Besides, somebody needs to look out for you."

I hugged Oma again, burying my face into her warmth. "Oma. You said Dad kept all my drawings. Can . . . can we go look at them?"

She softened and wrapped her arms around me, blanketing me in her kindness. "All right," she said. "We can dig out some old family pictures too."

"I'd like that." So much time had passed since I'd seen a picture of Mom and Dad. Sometimes I worried I'd forget them, forget the curves of their faces and the shapes of their smiles. I was more afraid of hurting Oma, so I never admitted it. I stayed away from the room with the boxes, with the pictures and memories. Funny how she was afraid of doing the same to me.

My heart ached more than it had in months. Yet I also felt better, like those bottled emotions had been squeezed out, and now my beast was a little smaller. A little less scary. It was still there in my heart, waiting, but maybe for Oma's sake I could manage it. And not fail this time.

I wanted to try.

"Allie, you need to make things right on Monday." I stiffened in Oma's arms. She pulled out of the hug and looked me in the eyes. "Breaking that robot was not okay."

I nodded, looking down at the couch with its faded floral pattern. "Okay. I'll apologize to Evelyn."

"And?"

"I'll talk to Mrs. Macquarie at school. And I'll make things right with the broken robot. Somehow." I kicked at the ground with my foot and glanced at Oma from the corner of my eye. Stuck-up Evelyn was the last thing I wanted to think about, but I wouldn't argue with Oma.

Oma smiled again and wiped at her eyes. She rose from the couch and reached for her walker. She shuffled toward the hallway, one shaky step at a time.

"Come on," she said, smiling over her shoulder with shining eyes. "Let's go find those pictures."

Oma and I laughed and cried as we flipped through picture albums and opened boxes of Mom and Dad's old stuff. By the time night arrived, I felt drained and tired, like watercolors thinned too much. I expected to fall asleep right away.

Yet when I laid my head on the pillow and closed my eyes, I thought of the fight again. Then I thought of Oma, and what she had said earlier. I had to make things right at school. With Evelyn. I'd promised.

Evelyn, obsessed with robotics. Obsessed with the tournaments and college and all that stuff she talked about today. She loved the world of robotics. I couldn't understand it.

But she was afraid to disappoint her family.

I understood *that* just fine.

Her anguish played in my mind. My beast had been growling and snarling, pushing me to get out. To leave the classroom before *I* started crying again. So I hadn't really cared how upset she was. Now though, with my raging emotions dulled by my talk with Oma, I thought about Evelyn again and again. Her face flashed before my eyes when I closed them, tears painting her cheeks and shimmering with the reflection of the bright lights against the silver metal tables.

I rolled over and shoved my face in my pillow.

The broken robot clattered through my vision, with Evelyn looking at it like a lost friend. Metal pieces decorated the floor with slashes of silver. Bright green spots where the gears lay scattered across the linoleum. The stark black of the motors, with their wheels rolling away. It was like a horrible painting, and it was all my doing.

You broke the robot. Our programmer quit. Our design notebook is empty.

I groaned and sat up. Guilt rolled in my stomach, making it impossible to sleep. I rubbed at my eyes and blinked around the room.

Our design notebook is empty.

I felt bad. I did. Breaking the robot was a terrible idea. Would I have still done it if I knew how bad it would be? Probably. But I regretted it now. Yet regret was useless, a dry brush leaving no color behind. I couldn't fix the robot. But there was something I *could* do.

I stood up and tiptoed across the carpet in the darkness. My hands brushed against my desk, and I reached for the drawer where my empty notebooks lay. Then I flicked on my desk lamp and booted up my computer. It was time to see what a design notebook was and how much drawing it included. Maybe Oma was right. Maybe there was art even in boring robotics.

CHAPTER NINE
EVELYN

My cereal was shaped like robots. Mama found it last week at the dollar store, and before that disaster tournament, it had seemed like a sign that my team would do great. Now the little blocky marshmallows taunted me.

I stabbed my spoon through one, watching it break apart like my robot on Friday. I'd agonized over it all weekend, avoiding Mum's and Mama's looks. I couldn't understand how it broke that easily, even after being pushed off a table. The robots were supposed to be stronger than that.

But Naiely had given me the answer over the weekend. Her email played through my head again.

Hey Ev,
Sorry to hear about the fight. That girl sounds terrible.
I hate to say it, though, but if the bot broke that easily, it probably didn't have enough connection points. Maybe this is a good thing? Now you know it's weak, so you can improve

it before your next tournament. Imagine if it fell apart like that in the middle of a match! That would be embarrassing.

I know you'll figure this out and get it fixed in time. You have to! My new team already qualified for the California State Championship. We are determined to win and make it to Worlds. I'll be waiting for you there. We can hang out every day of the tournament, and I'll introduce you to my new friends. It'll be fun.

I miss you so much! Promise me you won't give up, okay? Oh! And let me know when you aren't grounded so I can borrow Dad's phone and call you again. I need to tell you about the Raspberry Pi I'm programming. It's like a mini computer, and it is COOL.

Your bestie,

Naiely

PS You are trying to make friends without me, right? I know you. Don't be a hermit!

I stabbed another marshmallow and swirled it around in the milk, fighting back my misery. She was right. The robot stunk. Maybe I wasn't as good as I thought. If I were better at robotics, I would have noticed the weak connection points.

Her last line stuck with me too. She knew me well. I should be trying to make new friends. But I wasn't good at that. I tried before. I really had, but I never knew the right things to say or how to make people like me. I never knew how to fake being "normal" enough. It was always easier to just have Naiely, my one friend who never judged me and liked me for who I was.

Except Naiely was gone, and now I had nothing. While I was getting in trouble and everything fell apart, she was having a blast. That was like her, though. She was friendly and happy all the time. People *liked* Naiely.

She wasn't coming back, no matter how much I wished it. I should be getting to know the other kids and trying to make middle school a little less miserable. But every time I thought about that, my mind drifted to the days spent with Naiely. It felt like it would be a betrayal of our friendship in a way. Besides, other kids didn't get me.

No, I didn't need new friends. I just needed to win my way to Worlds. The bot was step one. My robot broke because it was badly built, so I had to find a way to fix it.

Mama walked into the kitchen, her boots clicking against the tile floors. She'd scolded me on Friday night when I got back from school, after she got a call from Principal Gilbert. I was grounded for the entire next week; no staying late at school, no playing with the computer all week, no going out with friends. Not that the last one mattered.

Now, on Monday morning, Mama looked at me with pursed lips and a tight disappointment in her eyes. When she saw me peeking at her from my cereal bowl, she looked away. Her eyes latched onto her cross wall instead.

The cereal turned bitter in my mouth. I had never made Mama this upset before.

I looked at the cross wall too, staring at its deep blue paint and the dozen crosses from a dozen unique places that Mama had hung on it. It was the prettiest wall of our apartment, full of so many different crosses. The cross my grandma gave Mama the day I was born. The cross I bought her from that gift shop in Tucson. That hung next to a big cross, one she found when she was my age. My favorite was always the tiniest of them, the little beaded one Mum had made for Mama when they first met.

As if drawn to it, Mama walked over. She straightened the little cross, running a hand along the shining, silver beads. The silver reminded me of my robot, and my robot reminded me of the fight.

"Mama, I'm sorry." I dropped my spoon against the rim of the bowl and clenched my fists, staring down at the tabletop.

Mama took a deep breath and pulled her hand away from the cross wall. "I know." She sighed and walked over to the table. Her chair scraped against the floorboards as she pulled it out. She sat and gazed at me with serious eyes. "I'm still disappointed. Fighting, Evelyn? You're better than that."

I sniffled. "I'm sorry. I got mad and didn't think."

"Of course you didn't. If you had been thinking, you wouldn't have gotten into a fight."

I stared at my cereal, at the marshmallows that we usually couldn't afford. We had this conversation on Friday too, and it had hurt. I had disappointed them. Like with the tournament. I had to be better than this. I had to be perfect so that Mum and Mama wouldn't have to worry about me, like they worried about the bills and Mum's job hunt and everything else they talked about late at night when they thought I was asleep.

"Allie broke my robot," I said. "But I insulted her too. It was wrong of me, and I'm really sorry."

Mama stared at me with her dark green eyes, and I forced myself to look even if it hurt. Her red hair, thick like my own, settled around her shoulders. "Are you going to tell her that?"

"I did! Kind of."

Mama raised an eyebrow.

"I mean, I told her I shouldn't have done it," I said. I stuck a strand of hair in my mouth, pulling it between my teeth. "But I guess I forgot the apology part."

Mama cleared her throat, and I spit out the hair, looking back down at my robot cereal. The marshmallows were getting soggy, breaking apart into little bits. Probably not worth the money Mama had spent. I took a bite so I wouldn't waste them.

They were mushy and gross, the texture all wrong now that they had soaked up the milk. I shoved the bowl away.

"I guess I can apologize again today," I mumbled.

"Good. Taking responsibility is important." Mama looked back at her cross wall, but this time she let a brief smile onto her face. The knot in my gut loosened.

A chiming sound echoed from the hallway, and a moment later Mum swept into the kitchen. Her many bracelets and earrings chimed as she moved. She paused when she saw us.

"Are you done interrogating our daughter?" she asked, her voice light and musical.

While Mama was always very serious, Mum was quicker to forgive and smile. With her flowing skirts and handmade jewelry, and shimmering golden hair that fell almost below her bottom, Mum often looked like something out of a fairy tale. I loved Mum and her musical walk, even if her bracelets did get painfully loud sometimes. Mama's stern face softened as Mum entered the room.

"I'm not interrogating her," Mama said. "I'm making sure she knows what she needs to do."

"I do, Mama. I promise." I traced the scratches in the table with my fingers.

"I, for one, would feel quite upset if somebody damaged my jewelry," Mum said innocently. She walked across the room to the kitchen and began rifling through the cabinets for the cereal boxes. "Especially if someone pushed it all off the table. In that case, I'd probably end up getting in a fight too."

"Hey, now!" Mama cried. "You're supposed to be setting a good example for our daughter." But Mama smiled as she spoke, so she wasn't really upset.

Mum pulled out a cereal box and shook it, then frowned. It sounded empty. Tossing it into the recycling, she came to sit at the table instead. I pushed my own bowl of soggy cereal her way, and Mum smiled.

"Bad texture?" she asked.

I nodded. "It got soggy." Mum and Mama always understood, which made disappointing them feel even worse. I looked back down at the table, avoiding my moms' gazes. "I really am sorry about last week. I was upset, and I acted without thinking."

"Evelyn," said Mum, pulling my abandoned cereal bowl over, "we want you to do well and enjoy yourself, and the fact that you got that upset worries us. Is robotics class still where you want to be?"

"Yes!" I shouted, before she could say more. "I mean, it's kind of tough with my teammates, but I like building the robot, and we have the tournament next month, so I'll have another chance to win, I promise."

Mama and Mum exchanged a look.

"We want you to be *happy*, sweetheart," said Mama after a moment. "But if robotics is what makes you happy still, then I'm glad. No more fights, though, understand?"

I smiled weakly. "I promise I won't get into any more fights. Even if my robot gets broken more. I promise. You're the best moms ever, and I won't let you down again."

Mama shook her head, but her eyes were warm now and her shoulders relaxed. "Flattery gets you nowhere," she teased. "Now, I believe it's time for school?"

I looked at the clock on the wall, and my smile fell from my face. Today was my first day ever of in-school suspension. My nerves ramped up as I thought about it. My hands trembled even as I hugged Mum goodbye, grabbed my backpack and headphones, and followed Mama to her car.

***

By the time we reached the school, I was stuck in a constant loop of stress. I trudged slowly toward the ISS room. The closer I got, the more people looked at me, noticing, watching. I had never gotten in trouble before.

I kept my head down and hurried toward the door. I put my hand on the door handle, then froze when I heard laughter, muffled only slightly by my headphones. Jeremy Jacobs and his goons sat on a bench three feet away.

"Wow. Evel-loser has detention?" Jeremy started laughing again, so hard that he bent over.

"What did you do, Evelyn?" D'Angelo snickered as he spoke. "I bet it was terrible!"

I blushed and turned away.

Deep breath in.

There was nothing I could do now. I had made my mistake and was paying for it.

Deep breath out.

I had to be calm. I'd get through this.

"Oh! Oh!" cried Mike. "Maybe she forgot to do her homework!"

"No, wait." Jeremy held up his hands, and his friends fell silent. "Maybe she stole everyone else's homework because she's such a loser that always wants more work to do!"

Jeremy and his friends howled with laughter. I squeezed my hands against my headphones, squishing them against my ears, and tried to breathe, to focus. I couldn't handle any more of this. I pushed my way inside the ISS room, letting the door close behind me and silence their laughter.

The room inside was small and dim, lit only by fluo-rescent lights above. There were five desks set around the small space, and a larger teacher desk in one corner. The lady sitting behind the teacher's desk frowned. Her eyes narrowed as her brows drew together.

"I don't believe I know you," she said. She looked me up and down. I gulped.

"I'm Evelyn. I think I'm supposed to give this to you?" I stared down at her desk and thrust the hall pass toward her, my hands trembling.

"Look up, please," said the lady. "It helps to see your lips."

I hesitated, then lifted my eyes to meet hers. It was too hard. I looked at her hairline instead. Only then did I notice the silver hearing aids peeking out from behind her ears.

"I'm Evelyn," I repeated.

"Much better." The lady took the hall pass and nodded. Her dark hair moved with her, like a halo reaching out from her head. "Welcome, Evelyn. I'm Miss Hawk. I won't ask you what you're in for. If you're here, it means you messed up, but we can learn from our mistakes. Find a seat and pick some work to do." She glanced at a note on her desk. "I see here you are allowed breaks as needed and to wear the headphones in class as long as you aren't using them for music?"

I nodded, trying to show I was listening. I never used my headphones for music. It sounded tinny in them since they were so old. They didn't have fancy sound-blocking technology, either, or anything. All they did was muffle sounds a little, enough that I could focus better on the conversations I was having and not get overwhelmed when stuff got too loud. But I didn't think Miss Hawk wanted me to explain, not when I was there because I was in trouble.

I rocked on my feet and waited, wishing once again that I hadn't messed up so badly.

"Very well," continued Miss Hawk. "If you behave, I'll let you go on your phone at the end of the day. At the end of the week, we'll reflect on what you've learned and how to avoid having to spend time with me again. Not that I mind the company."

She chuckled, a warm sound that brushed away some of my worries. Miss Hawk seemed okay. She wasn't at all what I expected the ISS teacher to be like.

I offered her a weak smile, then shuffled over to a desk and dropped my backpack beside it. I sat down and pulled out my packet of homework. I had gotten my homework from all my teachers on Friday afternoon, but now as I stared at it, I couldn't make myself focus.

Jeremy's laugh kept echoing in my head. I saw my mama's disappointed face again and again. My mind latched onto how many days I'd be losing. How impossible it would be to win at this point with only a month left to rework the robot. And it needed to be reworked, I knew now. My original design had a lot of flaws.

My robot was a colossal failure.

I was so lost in my misery that I didn't even notice the door open again, not until a notebook slammed onto my desk. I jumped and stared at Allie.

She placed her hands on her hips and looked at the notebook.

Mama's words echoed in my head. I had to apologize again. I had to be a better person.

"I'm sorry about Friday," I said. My voice shook as much as my hands did. "Sorry I got you in trouble and said such mean things. I shouldn't have picked a fight."

"No duh," said Allie. "But you did, and here we are." She made a face and shrugged. "I've been here before, anyway."

She looked pointedly at the notebook again. I glanced at my desk. The notebook she had dropped there was simple and red—a plain spiral-bound. Allie looked at it like it meant something. Hesitantly, I flipped open the cover.

My heart thudded.

On the first page was a beautiful drawing of my little clawbot. It looked perfect, down to the texture on the plastic wheels. Allie had even sketched the claw, with its gears and hinges perfectly detailed. The whole drawing looked ready to pop off the page. It wasn't realistic, but it wasn't cartoony, either. Somehow, she had drawn a brilliant mix between realism and not. She must have drawn it from memory, from those few times she saw the robot. It was better than perfect!

I flipped the page and gasped. On the next page she showed the robot from many different angles. There was a view from the top, from the right, and even from behind. It made a flawless multi-view sketch. When did Allie learn what a multi-view sketch was?

"Allie. Did . . . When did you draw this?"

Allie shuffled on her feet and looked away. A bit of red colored her freckled cheeks.

"Last night." She shrugged. "Look. I'm sorry I broke your robot. That wasn't cool of me. You were a total jerk yesterday, but you didn't have to say what you did to Principal Gilbert, so I guess . . . I dunno. Call this a truce?"

I stared at Allie, my mouth opening and closing. Allie had just apologized. Allie was offering to make peace with me. Allie had started the design notebook.

Maybe I had misjudged her.

I flipped back to the first page, looking at that beautifully drawn robot.

Allie kept talking. "It's not perfect. I read that we're supposed to show how the robot got built, but I wasn't here for all those steps, so this is all I have. Also, you'll have to do the math stuff because I don't know what half of the things they want written down even are."

Allie crossed her arms and made a face.

I couldn't believe it.

Then it hit me. I was so oblivious. I had been making Allie go get parts all week long and had been begging Varsha, who hated drawing, to do the notebook. Yet, the answer had been there all along. *Allie* should have been doing the notebook from the minute I learned she liked art. Maybe she would've been more willing to take part in robotics. What kind of team leader was I if I hadn't even realized that?

"This is amazing," I said to Allie. "If I describe the way it looked when we were building it, do you think you could do the in-progress pictures too?"

Allie nodded, though she pursed her lips and didn't look thrilled.

A thought occurred to me. I glanced over at Miss Hawk. Would she care that we were sitting here talking? Allie's gaze followed mine. The teacher was sitting behind her desk, but she was watching us with her eyebrows raised.

"Hey, Miss Hawk." Allie waved at the teacher. "If I promise to work for once, can I work with Evelyn? We have robotics stuff to finish."

Miss Hawk smiled. Her face lit up again, making those harsh eyes seem beautiful in that moment. "I think that would be fair. I'm glad to see you motivated today."

"Thanks," said Allie, making a face. She turned to look at me. "Let's finish this design notebook. That way you can do the whole robotics tournament stuff you were crying about."

A little hope clicked into place. I bit my lip and looked at the notebook. This might work. If Allie helped me . . . if we got the notebook done . . .

There was a month to go. Maybe, just maybe, there *was* time to rebuild the robot.

Except for one thing.

I closed the notebook and sagged in my chair. "It doesn't matter," I said. "Our programmer quit. Without Alex's programming skills, even the best robot in the world will be useless."

Allie shrugged. "Leave Alex to me." She grabbed the desk next to mine and dragged it over, then sat. She leaned forward and looked me dead in the eye. My neck prickled, and I glanced away, then back at the bridge of her nose.

"Listen up," said Allie Wells. "I can help you get your team back together. But if you drive them away again, that's on you."

I nodded, not trusting myself to speak.

Allie continued, "I'll even point out when you are being overbearing. And I'll help you with the notebook. But no more fetching parts and stuff. I don't like all the math and science-y stuff, but I'm not useless, either. I want to draw the notebook pictures, and then I want to draw my own stuff whenever I'm done. Do we have a deal?"

Cogs turned in my head. I felt a little hope crank into place. It wasn't all over. There was still time to win. I had a chance again, to make it to Worlds and to see Naiely. I'd show my moms that robotics does still make me happy, and I'd make it onto the Tech Tigers' team, taking that first step to my perfect future. The idea was so wonderful, I was almost afraid to let myself dream it.

I bit my lip and looked at the notebook. "You've got a deal."

CHAPTER TEN
ALLIE

I would never admit it to Evelyn, but working on the notebook was kind of fun.

Normally, I drew people or the things I noticed around school. I drew anime, fan art with my favorite characters, and whatever else popped into my head. Trying to draw the robot was hard. It had so many little parts, and I had to show each accurately. If the robot wasn't accurate in the notebook, it would lose points during tournament judging. Every detail had to be on point.

It was the hardest art I had ever done.

I liked it.

Not that I wanted anyone to know. I kept my mouth shut as we hunched over the notebook, adding in measurements and drawing more pictures here and there. By the time the school day ended, we had five pages filled out. I didn't understand half the stuff written on them. Gear ratios, cartridge sizes, C channels, and brackets. It was like a whole different language.

Still, I appreciated the way Evelyn's eyes widened as I sketched out picture after picture for her. As the robot took shape on the page again and again.

"We actually have a chance," said Evelyn breathlessly when the school bell rang and Miss Hawk said we could leave. Evelyn grinned at me, even as she put on the large blue headphones she always wore. "We should get the team together tomorrow. I know we're suspended, but maybe we can convince the others to come in and work a little before school. Say an hour before school starts?"

I groaned. Work before school? Sounded like misery.

Oma's smiling face flashed behind my eyes. I remembered my promise to her, that I would make things right. Something told me the notebook wouldn't be enough. I broke the robot, so I had to help Evelyn fix it.

"Sounds boring," I said. Evelyn gulped, and she rocked back on her feet. "But whatever. I'll see you before school tomorrow."

I stuffed the sketchbook into my backpack and slung it over my shoulder. Evelyn grabbed her backpack too and looked up at me. I winced and slouched slightly, remembering how much I towered over her. Next to Evelyn, I really was a beanpole.

"Thank you," said Evelyn, smiling wide. It was the first time I had seen an actual smile from her, and not the fake, pretending-to-be-nice ones she usually wore.

I frowned and looked away. I didn't need her thanks. I was only in the situation *because* of her. "Whatever. I'm going to get your programmer back. Where does he hang out?"

"Try the computer lab. I'd see him there sometimes when Naiely and I went there after school, and . . ." Evelyn fell silent. When I glanced back over, she was biting her lip and staring down at the desk.

Naiely? Evelyn had mentioned the name before too. Something about Naiely being her best friend and moving. It was strange to think that annoying Evelyn actually had friends.

I shrugged and pushed my way out of the ISS room. The sun beat down in the courtyard beyond, casting sharp shadows across the buildings and lighting up the concrete with glaring brightness. Sweat tickled the back of my neck. The air hung heavy from the heat, even though it was late September. It was the sort of hot that made you feel like you were melting. Still, compared to the heat when school had started in July, it almost felt nice.

Students rushed every which way, hurrying to the buses or parent pickup. It was a sea of faces, the sort of crowd you could get lost and forgotten in. I squinted into the chaos, searching for any sign of Alex.

Evelyn specifically mentioned the computer lab, so I headed there first. I wove through the crowds toward the lab, scanning for Alex.

Only, Alex wasn't anywhere inside the small, brick room. He wasn't over by the library near the cafeteria, either. I frowned. Where was he?

I crossed my arms and scowled. For all my bravado back in the ISS room, I didn't actually have a plan. I was winging it here, and that didn't seem to be working.

Okay. I knew that Alex was a nerd, specifically a robotics nerd. He was usually found with Santino, 'cause those two were a *thing*. I tried to imagine where else they could be. Maybe walking hand in hand somewhere, talking about robotics and nerd stuff? Maybe kissing somewhere, since that's what people did when they were dating, right?

The mental picture made me feel kind of funny. When I tried to imagine holding hands with somebody or asking somebody out, it felt wrong. Not in an "Ewwww, cooties" way. I was in eighth grade now. I was more grown up than *that*. But every time I overheard my classmates talking about crushes and dates, I just didn't get it. Why would I *want* to have a crush on anyone? It sounded exhausting.

I shook my head and focused back on Alex and Santino. They were the type of kids that liked to stay after school. They could be in the robotics room. I slipped out of the library and walked around the building. The school emptied out, students disappearing like rivulets of water running off a shiny outdoor table.

I was almost past the cafeteria when I noticed a small group standing nearby, in the hidden corner that teachers didn't always remember to watch. I often liked to hide away in that corner, when the cactus garden got too busy, and I wanted to be away from the world. For me, it was a peaceful place.

Alex probably wouldn't agree. He stood in the corner,

no Santino in sight. He held his hands clenched into fists and had an angry glare in his eyes. Jeremy Jacobs, Mike Willows, and D'Angelo Tapia surrounded him.

I scowled. Jeremy Jacobs gravitated toward trouble more than I did. I had spent multiple days in detention with him, and Jeremy learned early on not to mess with me. If Principal Gilbert wanted to send somebody to Sunrise, he should consider Jeremy. At least *I* wasn't a bully.

Jeremy took a step toward Alex and shoved him back against the faded red bricks. Behind him, Mike and D'Angelo laughed. For a second, I wondered if I should leave. If I got into a fight, Principal Gilbert wouldn't be able to ignore it a second time. Especially not when my last fight was *literally* just last week. Sunrise would be closer than ever.

I gulped. But then I imagined Mom beside me, tutting and asking me if I was really going to let this happen. Mom used to face down criminals and grown bullies every day in the courtroom. She'd be disappointed if I ignored Jeremy now. I couldn't let this go.

"Hey!" My voice rippled across the quiet courtyard, like a splatter of paint across a clean canvas. Jeremy froze. He looked over his shoulder, and his eyes widened as he saw me. I stormed over.

"What are you doing?" I asked, raising an eyebrow.

"We're just talking." Jeremy crossed his arms and glared at me.

I looked at Alex. He held his shoulders tense and his eyes cast down. I didn't really know Alex. He was always playing games on his phone, and we never talked much in class. But I knew that look on his face, that fear and sadness. Like he was caught in a nightmare he just wanted to end.

My anger uncurled and stretched.

I took a step toward Jeremy. Jeremy flinched.

"I'm sure you were," I said, anger seeping from my voice. It rolled through my bones, crawling out from the hole I had shoved it in last night. Smaller than it was but still burning. Dangerous. "Conversation is over now. Go away."

"Seriously?" asked Jeremy. "Butt out, Allie. This has nothing to do with you."

He glanced at Mike and D'Angelo to back him up. Neither would meet his eye. Instead, both gazed at the ground and shuffled their feet.

"Oh, but it does." I took another step toward Jeremy, clenching my fists. He flinched again and took a step back. "See, Alex is on my robotics team, and I care *deeply* about robotics now. So when you upset Alex, you upset me. Got it?"

"Jer . . . ," muttered D'Angelo. "Let's go."

Jeremy shook his head.

"Jeremy. You can't pick a fight with Allie Wells," hissed Mike through clenched teeth.

Jeremy hesitated a moment more. Then his shoulders slumped.

"Fine!" he snapped.

He hurried away, giving me a wide berth. His friends followed. I waited until he had made it to the circle of outdoor tables a few yards away before I called after him.

"Hey, Jeremy. If I see you bugging Alex again, you and I will have a fun conversation." I faked a smile and hit my fist against my hand, telling him what sort of conversation it would be. Jeremy's face flushed. He glared at me for a second more, then turned and ran, his friends following.

I grinned. It felt good to send Jeremy running away with his tail between his legs.

"Um . . . thanks?" said Alex. He walked out of the alcove and sat down at a table. He glanced at me nervously, scratching at the back of his neck.

I shrugged. "No problem. Those guys are the worst."

"Yeah." Alex looked down at the table, then back up at me. "Why are you helping me? You hate robotics."

There it was, *the* question. "Yeah, well, I also hate bullies," I said. "You looked really sad, and it sucks to feel like that."

I stared at the cafeteria windows, watching the way they distorted reflections, turning the bright sidewalks and green plastic tables into shimmering blurs.

"Oh. Well, thanks again," said Alex.

His reflection was looking up at me, and I stared at him in the warped windows. It was easier to look at the reflection than at the actual person.

I took a deep breath and said, "Actually, I was looking for you for a reason."

"Yeah?"

"Will you give robotics another try?"

Alex sat silent for a while. His wavy reflection stared down at the wavy table. When he spoke, it was almost in a whisper. "I like robotics. I do. But it's not fun anymore, and I don't want to go back. Mrs. Powell said I can change my schedule if I stop by the office tomorrow."

I sighed. "I get it. Evelyn's super annoying."

"Tell me about it," grumbled Alex. "She wasn't that bad at the start of the year, but then Naiely left, and Evelyn's been the worst for the last few weeks. Did you know, at our tournament last week, she wouldn't even let DJ drive the robot? He wanted to practice in the arena before the match started, and she wouldn't let him. He's our team driver, but she still refused to give him the controller! Then when we got bored and wandered off, she got mad at us. What were we supposed to do when she wouldn't even let us *touch* the bot? I don't want to deal with that anymore."

I winced. That did sound bad. I had made a deal, though, and I had to convince Alex. I shrugged and turned around to face him. "I know, but I think she's going to try to be better. Give her one more chance. If she keeps being terrible, then you can quit."

Alex traced the plastic on the table, his brows drawn together in thought. "Why would she be any different now?" he asked.

"Because," I said, crossing to the table. "I'm helping her. And I'll call her out on it when she's being bossy." I raised an eyebrow and stared at Alex.

He hesitated a moment more, then shrugged. "Fine," he said. "But she needs to let me test the code on the robot. I can't fix the programming if I never get to see it in action."

I nodded. "Great. We're going to meet before school tomorrow, since she and I are in ISS all week and won't be in class. Can you let Santino know?"

Alex stood and reached for his phone. "Yeah. We're hanging out later. I can also text Varsha and DJ if you want."

"Perfect. Tomorrow. Before school. Make sure to be there." I turned and walked away, leaving Alex and the cafeteria behind. Getting to school early sounded miserable, honestly, but I wasn't going to say that. I needed Alex and the others to buy into this. To show up and give Evelyn one more chance. I promised Oma I'd make things right, and this seemed like the easiest way.

I just had to get the robotics team working together.

Mom used to always say that teamwork wasn't bad, especially whenever Dad was grumpy about something his coworkers did. You just had to show people what they had in common and help people find what they were good at. She did it all the time when managing her clerks and interns. Surely, I could do it too.

The team was like a picture done in five unique styles, none of which matched. I didn't think it was possible to meld the picture together . . . but it could be entertaining to try. As I started walking back to Oma's house, I imagined how I'd draw the team. A way to show the chaos they were.

Perhaps this would be a mistake, a headache worse than any class, but I could at least try to make things interesting. Mom would have approved, anyway.

CHAPTER ELEVEN
EVELYN

My heart was thumping at a million rpms when I got to school the next morning, racing faster than a battlebot in the final round. What would I find inside the robotics room? Would the team be there like Allie promised? Or would the room be empty?

I stopped in the cactus garden outside the blue door and hesitated. My hand froze on the door handle, and I rocked back and forth on the balls of my feet as horrible thoughts hit me.

What if Allie fails to get the team together? Alex was so mad at me the other day. I can't imagine him coming back, whatever Allie claims.

I took a deep, shuddering breath.

There was only one way to find out. Only one way to see if Allie could really work the miracles she claimed.

I rolled back my shoulders, trying to muster all the confidence of Mum making a tough sale at a craft fair. Then I pushed open the door and stepped inside.

Allie was already there. She sat back by the robotics table, her sketchbook in her lap and her pencil flying across it. I waved to Mrs. Weir at her computer and walked over to join Allie.

"I've been thinking about it," said Allie. She didn't glance up from her drawing as she spoke. "And I think you will have to make some big changes if you don't want the team to run away again."

Allie sounded so matter-of-fact. So straightforward. I stuck a strand of hair in my mouth. "What changes?"

"For one thing, you can't do any of the building this week. Or the planning. Point everyone to ideas and do that team leader-y stuff, but if you start planning, you'll take over like you always do and drive them away. So you know . . . Don't do that. This week, you leave all the important stuff up to the team."

I pulled my hair through my teeth and stared at the ground, kicking my foot across the linoleum. What Allie said sounded close to what Mrs. Weir had told me the other day.

"Okay," I said.

"I'll call you out on it if you're getting controlling," Allie said. She frowned at her drawing and erased a bit. "If I have to do this boring robotics stuff, then I want it to at least be tolerable."

I opened my mouth to retort. Robotics was *not* boring! I stopped myself with the words on the tip of my tongue. I needed Allie to help me. I couldn't do this alone. Instead of snapping back, I closed my mouth and nodded.

"That's fair," I said instead.

I looked around the big empty room. The 3D printers were already running; Mrs. Weir usually ran prints for her engineering classes in the morning. Along one wall, the robot batteries blinked red as they charged, and the AC had kicked in, making loud, rattling noises. The robotics room came to life, like it did every day, loud enough I was thankful I had my headphones to muffle the noise.

But other than Allie and Mrs. Weir, nobody else was there yet. It was almost an hour before school started. I wondered if the others would even show up.

I glanced nervously over at Mrs. Weir. She sat at her computer, rapidly typing something. When she saw me looking, she smiled and waved, then went back to her computer. I almost expected her to call me over to tell me I had lost my job as Team Lead. After all, I got into a fight and drove Alex away.

But Mrs. Weir said nothing. She kept working at her computer, her brows furrowed and dark shadows under her eyes. There was a rumor that she had two jobs. I had once overheard some kids in math say they saw her working at the local coffee shop, and before she moved away, Naiely swore she once saw Mrs. Weir stocking shelves in the grocery store. It did seem like our teacher was always really tired. Maybe she was so busy, she forgot to be upset with me.

Still, Allie and I had gotten into a fight, and fights never happened in Room 303. I frowned. Mrs. Weir should have at least been a little angry.

"Did you say anything to Mrs. Weir?" I asked Allie suspiciously.

Allie shrugged. "I apologized for breaking the stuff." She made a face, looked at her sketch, then rotated the sketchbook and started drawing again. "And I might have asked her to wait until after she sees how we work together this morning before deciding anything with you and the Team Lead stuff."

I stared at Allie again, really stared at her. This was . . . cool of her.

The door clicked open, and I spun around. Alex, DJ, Varsha, and Santino all filed into the room. When they spotted us, they walked over hesitantly.

"Hey," said Alex. He held Santino's hand, and Santino gave him a comforting look. My stomach sank more. Were they really dreading being here *that* much? Was I that terrible of a Team Lead?

Allie grinned. "Hey. You got everyone!"

Alex shrugged. "Now I don't owe you anymore," he said. Allie nodded, and once again I wondered what she had done. How had she convinced them to come here?

The others gathered around the robotics table. The silence stretched out, broken only by the sounds of machinery around the classroom.

"I wasn't going to come," said Varsha. "I've got a new fanfic I need to post, and I *was* going to go hang out with my friends before school. But my mom saw Alex's text to me and made me." She sounded annoyed. I blushed and looked at the table. Our broken robot was in a plastic bin on top of it.

"I'm sorry," I said, staring at the blurred shape of the bot through the dark plastic. "I've been cruel to the entire group, and I'm gonna try to be better."

Nobody said anything. I rocked on my feet, waiting. What now? I didn't know where to go from here.

"I need to be honest with you all," said Allie. She leaned back in her chair and kicked her legs up on the robotics table. "You guys are kind of a joke. You're a mess. I would know, because I'm a mess too. But it doesn't need to be that way."

Allie added a few more strokes to her drawing, ignoring how everyone bristled at her words. I wanted to be mad. What she was saying was mean, but it was also true. I couldn't come up with an argument.

"This is how I see you guys." Allie flipped over her sketch-book and held it out so we saw what she had been working on. It was a fantastic, anime-style drawing, showing all five of us gathered around the table. Heat rushed to my cheeks as I noticed the character that represented me. The short girl with her fists clenched and hair practically standing on end as she yelled at the other kids.

Alex ran a hand through his curly hair and let out a breath. His depiction wasn't much better. His character sat at a computer, hunched over his phone and unaware of the world around him. Allie had drawn him with spirals for his eyes, as if the phone screen had hypnotized him. Santino stood behind him, blinded by little hearts in his eyes. Varsha and DJ, meanwhile, were shown goofing around, throwing parts through the air and looking ridiculous.

"Ouch," said Varsha. She drew her long brown ponytail over her shoulder and ran her hands through it. "That's harsh."

"Look, I'm assuming you're all here because you *like* robotics, or liked it when you joined. You're the smart kids. The good kids." Allie made a face. She snapped the sketchbook closed. "Maybe it's time for you to do the robotics thing again. Try to be a team that isn't a giant mess."

"That would be easier if Evelyn let us work on the robot," said Alex.

"And have fun while doing it," added DJ. He frowned and leaned back in his seat. "Robotics is about as fun as hugging a cactus right now. And I'd know. Alex dared me to do that last week."

Everyone looked at me. I gulped. I tried to think of what Naiely would do. She got the team assembled at the beginning of the year. She was the people person, the glue that held everyone together. I was the brains of our operation. Together we were a great team, but alone, I *had* been overbearing. I was so focused on my dreams. On Worlds. On Naiely. On becoming an engineer one day. I forgot that not everyone could be so driven.

"I'm sorry," I said. "If you give me one more chance, I'll try to be a better Team Lead. I'll let you build the bot, and test it and drive it and do everything else."

Varsha crossed her arms and looked me up and down. The others looked to Varsha. I saw them now, watching her to see what she decided. They would follow her lead. If I could convince Varsha, then we had a chance.

"I promise." I ran my fingers through my hair, twisting around the strands. "It'll be like at the start of the year, when we still had fun. When we had Nai—well, you know."

Varsha's harsh gaze softened. "Fine," she said, slowly. "I'm willing to give you a chance."

Beside her, Alex nodded. "My mom won't let me swap classes, anyway," he said. "So why did you want us here? It's early."

I let out a breath. It worked. It really worked!

"We asked you here to work on the robot," said Allie. She nodded at me before turning back to her sketchbook.

"I need to—" I stuttered to a halt as Allie raised an eyebrow. I cleared my throat, started again. "We should start by replanning our robot. My design didn't work."

"No duh. Though it could have if you had let everyone help you with it." Varsha stared me down with her intense brown eyes.

I tugged nervously on the red strands of my hair. "I— we should brainstorm some ideas for a new bot. We don't have time to make it complex, but we can at least make something that works better."

Varsha nodded. "We, huh? Do you mean that, or are you going to take over again?"

My palms broke into a sweat as all the members of my team stared at me. I knew what I had to say, but the words got stuck in my throat. Could I really do this? Give up control? What if they messed up? What if they ruined everything? What if—

Allie saved me from having to answer. She pulled out the design notebook and slammed it onto the metal table. She flipped to a blank page.

"She means it," said Allie, clicking open a pen. "Let's brainstorm. Tell me what to draw."

I took a deep breath while everyone was looking at Allie. Calm. I had to be calm. There was no way to win without the rest of the team, and the team would leave again if I voiced my thoughts. I closed my eyes and took another breath. Hold for four seconds. Let it out. I opened my eyes.

Allie gave me a quick smile, and I forced back my surprise. Allie was acting like an entirely different person today. She must really want our deal. She would help me and in exchange, I had to let her do her own drawings in between. No more supply gopher. Just Allie participating on *her* terms.

If it helped us win the tournament, I could do that.

"You heard Allie," I said. "What ideas do you have?"

Santino sat up in his chair and ran a hand through his mop of hair. He leaned in to stare at the design notebook. "Hey," he said, "what if we make a reverse stacker like the ones on YouTube?"

DJ hesitated a second and nodded. "Yeah. Like the one the Tech Tigers have!"

I sighed at their name. The Tech Tigers. The best robotics team in all of Phoenix. Their robot had been perfect. Their *entire team* was perfect.

Allie snorted, and as I looked around, I realized that everyone else in the group had the same expression as me. That longing want.

"Okay." I blushed. It was time to focus, not to daydream. *Be a leader, Evelyn. You can do this.* "Alex, can you find the Tech Tigers' YouTube channel?"

"YouTube's blocked on the computers, remember?" Alex shrugged.

"Yeah, but don't you have an amazing data plan?" I asked. He had to have a good one with all the games he played.

"Right. Give me a sec," said Alex, drawing out his phone. His fingers flew over the screen as Santino walked over to watch.

"Hey," said Varsha. "Can we try the new wheels on this robot? I know they're not as big, but they have the omni-directional parts on them, and it will make the robot move better if we use them."

I frowned. The new wheels were too small. Omni-directional or not, the old wheels were bigger and would give it more traction. I opened my mouth to say that, but behind Varsha I saw Allie. Allie flipped over her sketchbook again and held it up, showing me the picture of the dys-functional team. I gulped.

"All right," I said. "But if they don't work, then we're swapping to the big wheels."

Varsha smiled, a bright smile that showed all her teeth. "Well, duh." She laughed. "Isn't that the point of robotics?

We try something, and if it doesn't work, we try something else? That *is* how the design process works."

I shrugged. I'd rather get things right the first time. Still, I told Allie I would let the team decide everything important for the week, and I was sticking to that. Even if it meant the robot was a disaster. I knew how to build a simple clawbot, so worst-case scenario, I'd rebuild mine right before the tournament. And this time I'd make sure it couldn't fall apart so easily.

I had to. There was no room for anything less than perfection. I couldn't disappoint my moms again. Not with how hard they were working to provide for me.

I took a deep breath. "I guess."

"Hey, look!" shouted Alex. He held up his phone and waved it around. "We found it. The Tech Tigers have a concept video for their bot here. Also, it looks like the Phoenix Wolves have a build video uploaded. There are all sorts of good ideas!"

Allie grabbed the design notebook and stood up. "Cool," she said. "Now what?"

I took a deep breath. *Be a leader.* I crossed over to Alex and the others. "We don't want to copy another team directly. That would be cheating, but we should sketch down any parts of the robot that look good, and then if we want to try it ourselves, we can add our own spin to it. We can take all the ideas we like and put them together into one awesome bot of our own."

"Great," said Allie. "Let's go. We only have so long before the bell rings. Tell me what to draw."

CHAPTER TWELVE
ALLIE

When I agreed to help Evelyn, I thought having to do robotics before school would be the worst. Oddly enough, it wasn't terrible. Annoying, yes. But not the nightmare I had expected.

We met again the next morning and brainstormed as many ideas as possible. Alex pulled up YouTube on his phone again, and we spent part of the morning watching what other teams had built. The best teams liked to post reveal videos, made to show off their robots. They had some intense-looking bots and paired the videos with electronic-sounding music. Some almost made robotics seem cool.

The others pointed out robot parts they liked from the reveal videos, and I sketched each part out so we wouldn't forget them. By the end of the morning on Wednesday, I filled over ten pages with designs for us to choose from.

At one point, we even looked at Team A's robot to see what they did right. They worked so well together that they had to have a good design. Yet, when we looked at their bot, Evelyn scoffed and showed us eight things that they should fix. Then Varsha pointed out that at least their robot worked, and Evelyn fell silent after that.

It was strange, really. What would Mom and Dad think, to know I was actually helping a robotics team?

They'd probably be proud of me. When I closed my eyes, I could almost imagine us sitting around the kitchen table at my old house, with Mom and Dad talking about how soon my math scores would improve too.

Oma was proud. When I asked her about going to school early for robotics, she started crying. Then she explained they were happy tears, and I thought my heart would break in that moment. If it made Oma *that* happy, helping Evelyn's team for a while was doable.

I'd help Evelyn and her team not to turn into a giant dumpster fire, and then once they weren't falling apart, all I'd ever have to do was work on the notebook. Do a few sketches when needed and draw my own stuff the rest of the time. Who knew, maybe robotics would become my favorite class, once I no longer had to do as much work.

My thoughts danced around that when I went to get my lunch on Friday. On a normal day of in-school suspension, we ate lunch in the ISS room. Since Evelyn and I had been working hard and doing well, and since another kid had thrown a few desks across the room, making a bit of a mess in there, Miss Hawk let us go have lunch in the cafeteria.

Not that I would ever eat in the cafeteria itself. With

its square brick walls and countless tables crammed close together, it was poorly designed chaos—a blend of colors and voices and smells and noise so loud you couldn't hear yourself think. Even the outdoor tables, scattered around under the shade of several pavilions, weren't much better.

Normally, I ate my lunch in the quieter calm of the cactus garden. I'd sit and munch on rubbery cafeteria food while staring at the saguaro, imagining myself at the arboretum with Dad beside me. He would point out the birds that had made a hole in the cactus and the splotch of brown peeking out. A nest, abandoned when summer hit. I would sketch a picture for Dad to add to his office, and he'd tell me stories about the animals that live in a cactus.

Then I'd tell him about robotics, and he'd laugh with me about how ridiculous the team could be. Or maybe he'd shake his head and tell me I should give robotics an honest try, that it's good for me. The daydream faltered there, leaving me empty and unsure. It was just a daydream. Dad was gone. It would never be possible to find out what he thought about robotics, or any of this.

I bit my lip, fighting back the emotions as I snagged a pizza from the cafeteria line and hurried through the chaos. With my lunch tray in hand, I headed toward the cactus garden.

I was halfway out of the cafeteria, passing by the tables outside, when I noticed Alex and DJ. They sat alone at one of the tables. DJ was working on homework, and Alex huddled over his phone. That was nothing unusual, but two tables away sat Jeremy Jacobs and his friends. They watched Alex intently. Mike nudged Jeremy, as if encouraging him to go do something.

I scowled.

This was none of my business. I was trying to stay out of trouble. The only reason I helped Alex before was so he would give Evelyn another chance. That was it.

I shook my head and kept walking. The cactus garden was my calm spot, my favorite area in the school. I wanted to get back there.

I only made it three steps before I hesitated again. I glanced back at the robotics boys and at the table beyond. Jeremy got up from his seat, a wicked grin on his face.

Mom would be disappointed if I ignored this. She wouldn't care that I already stepped in last time or that I wanted to be alone today. I imagined her now, frowning at Jeremy. *Will you let this slide, Allie? You're not going to stand up for Alex?* I wasn't sure what hurt more: thinking about Mom or imagining her disappointed.

My beast stirred and growled, shaking at the leash I had been securing around it these last few days.

I wanted to hide in the cactus garden, sit with my memories of Dad and better days. But here was Jeremy causing trouble once more. I couldn't ignore it. Not with Mom's memory looking over my shoulder again, and my beast pawing at the ground, waiting for me to act.

I spun on my heel and stormed over to the table. Alex looked up in surprise as I dropped my tray by him.

"Oh. Hello," said Alex.

DJ blinked, then also said, "Hey."

"Hey," I mumbled. I didn't want to explain myself. Instead, I reached for my backpack and pulled out the design notebook. Without looking at the boys, I got to work finishing up a sketch I had started earlier that day. After a few moments, DJ shrugged and turned back to his homework. Alex watched me a moment longer, then kept playing his phone game.

When I glanced up from under the screen of my blonde hair, I saw that Jeremy had backed down. He sat at his table again, pretending to not see us. Good.

"What are you working on?" asked Alex after a moment.

"Remember how you were talking this morning about combining the arm thing from that one robot with the wheels from the original one you guys built? I'm drawing that."

I frowned at the page and flipped over my pencil to erase a bit. My hair fell around me, like a golden curtain between me and the world. Normally, I'd like that. Right now though, it was in the way.

I tucked my hair behind my ears and kept working.

"The arm thing is called a lift mechanism," DJ said, pushing his homework aside and leaning over to study the picture. "Wow. That looks good. Alex, check it out."

Alex looked over and whistled. "Okay, that's impressive. Though, weren't we doing three wheels on each side, not two?"

I made a face at Alex.

"Yeah, yeah," I said, dragging the eraser across the page. "Whatever."

Alex snorted. "Really, though. You're good at that. I can't do more than stick figures."

"I can't draw at all." DJ laughed.

"Thanks." I blushed a little, even as I began redrawing the wheels. "I've been drawing since I was three. That's what my mom used to—what my oma tells me."

"I believe it. Your art is cool," said Alex. He smiled and turned back to his game. I worked for a couple more minutes, drawing in the wheels and the gears and labeling the parts I remembered the names of. DJ kept watching me, and I was highly aware of his eyes following my pencil around the page.

I looked up and frowned.

"Sorry!" DJ held up his hands. "It's just so cool to watch you draw." He laughed again and reached down to scratch at his leg, right above the leg splint he always wore. I stared at it for a second. I'd noticed it that day I joined robotics, and at first I just thought he had a sprained ankle or something. But the splint was made out of a thin plastic that hugged his ankle, rising to just a few inches below his knee. It secured over his sock and tucked into his shoe. It didn't look like any cast I had seen before, and now that I was actually talking to DJ more, I kind of wanted to know what it was.

I opened my mouth, then closed it again. Was that something I could ask about?

DJ noticed my struggle and laughed again. "It's okay. You can ask me."

"What is that?" I asked.

DJ shrugged. "So I have cerebral palsy. It means my muscles get too tense sometimes. I can't really grip things with my right hand, and I have to wear this splint to walk. Without it, I'd be pointing my toes at the ground all the time and messing up my ankle long-term."

I stared for a minute, then asked, "Do you have to wear it forever?" It didn't look very comfortable.

"Naw," said DJ. "I've had some surgeries to help, and my physical therapist says I might not need it anymore after this year. I'll lose my favorite fashion accessory." He sniffled dramatically and pretended to wipe at his eyes. Beside him, Alex chuckled.

"Is it comfortable?"

"Eh, sometimes?" DJ reached down again and tugged on the straps. "I'm used to it most of the time, but it can make me sweat through my socks more and that gets itchy. I sweat a lot."

I snorted. We lived in Arizona. Who didn't?

"I might have to get it replaced soon," added DJ, taking a bite of his burger.

"That's cool," I said.

"Are you still thinking of changing the strap color?" asked Alex.

"You know it. I want red for my new one, to match the robotics shirt!" DJ grinned. "But mostly I just want it to not pinch so much. I've been going through a growth spurt, you know."

"You're still shorter than me," said Alex.

"Liar. I'm at least as tall as you now!" retorted DJ.

"Prove it!"

I groaned and turned back to the notebook, slouching down in my seat. Why would anyone *want* to be tall? I tried to tune out their bickering and draw instead, adding more details to my picture of the robot.

Then I paused. I flipped to the front of the notebook, where I had pasted in a rubric I'd found from the tournament—robotics rules. Then I flipped back to my drawing and gulped.

"Hey," I asked, interrupting Alex and DJ. They were sitting back-to-back, trying to compare their heights without having to actually get up. "According to the notebook rubric, I'm supposed to label the *gear ratios*? What even are those?"

I tried not to look at the boys as I asked. Alex was in the same math class as me, and he probably saw how bad I was at the smart stuff. Last week, before the fight and my in-school suspension started, I butted heads with my teacher almost every day. I didn't get math, and Mrs. Vern—the math teacher—moved way too fast. But I didn't want people to know that.

Alex leaned over. "Oh! See how the wheels have gears attached?"

He pointed to my picture. I had drawn several gears in a row. One attached to the robot's motor and another to the wheels. It looked simple enough. I nodded.

"Okay, so look," explained Alex. "To make the wheels move faster, you have to have a big gear on the motor and a small gear on the wheels. When the big gear spins, it forces the small gear to spin faster to keep up, and that makes the wheels move faster. That's because of how the teeth, the notches you drew here, lock together."

I dropped my pencil onto the table.

"Please," I said, giving Alex the stink eye. "Not a robotics lesson during lunch."

He snickered. "Sorry! I get excited about this."

DJ laughed. "You're such a nerd."

"That's rich coming from the kid with gears shaved into his hair." Alex leaned over to elbow DJ. DJ laughed and ran a hand over his hair.

"Anyway," continued Alex, "the big gear has sixty teeth, and the small gear has twelve. So write down sixty and twelve. Those are the gear ratios."

I quickly scrawled the numbers down.

60   12

"Don't forget the colon," added DJ.

I added it in, then drew an arrow over each number pointing to the gears.

60 : 12

My head already pounded from the mini lesson, and my cheeks burned. Did they see how little of this I understood?

Shame flooded through me, crashing against the cliffs in that empty hole in my heart. Why had I sat down here? Why didn't I just ask Evelyn to do that part of the notebook later? My hand curled into a fist around the pencil.

"Oh!" cried Alex. He didn't seem to notice my raging emotions as he leaned over the notebook. "Oh, you also need to simplify the ratio using greatest common factor. Ummmm . . . it's either one to five, or five to one." He scratched sheepishly at his hair. "I don't remember which comes first, actually."

I stared at Alex, startled out of my frustration. He was a robotics kid, one of the smart kids. Alex was a genius programmer. How did he not know this?

Alex saw the expression on my face and grinned.

"What?" He laughed. "Not everyone is good at math. It's okay to struggle sometimes."

"Yeah. I have a C in math right now," added DJ.

I couldn't believe it. DJ acted so casual as he said that.

I always got in trouble in math, but my teachers thought it was because I didn't care. Not caring was better than them knowing how bad I was at it. Yet here DJ and Alex sat, openly admitting that they struggled with something.

"Wait," I asked. "How are you in robotics if you aren't good at math?"

DJ shrugged, "I like the driving and building parts. That stuff is easy."

"Yeah," added Alex. "There's a lot more to robotics than just math."

Like that, my rising frustration fled. I breathed a small sigh of relief. They didn't care if my math was bad. They really didn't care.

"So which one should I write?" I asked. I tried to make my voice sound normal as I spoke.

"I don't know." Alex bit his lip and glanced around. "Normally, I'd ask Santino. He's good at math stuff, but he got sick and went home early. Do you know, DJ?"

"Don't look at me. I just told you I'm bad at this."

"Hmmmm, maybe Varsha would know?" asked Alex.

We all looked across the cafeteria, to where Varsha was sitting with her friend group, off in the corner. She and her friends all seemed to be deep in conversation.

"They look busy. I don't want to interrupt," said DJ.

I frowned at the notebook. Everything I read online said that it had to be accurate, as accurate as possible. If we put the wrong gear combo, that would lose us points.

I was stuck on this team, and I didn't want us to seem like losers that couldn't even follow directions. I had enough of that in my other classes, like in math, when I'd answer every question wrong and could *feel* the other kids staring at me.

That's when I noticed Evelyn. She clutched her tray of pizza close to her chest and hurried out the cafeteria doors. She had her headphones over her ears, and her eyes locked on the library. I bit back a laugh. Of course she would go to the library for lunch.

"I bet Evelyn would know," said DJ, following my gaze.

The words held heavy in the air. It was one thing to work with Evelyn during class. But lunchtime? Lunchtime was sacred. I wasn't even sure what *I* was doing, sitting there with Alex and DJ. Like we were friends . . . or something. I could always wait and ask Evelyn about the gear ratios later. In half an hour when lunch ended, I'd be right back in the ISS room with her.

But there was something about the way she wove through the tables toward the library, trying to focus on the path in front of her and not make eye contact with anyone. She looked . . . lost. Lonely. I knew that feeling well.

Something stirred in me. Not my beast. This was softer, kinder, painted with sunset-yellow worry and memories of slate-gray loneliness.

At my old school, I didn't have many friends, not like I saw the other kids with. I didn't have my beast yet, that temper that constantly betrayed me, but I was quiet, liked to draw, and kept to myself. Sometimes it was lonely. It never felt good.

It couldn't feel good for Evelyn, either.

"Evelyn!"

I waved to her when she glanced over and motioned for her to come join us. Evelyn's eyes widened in surprise. She hesitated, and I imagined her thoughts like a scene from an anime. Her gazing across the cafeteria with ominous shadows on every side and us in the distance. Our table lit up more than anywhere else, drawn from softer lines than the rest of the students, but with our own shadows and uncertainty. I wouldn't blame Evelyn if she turned around and kept going, ignoring us. She had no reason to like me or the boys right now.

She bit her lip, and her fingers tightened around the lunch tray. Her shoulders heaved, like she was taking a great, big breath.

But then Evelyn relaxed her shoulders and walked over.

"What's going on?" She set her lunch tray down on the table and tugged nervously at a long strand of her deep red hair that fell over her shoulder.

"We need your help with ratios," said Alex. He pointed to the notebook. "Do you remember if we write the big gear first and then the small gear? Or is it the small gear and then the big gear?"

"Gear size doesn't matter. It goes output to input." She pursed her lips and leaned over the table to look at my diagram. "In this case, since the big gear is attached to the motor, the big gear is the input. It's the thing that's making everything else turn and move, you know? The small gear is the output, since it's attached to the wheels."

I blinked and stared. This was *way* too technical. "Why does it being attached to the wheels make it the output?"

"Oh, um"—Evelyn twisted a strand of hair around her fingers—"it's the output because it's being turned by the input, and that makes the wheels turn. It's kind of like cause and effect. Because the input gear—which is attached to the motor—is turning, that causes the output gear—the one controlling the wheels—to rotate. But when you write the ratios, you always write output first, so it would be one to five." Evelyn leaned forward and pointed at the picture, where I had drawn three gears in a row connecting the wheels.

"Ugh. So it's almost backward?" I asked.

Evelyn nodded. "Yep. Write output first, then input."

I hesitated, then crossed out my earlier numbers and added to the notebook:

~~60 : 12~~

12 : 60 becomes 1 : 5

"Does that look right?" I asked.

"Perfect!" said Evelyn.

Huh. That actually kind of made sense once it was written down. The small gear was the output and had twelve teeth. And the big gear was the input. It had sixty teeth, so the ratio was twelve to sixty. After simplifying the numbers, just like simplifying a fraction, it became a ratio of one to five.

Evelyn offered a quick smile, then grabbed her lunch tray again. "Let me know if you need any more help later."

"Cool, thanks," I said.

"No problem," she said. She turned away.

"Wait. Eat with us." I wasn't sure why I said it. It's not like I normally hung out with the boys at this table, either. Who was I to invite Evelyn to crash the party? Yet when I glanced to DJ and Alex, they nodded.

"Are . . . are you sure?" asked Evelyn.

I nodded. Evelyn smiled, then sat. For a moment, all was silent.

Awkward, unending silence.

We shuffled in our seats. Evelyn poked at her pizza, and Alex stared at the table. DJ cleared his throat and started fiddling with his homework again.

I bit my lip, then closed the notebook and leaned forward. "Hey, Alex, what game are you always playing, anyway?" It was a weak way to break the silence, but I couldn't think of anything better.

"Huh?" Alex pulled out his phone. "Well, it's actually about robotics. You play as a robot, and as you beat the other robots, you get parts to level up."

"Oh God. More robotics." I groaned. But Evelyn leaned forward to look at his phone.

"What's it called?" she asked.

"Robot Battles 23000."

"Oh!" cried Evelyn, clapping her hands together. "I've heard of that one. Naiely told me about it. Except she plays it on the computer."

Alex nodded. "Yeah. It started on the computer. But the mobile version is way, *way* better. See here, it has better controls thanks to the touch screen, and . . ."

For the rest of lunch I sat there, listening to them babble about robots and video games. When the conversation turned to analyzing how accurate the game was, I rolled my eyes and pulled out my sketchbook again. Yet as I sketched the pictures, lunch didn't seem so terrible, so long and alone. Evelyn, Alex, and DJ's chatter filled the air around me, leaving no room for anything else.

They weren't the cacti I usually hid among. They weren't the memories I danced between avoiding and seeking out. But maybe they could be my friends.

CHAPTER THIRTEEN
EVELYN

Monday morning marked the end of ISS and a return to normal classes. Like usual, I got to school early on Monday.

There was no guarantee the team would be there, no reason for them to all keep meeting before school. Not now that we would see one another in class. But I dreamed about the robot all night, and even if nobody else was there, I wanted to poke and prod at it.

I had an idea for a lever mechanism that would pick up five cubes at once. It was a variation on the clawbot we had made at the start of the year, but with a better claw and way more advanced. It would be heavier than the reverse stacker and make our robot slower, but if it worked, it would push us ahead in the competition. It could stack the cubes way higher than our reverse stacker plan, anyway.

Mama drove me to school that morning, like usual. Since Mum was still job hunting and didn't need to go out much,

Mama used the car most days. She always did daytime shifts at the restaurant where she worked so she could drop me off at school on the way. Sometimes we talked. Sometimes, when Mama was stressed, we said nothing the entire drive. Today though, Mama was happy.

"Evelyn, I'm proud of you," said Mama. "Not about the suspension, of course. But about how maturely you handled it."

I smiled at Mama, and she smiled back at me. We had the same smile, the sort that brought out dimples in the corners of our cheeks and crinkled our eyes. I loved that I had Mama's smile and Mum's determination. I nodded to Mama, clutching the plastic container I held tightly.

"Thank you, Mama," I said. "I love you."

"I love you too, sweetheart."

Mama pulled the car up to the curb at parent drop-off and pickup. Only a few kids hung around the school this early. It was an hour before school started.

I hopped out of the car and hugged my arms around the plastic box. My stomach twisted and turned in that way I was getting used to but still hated. I couldn't blame my classmates if they didn't want to keep coming early in the morning. We had only agreed to do it while Allie and I were in ISS. But a part of me would be disappointed if I walked inside the robotics room and found it empty.

I took a deep breath and hurried toward the school gates, past the many outdoor pavilions, and all the way to the 300 Building in the very back. I hesitated again outside the little blue door.

Like always, I wished Naiely were with me. We had chatted on the phone for an hour yesterday, and the box I held was her idea. She told me I needed to do something nice, something to show the team I liked them. Naiely was way better at social stuff than I was, so I always took her advice. Mama and I woke up extra early just to bake everything. I took a deep breath, remembering the way breathing could calm my nerves.

Deep breath in.

The last few weeks with my team had been full of frustrations and problems. But Naiely was right. If I wanted things to change, I had to change too. I had to show them I cared. Maybe, just maybe, the robotics team could become my friends. Maybe I could make friends without her. I had to try.

Deep breath out.

It wouldn't matter if I walked into an empty room, though. What if none of my teammates cared enough to be there? The thought made my heart pound again and my head feel buzzy. I gulped and rocked on my feet. There was only one way to find out.

I balanced the box on one hand so I could pull on my headphones with the other, rolled my shoulders back, and pushed through the door.

For a moment, I froze. My heart raced, and I was tempted to turn around and bolt back outside. The rest of the team filled the room. Alex huddled up in front of a computer, and for once he didn't have his phone out. DJ helped hold the robot steady while Varsha slotted wheels onto the frame we had built. Allie sat at the edge of the robotics table, her feet up on it and her sketchbook in hand. Only Santino was missing, but he had been out sick since Friday.

"Wow," Allie called out when she noticed me. "You're later than normal."

All the others turned to look, but I was afraid to meet their gazes. Afraid they would be rolling their eyes and giving me *that* look. The one they always gave me when I acted overbearing and annoyed them.

"Finally." Varsha tossed her long brown hair over her shoulders and grinned. "We were waiting for you. We're about to build the lift mechanism, but it turns out we don't have any of the parts we need for our plan."

DJ laughed. He made a dramatic flourish with his hands and said, "¡Ayúdandos! Help us, Evelyn Cole. You're our only hope."

I hesitated but finally looked up. Were they making fun of me?

"Seriously," said Varsha. "We're stuck. The reverse stacker relied on having tank treads, and Team A used them all. You have a backup plan, right? You usually do."

They needed me. They actually *needed* me. For the first time this year, my team wanted me to give them ideas. I ran my thumb along the edge of the plastic container and took a deep breath.

"I do have an idea for a claw mechanism that could pick up four or five cubes," I whispered.

"I knew it. You always know what to do!" Varsha cried. She spun to face DJ and held out her hand. "You owe me."

DJ made a face. He pulled a dollar out of his pocket and slapped it into Varsha's open palm.

"You were right," said DJ. "Waiting for Evelyn was a good call."

"Hey, I didn't doubt Varsha." Allie yawned and stretched. She kept her feet up on the table, balancing the design notebook on her knees. "Oh, Ev, when you have the design figured out, show it to me so I can add it to the notebook, cool?"

I smiled. The knot in my stomach unwound. They believed in me. Well, Varsha and Allie did, anyway. That was enough for me. I stepped farther into the room and held out the box.

"I brought some snacks if anyone wants them. Mama and I baked them this morning. We made muffins *and* cinnamon rolls." I dropped the Tupperware onto the robotics table and stepped back, wiping my sweaty palms on my jeans.

"Okay, *now* you're my favorite person ever," said Varsha.

"Dibs on a cinnamon roll," cried DJ, lunging forward.

"Hey, are those chocolate muffins?" asked Alex. "Bring me one. I have to show you something. I figured out the new code for our robot."

"Oh, I should bring conchas tomorrow," said DJ as he reached for a muffin. "Have you ever had them?"

"Yes! Soooo good," said Varsha. "If you do that, then I'm bringing a snack the next day. Ummm . . ."

DJ grinned. "Have your mom make gulab jamun again. Those were delicious."

"Naw. I'm saving that for when I make you all come hang out one of these days. You know what, I'll bring doughnuts." Varsha grinned and tossed her hair over her shoulder.

"Fair," said DJ. He turned to Alex, his words slightly muffled by the cinnamon roll he was shoving into his mouth. "Oh, did I ever tell you that my abuelo knows how to bake orejas too? They're these amazing Mexican ear-shaped pastries. He makes the best ones."

The next thing I knew, my teammates were talking food and laughing as they headed back toward the robot. Alex waved me over to his computer, and soon we had emptied the entire box of muffins. The rest of the morning became a whirlwind of food and robotics.

For the first time since the beginning of the school year, I wasn't as nervous.

I didn't need to breathe in and out to calm myself. I felt good, as good as the days when I'd work with Naiely late into the night, giggling over robotics and half-failed engineering projects.

DJ, Varsha, Alex, Santino, and Allie weren't that bad to be around. I had been so worried for nothing. Of course they wouldn't reject me, now that I was giving them a fair chance too. They were my team. And maybe they were my friends.

I'd like it if our team was friends.

CHAPTER FOURTEEN
ALLIE

New schedule or not, math class was torture.

I groaned and leaned back in my chair. At the front of the room, our math teacher, Mrs. Vern, babbled on and on and on and on about graphs. Only a smattering of it made sense, but nobody asked questions, so I sure wasn't going to start. Instead, I closed my eyes and let my thoughts drift.

Once, I asked Dad why math mattered. I mean, I planned to be an artist. It's not like I needed it. Math was always my worst subject. I meshed with math like crayons and watercolor. I hated it. Dad used to chuckle and say, *Allie, math is everywhere. You wait and see. Knowing math will help you understand so much more about the world.*

He was wrong. A year later, and I still didn't understand why math mattered.

A twisting of my heart reminded me I shouldn't think things like that. If Mom and Dad were around, would I think

Dad was wrong? Or would he have explained it to me by now in a way that I could understand?

That painful and hollow emptiness began to wind through my bones again, like it always did when I thought of my parents. I snapped my eyes open and looked around the room, searching for anything to distract me.

The teacher was going on and on, covering the whiteboard with graphs and formulas. I shuddered. Out of the corner of my eye, I spotted Alex. He glanced at the board and made a face.

My thoughts drifted back to Dad and Mom, to those days we would sit around the kitchen table. To them looking at my report cards and talking about getting me math tutors.

I imagined Mom saying, *It's not so bad if you give it a chance.* Then she'd wrap me in a hug and tell me to keep trying.

I frowned and pulled out my sketchbook, trying to redirect my thoughts.

I ended up drawing the cactus that used to be in our backyard . . . before I moved in with Oma. A prickly pear with a dozen different, round, flat pads. For a while I lost myself in the art, and everything else became background noise. The murmur of the teacher above me, the rustling of papers, the scratching of pencils. It blurred together into a melody that I barely heard.

I was shading in the cactus's spines when a shadow fell over my paper. I looked up. Mrs. Vern stood in front of my desk.

"Allie, I asked everyone to start their homework ten minutes ago. Please put the drawing away."

Mrs. Vern didn't like me. I could see it in the way her lips drew down, in her rigid stance and crossed arms. She resented that they added me to her class late in the year, all because of that horrible schedule change Principal Gilbert had made.

I pursed my lips and stared down at my picture. Beside my sketchbook lay a math worksheet that somebody had dropped onto my desk. I hadn't even noticed when Mrs. Vern had passed them out.

"I'm getting started," I lied.

Mrs. Vern raised her eyebrow. "Do you need help with any of the problems? Is that why you aren't working?" she asked. Her voice echoed through the quiet classroom, and some of my classmates glanced over.

Heat raced to my cheeks. My palms broke out in a sweat.

"I am working," I said. I glanced around the room, hoping my classmates would look away. My blush deepened, and I slid my sketchbook aside so I could grab the math worksheet. "See? I'm fine."

"It's okay if you don't understand it," said the teacher. She smiled wide and leaned over my desk. "Here, why don't you do problem number one for me?"

"I'm fine," I snapped. More kids looked now, not even trying to hide it. I wanted her to leave me alone. To not point out how bad at math I was. I sank down in my chair and stared stubbornly at the worksheet. It was all those graphs, the ones I didn't get.

"Allie, I'm not sure I like your tone." Mrs. Vern stood up and crossed her arms again, looming over me like a towering statue.

"I'm starting the work. I *don't* need help!" I wanted her to go away, to take with her those heavy gazes of the watching students. The whispers in the room had died out. Everyone was watching, waiting. Maybe they had heard the rumors and wanted to see me blow up again. Maybe they thought this was better than doing math homework.

It didn't matter. My fist tightened around the pencil, and I felt that beast of anger stirring. I glared around the room, daring the other kids to say anything.

Then my eyes locked onto Alex. He shook his head, his eyes wide. *Don't*, he mouthed.

Why did Alex care?

It surprised me enough that, for a second, I froze, my beast hesitating.

Mrs. Vern looked annoyed. "Listen, Allie. I know you are struggling. Principal Gilbert briefed me on what happened last year, and I am sorry, dear. It's okay if you need extra time, or a little extra help. I can—"

I clenched my fists and bit my tongue. Her words turned to a blur in my mind. My emotions warred within me. Anger and shame. Guilt and frustration. How dare she say that! How dare she believe I would use my parents' death as an excuse! How dare she even mention it!

"Miss?" Alex raised his hand as he called out. Mrs. Vern fell silent and looked over.

I barely noticed. I spiraled down, down, down into that dark place. My beast spiraled with me, breaking from its leash and expanding back into that thing I could never control as it crouched for the lunge.

"Miss? I'm stuck on this problem and really, really need help." Alex waved his hand in the air, trying to catch her attention.

"Alex, dear, please don't interrupt." Mrs. Vern's tone softened.

"But I'm really, *really* stuck. Please, can you help me?" Alex looked up at her, his eyes practically shining. For a moment he looked like a lost puppy, helpless and in need.

Was Alex distracting her? For me?

I stared at Alex, at the boy I had protected from Jeremy, sat with at lunch, and maybe even enjoyed talking to. Alex was helping me.

It slowed my descent, slowed that rage.

"One moment, dear," said Mrs. Vern. She turned back to me and sighed. "Please get started on your worksheet, Allie. We'll talk about this when I return." She turned and hurried to Alex.

I stared at the paper, letting my hair fall around my eyes to hide me from the looks of my classmates. I counted to ten, then thought of Oma and the promise I made her. Anything to pull my beast back, to force it calm and back in its box. I held my hands in my lap, clenched into tight fists, and squeezed my eyes shut.

Several long heartbeats passed. My beast retreated, taking one slow step after another, back to its box. It was still there, spots of red coloring the corners of my heart. But it wasn't ready to explode anymore.

A few more heartbeats, those long strokes of time, and I could uncurl my fists. I glanced up through the screen of my pale hair. Alex kept distracting Mrs. Vern, pointing at his paper as he shrugged helplessly. He caught my eye and grinned, then went back to shaking his head and pointing at the page.

Another long moment passed. I let out a shuddering breath.

By the time Mrs. Vern got up and walked back to my desk, I held my pencil in hand and started the first problem. I didn't get it at all. But if I at least wrote in some numbers, it would look like I was trying, right? My hand shook, and the pencil with it.

"I figured out how to do it." I refused to look up at her.

Mrs. Vern glanced at my paper. "Wonderful," she said. "Keep working and please let me know if you need help. It's okay to ask questions." She paced away to check on the rest of the class. I sighed and sagged in my seat.

When the bell rang, it was a blessing.

I rushed to shove everything into my backpack and hurried out of class. Alex caught up to me as I stepped out the door.

"Thanks," I said. I stared at the cracks in the concrete ground and slouched. Alex was one of the tallest kids in robotics, but somehow I *still* towered over him. Why did I have to be so freakishly tall? And bad at math?

"No problem. You know, she was trying to help you." Alex kept pace with me as he talked. I glared at him, and he smiled innocently. "What? She was."

"Yeah, well, she didn't need to tell everyone how pathetic I am. Or mention—never mind." I wasn't going to tell Alex about that. Last year, at my old school, everyone knew about my parents. All the time, people told me how sorry they were. People looked at me funny, like they felt bad for me. Pitied me. I hated it.

I kicked at a rock, then ducked around a group of students talking in the middle of the sidewalk.

Alex caught back up to me a second later. "Come on. It's math. Not everyone understands it, and nobody would think you're pathetic for needing help."

"Evelyn understands it fine."

"Sometimes. And sometimes she gets stuff wrong," said Alex.

I made a face at him as we dodged another group of students.

We turned around the corner of the 400 Building and started toward the 300 Courtyard with the cactus garden. Alex wasn't done.

"You know," said Alex, "I couldn't figure out the gear ratios the other day. Does that make me pathetic?"

I stopped and stared at him. "What? No! You're not pathetic at all."

"See?" Alex smiled and reached up to run a hand along his dark curls. "Needing help is normal. Nobody was watching you because they think you're bad at math. They were watching you because they wanted to see if you'd yell at the teacher again."

I blushed. He was right. The other kids here didn't know about my parents, but they knew about my temper. About how I always exploded and yelled or broke things. They were judging me, but at least it wasn't with pity.

"Whatever. Thanks for helping me," I said.

Alex shrugged and turned back to the robotics room. "I'm sure I owe you, anyway. Jeremy has never left me alone for this long before. Besides, we need you. Can't have you stuck in ISS again!"

I looked away, not sure what to say to that.

"Hey," added Alex. "If you don't want people to see you ask for help, you could ask Mrs. Vern in the morning. Or after school, when nobody else will see. Math will only get harder, but it is possible to learn. Some of us just need extra practice."

I scowled at the ground and said nothing.

"Welp," said Alex. "I'm going into class. I can cover for you if you need a few minutes. See you in there!" He pulled his cell phone out of his pocket and headed inside.

I hesitated a moment, then crossed to the bench inside the cactus garden. I was mad at Mrs. Vern, but the real anger was gone. It left me with only the hollowness and the frustration.

I bit my lip and stared at the saguaro.

Mom would say Alex was right. She would hug me and tell me she understood, then smile at me and argue that it was a teacher's job to help me. But did Mrs. Vern have to be so loud? To let everyone know that I didn't get it? To almost tell the entire class about my parents being gone?

Maybe I should get help on math. Not from Mrs. Vern, though. I bit my lip and kicked at the ground, thinking about my options. I could ask Miss Hawk. She was always willing to help with homework when I got sent to ISS. Or I could ask Evelyn. Even though she was annoying, she was pretty smart, and she had made the gear ratios make sense.

My head pounded from trying to think this through. I stared at the saguaro, waiting until the last moment before the late bell rang. I imagined I was back in Dad's arboretum, with him sitting beside me, giving me advice. Telling me that Mom was right and it's okay to ask for help. Maybe Dad would even be proud of me.

Math was frustrating but thanks to Alex, I hadn't exploded. I wasn't sitting in the office again, staring at Principal Gilbert. I wasn't kicked out. I had gotten mad, yes. But this time, I managed to not get in trouble. Alex had helped me, like I helped him the other week.

Alex didn't think I was pathetic or a failure.

He understood.

The saguaro cast its shadow across the bench where I sat. It stood tall and regal, despite the old holes bored in it by generations of woodpeckers looking for a nest and the many arms that should have weighed it down. It looked battered, worn out, yet still majestic. People understood it. They cared about it, despite its flaws.

Thanks to Alex, I kind of got what that might feel like.

"I get it, Dad," I whispered, tugging at the laces of my hoodie. "And maybe I will ask for help from somebody. Maybe."

CHAPTER FIFTEEN
EVELYN

The robotics tournament was in three weeks. Three short weeks.

Somehow, I was holding it together. It helped that our robot was halfway done. We had built the new base two days ago, forming a square of metal and wheels. Alex whipped up some programming for the wheels, Santino had made sure all the connections were secure when he got back to school, and DJ drove it all around the room for the last two days, making sure everything worked. By Friday afternoon, he was a pro at driving it.

"This might be the best robot ever," DJ cried, driving the robot toward Varsha. Its wheels squealed against the linoleum floor. Varsha shrieked and clambered up on a desk as the robot sped past where she had been standing.

"Watch it!" she said, even as she giggled.

"Careful," I called. I stood by the robotics table. In front of me were all the parts we needed for the lift mechanism, the part of the robot that would pick up the cubes. Allie leaned against the table as well, finishing up a sketch of the mechanism in the notebook.

We needed to build it. Once we did, it would look like a strange robot arm, but with two flat pieces of metal instead of hands. Like giant spatulas that pressed together. Those enormous pieces of metal would close around a cube, sandwiching it between them and lifting it up. They were big enough that they could hold several cubes at once.

Varsha hopped off the desk and ran over to join me at the robotics table. "I don't know about you, but I'm ready to build this thing."

She dragged over a chair and sat, pulling her legs up so DJ couldn't try ramming the robot into them anymore. She smoothed out the kurti she wore and made a face at DJ. Varsha didn't wear the pretty, tunic-like tops often, but when she did, she always looked amazing. I wished I had clothing that nice or could look that pretty wearing stuff. I blushed and got back to work sorting out the robot parts. DJ snickered and drove the robot away, whipping it through the chairs and toward the practice arena in the corner.

"Here," said Allie. She shoved the notebook our way so we could see the sketch. The page she showed us had a multi-view diagram on it. There were three pictures in all. One of the lift mechanism from the top. One of it from the side, and one from the front. On the next page was a 3D-style picture showing what it would look like when we connected it to the base of the robot.

The base that DJ currently drove in circles around Mrs. Weir's desk. I glanced over in time to see Mrs. Weir look up from her grading. She smiled as the robot base whirled around, then said, "Very good, though is it drifting a bit to the left?"

DJ stopped driving the bot to look at the motor, and I turned my attention back to Allie and her drawing, while making a mental note to check the motors myself later.

Varsha whistled as she looked at the picture, and I understood. Allie's drawings were amazing.

"Can you make me art for my fanfic someday? Pretty please?" Varsha asked. "I'm working on a *Legend of Zelda* fic right now, and I get almost two hundred views each week."

Allie shrugged. "Send me it sometime, and maybe I will. Though it depends on if I like the character."

"Oh, come on." Varsha laughed. "How can you not like *Zelda* characters? Link is always *adorable*."

I hesitated, listening to them talk. This seemed like the sort of thing I should join in. I did like those games too. Okay, so my Nintendo was a hand-me-down from my aunt, and my only copy of a *Zelda* game was old, old, old. But I'd watched playthroughs of all the new games on YouTube, including the remasters. And I did want to make friends, like Naiely said I should. I took a deep breath, then said, "He is really cute, especially in the latest game."

Varsha giggled and looked over. "Wait, I thought you liked girls?"

I shrugged. "I do. I like both."

"Ohhh. I bet you like Zelda too, then." Varsha grinned.

"Well, yeah. She's so smart." I blushed and looked down at the table. Princess Zelda was a researcher in the newest *Zelda* games, and she cared about science. Of course I liked her.

"Are we talking about *Zelda* games?" asked Alex, as he walked by the table. "I want to play the new one so bad."

Santino came up behind him, holding a handful of screws and Keps nuts. He dumped them onto the table and grinned at Alex. "Right? It looks fun. You could speedrun it. You're good at those."

"Oh yeah!" said Alex.

"Alex! The turns are sticky. Can we fix that with the code?" called DJ from over by the robot.

"Yeah, go away. Both of you." Varsha laughed. "We're having girl talk here, thank you very much."

"Okay, okay," said Santino. He grinned and grabbed Alex's hand. "Let's go."

Alex stuck out his tongue at us and let himself be led away.

"What about you, Allie?" asked Varsha as soon as the boys were gone. "Do you have a crush on any of the characters?"

Allie shrugged and pulled her drawing back. She looked down at it, letting her hair fall to hide her face.

"I dunno," she finally said.

"Well, *I* like Link," said Varsha. "He's the main character in most of my fanfics, except when I write about my OC instead." She tossed her hair over her shoulder, then straight-ened up, reaching for a pile of gears.

"He is great," I said. I reached down for a few gears as we talked, adding them to the stack we'd need for the robot arm. I itched to be working, to get the robot built. The itch traveled from my fingers to my toes, and I rocked on the balls of my feet. Varsha noticed.

She grinned. "We should get working, shouldn't we?"

I nodded. "But we can talk and build. Can you start on the arm part here?" I pointed to the notebook. "I'll work on the spatula hands, and we can connect them when done."

"Got it, Team Lead," said Varsha. She set to work.

It was getting easier to work with the team every day. DJ drove the robot everywhere, and Santino shadowed him around, learning how to be the backup driver. Varsha and I took over the building, while Alex worked on the programming.

Alex still played his mobile games, but he also worked just as much, which was nice. Already he had sat back down at the computer and was typing in a few lines of code.

"Try downloading that to the robot," he said to Santino and DJ after a moment, before turning to his phone.

Allie, meanwhile, continued to be in charge of the note-book. When she wasn't adding to it, like now, she would draw in her sketchbook while watching what everyone else was doing. I thought about telling her she needed to help more, but I didn't want to drive her away. Besides, the notebook wasn't all she did. Allie had one other important job that neither of us spoke about.

"Shoot. I think this gear is stuck," grumbled Varsha. She pulled on the pieces of metal she had connected, and the gears in between them let out a terrible *click, click, click* as they ground together.

Oh no. No, no, no, no. That was *not* a good sound!

We didn't have time for stuff to break! I winced and lunged over, snagging the piece away from Varsha. I dropped it on the table and bent over it, prodding at the gears. It looked like one gear had warped, and every time the robot arm lifted and the "elbow" opened, the gears would start grinding together.

Allie cleared her throat loudly. I glanced up and froze. She held up that picture again, the one where I was angry and taking everything over.

I blushed. Varsha glared at me with her arms crossed, even as Allie set her sketchbook back down. Oops.

"Sorry," I muttered, handing the robot arm back to her. "I panicked."

"How about you ask first next time?" snapped Varsha. My stomach sank, and I stared at the table. She was right to be annoyed. I did it again, that thing where I took over. Ever since Allie started calling me out on it, I noticed how much I did it. Sure, I would find the problem faster than Varsha could, but then Varsha would have nothing to do and would get bored. She'd wander off, Mrs. Weir would get upset that I had driven a teammate away again, and we would be back where we started.

"Sorry." I tugged on a strand of my hair and bit my lip.

"Whatever," said Varsha. Then she hesitated. "Did you see what's wrong with it, though?"

I looked up in surprise.

Varsha frowned at the robot arm. She poked at it and glanced slyly at me. "What?" she said. "I mean, I don't like you taking things right out of my hands . . . but you're also good at this whole thing. So? Why's it getting stuck?"

I gulped and took a deep breath before speaking, "Well, you built the arm perfectly, but look, that gear is warped. It means it will keep getting caught."

"Oh! So we should swap it for a new gear?"

"Yeah."

Varsha grinned and ran off toward the supply closet. I stared at the robot arm, sticking a strand of my hair in my mouth and pushing it around as I thought.

That gear came from the brand-new pack Mrs. Weir had ordered. If it was warped, some of the others might be too. What if we hadn't found that until the tournament? We would be in so much trouble. I hated that the robot had issues, but at least we knew to watch for the broken gears now. In fact, we probably should take extra gears to the tournament. If any others broke or got bent out of shape, we would replace them.

"Hey," said Allie. I looked up at her. She pointed her pencil at me. "You're doing better. Much less annoying."

"Thanks?"

Allie nodded, then stuck the end of her pencil in her mouth. "So," she said. "The notebook is missing a crucial part. I read last night that we have to have details on each team member and a description of how the team met. I'm no good at writing those things."

Right. That was a problem. I wasn't the best at writing, either, with a consistent B minus in English. It just was so boring, learning about similes and metaphors and analyzing stories and things. I liked hands-on stuff—like building robots—way more. Maybe another team member could do it, though?

I looked around the room. DJ was busy talking to Alex. I could hear their voices drifting through the room.

"Can you move the reverse button closer to the left? Then I can reach it easier." DJ gestured to the controller, and Alex nodded.

"Oh right," said Alex. "Sorry I didn't think about that."

"It's okay. I'll just hate you forever now. ¡Siempre!" DJ doubled over laughing at his joke even as Alex threw a spare robot wire at him.

I shook my head. He wouldn't be a good choice for the descriptions. DJ would get distracted making jokes and was too busy practicing the driving, anyway. Alex wasn't much better. Santino was good at math but not so much writing. Besides, he was busy learning to be the backup driver.

Then it hit me. We had a team member who loved writing.

A minute later, Varsha came back to the table. I waited until she dropped the gears, then asked, "Hey, can you help us with something? We need team bios written and a description of how we met as a team. It's for the notebook."

Varsha froze. She stared at me for a minute. A wide grin broke out on her face. "Can I make them like a story? All dramatic and stuff?"

I looked at Allie.

Allie shrugged. "The rules only say we have to have a bio for each team member and the group description. They say nothing about how it needs to look." She leaned over the table and pushed the robotics notebook toward Varsha. "Have fun."

"Oh, oh, oh! This will be great!" said Varsha. She grabbed the notebook and ran to her desk. "I'll finish the arm tomorrow! Evelyn, do you want to be described as a brilliant genius or an obsessive mastermind?"

I blinked. "Brilliant . . . genius?"

"Perfect." Varsha bent over the notebook, writing rapidly.

I took a deep breath and looked at the abandoned arm. Tomorrow. She'd work on it tomorrow. I hoped that was enough time. We had to be perfect. It was all that mattered. It was . . .

Breathe. I remembered Naiely telling me that when I was panicked over breaking the hair dryer. *Take a minute to breathe when you start worrying this much.*

I forced myself to stop.

Deep breath in.

If I finished the robot "hand," then it would be fine. I'd help Varsha connect the arm tomorrow. The notebook was important too, and one day wouldn't be too much of a delay.

Deep breath out.

"Hey," said Allie. "You okay?"

I looked up. Allie leaned forward on the robotics table and stared at me. I bit my lip and shrugged.

"I'm nervous. There's only three weeks left, and—"

"We'll be fine," said Allie. "The robot is almost done, *and* you have a good plan."

I nodded, though my heart seemed to beat like a countdown. Three weeks. Three weeks.

Allie rose and reached for her backpack. "Hey, instead of stressing about the tournament, can you help me with something?" She pulled out a purple folder covered in random drawings. As she kept talking, she stared at the table, refusing to meet my eyes. "I don't get graphs. Do you think you can . . . help?"

I looked at the robot parts on the table. I couldn't do much more with the robot hand until Varsha finished the arm, and helping Allie would be a good distraction.

"Sure," I said. "I like graphs."

"You would," grumbled Allie. She flipped open her notebook and pulled out her math homework.

"I'm surprised you don't," I said.

Allie glared at me, and I flinched. She started to close the folder.

"Wait. Sorry," I said. "That came out wrong. It's just, graphs are like art, and you love art."

"Graphs aren't art," grumbled Allie.

"I mean, they are, though? A graph is a picture that shows how the numbers work."

Allie groaned. "Yeah. Well, I'm not good at this like you."

"I'm not perfect at it, either." I shrugged and fidgeted with my headphones. "I'm solidly okay at math but not the best, and that's only 'cause Mama helps me with homework when I get stuck."

"So you can't help me?"

"I didn't say that," I said, leaning forward. I pushed the robotics parts aside and pulled Allie's homework over. "Okay, look here . . ."

For the next few minutes, we bent over the homework, Allie scowling and erasing stuff as I explained what to do. I wasn't a good teacher, but it was a distraction I needed. It almost kept me from noticing the constant ticking of time.

Three weeks to the tournament. Twenty-one days. We could do this. It would be fine.

CHAPTER SIXTEEN
ALLIE

The tournament was in two and a half weeks, and I sat in the Barton Junior High front office. Again.

I wasn't in trouble for once.

"Would you like to try the breathing exercises once more?" asked Mrs. Macquarie, the school counselor. Her room was nice and dim, with the overhead lights turned off and the room illuminated by a floor lamp that sent a golden wash across the walls.

"I think I've got it," I said.

Mrs. Macquarie had been making me practice pausing and breathing, taking three big breaths before reacting. It was boring to practice, but she claimed it could help me control my temper. I didn't want to participate at first, but then I thought about math class and how I was just barely keeping a leash on my beast . . . and my promise to Oma. So even though I wasn't sure about Mrs. Macquarie, I was doing what she asked me to. For now, anyway.

I hadn't been sure what to expect when she called me out of math class today. She was soft, like her room, and wore flowing blouses and pastels that made me think of Oma's favorite clothing. Her long, russet brown hair was held back by a loose clip, and several large strands had escaped to fall across her shoulders like gentle strokes of a paintbrush. When she smiled, it seemed real. She asked me all sorts of questions but didn't mind if I didn't answer them all and also didn't mind if I drew pictures while we talked. So maybe she was okay.

"I heard you've been doing better this last week," said Mrs. Macquarie. She smiled and leaned forward on her desk, grabbing a pen from a light purple cup. "That's what your teachers report. How have you been feeling, though? Do you feel you are doing better in your classes?"

I bit my lip, then nodded.

"I guess," I said as I stared at the page I was working on. I hadn't clashed with Mrs. Vern in math since class the other day, and the rest of my classes were whatever. I erased a line of my drawing, then glanced up. Mrs. Macquarie was doodling a picture in the corner of her own notes. She smiled, and I got the feeling she was waiting for me to say more. But in a patient way, and not in that bored way some teachers had.

"Robotics has been okay," I added.

Mrs. Macquarie chuckled. "That's wonderful. You know, anyone can see that you're trying really hard. I just met you, and I can tell that."

I shrugged. "Oh. Thanks."

Though Mrs. Macquarie's words did make a little warmth run from my fingers to my heart. Hues of oranges and pinks painted the walls where my beast usually roamed. Normally I didn't like talking to new people, especially more adults, but Mrs. Macquarie seemed *nice*. Plus, she drew doodles on the edges of her notes, like I always did in class. I'd never met an adult who did that too.

"I'm afraid we're out of time today," she added after a moment. "But remember to practice the breathing. If you get mad, you . . ."

"Three deep breaths in before acting," I said, parroting the words she had taught me twenty minutes ago.

"Wonderful." She reached for her desk drawer and riffled through it. "Let's plan to meet again in two weeks. Unless you need me sooner. You can come by at any time, even if you just need a place to sit and draw and calm down."

I nodded. "Okay."

"Hmmm," she added, staring at the desk drawer. "Looks like I'm out of hall passes. Can you wait outside my door while I get more? Then we'll send you back to class." She flashed me another smile.

I trudged outside and sat in one of the office chairs, the same ones I had waited in so many times to see Principal Gilbert. As Mrs. Macquarie hurried past to the staff supply room, I propped my notebook on my knees and kept drawing.

I was adding little doodles to the robotics notebook, small chibi pictures of the team at work. Right now, I worked on a picture of DJ: his deep brown hair ruffled, zig-zag designs shaved into his undercut, and his eyes glinting with excitement. Literally. I used my pencil to erase a patch on his eye and outlined the spot to add some sparkles to it. It helped show his wild happiness as his chibi robot raced around. Chibi DJ held a controller in his hand and pointed it straight at the drawing I had done of our actual robot yesterday.

Beneath him was the description that Varsha had written during class:

Wednesday, October 19

Today, Barton robotics reached new depths in their work to create a perfect robot. It started with their brilliant scientist, Evelyn, assigning the team tasks to accomplish. Evelyn and the wonderful Santino worked hard at connecting the robot claw to the base of the bot. The creative Allie used her scribe-like genius to sketch it out. Then, as the beautiful Varsha started working on writing this paragraph, our computer genius, Alex, downloaded the code to the robot. With the code downloaded and the claw connected, there was only one last task left for our fearless robotics team. DJ, our daredevil driver, picked up the sacred artifact: the Robot Controller. He rolled his shoulders back and prepared himself to test the robot. We all waited with bated breath to see how it would drive. DJ pressed the controller forward . . . and the robot lurched ahead. Unfortunately, the robot moved too fast, and with a tremendous crash, it collided with the table!

Underneath Varsha's writing was a bullet-point list that Evelyn had added later in the day. I snorted a little, remembering the expression on Evelyn's face when she read the description that Varsha had written in the notebook yesterday.

"What?" Varsha had said, with an innocent shrug. "The guidelines say to include a summary of our work each day. They don't say I can't be dramatic."

Evelyn had rolled her eyes and then made sure that after each of Varsha's paragraphs, she included a short summary in case the judges didn't care for fancier writing.

In Summary:
- *Evelyn and Santino connected the robot claw, using one-inch screws and Keps nuts as seen in figure B.*
- *Alex downloaded his code to the robot. See page 31 for a printed sample of the code.*
- *DJ test-drove the robot. The speed was too fast, and the robot crashed. See figure C for calculations of estimated speed and figure D for plan to adjust programming to increase driver control.*
- *Allie and Varsha worked on record keeping in the notebook. Varsha then joined Evelyn and Santino in building.*

It sounded a lot less exciting when described that way.

Our notebook was impressive. We filled every page with descriptions of what we did each day, drawings of the robot, labels, samples of the code, and more. My art tied it all together.

I grinned a little as I sketched in the curves of chibi DJ's face. Then I remembered where I sat and forced the grin away. I was having fun, but I didn't need the office ladies to know that.

I finished adding in the lines of the chibi DJ's controller, when the door to the office opened and Mrs. Weir walked in. She hurried across the office, then paused when she noticed me. I waved. Mrs. Weir waved back and walked over.

"That's looking really good," she said with an enormous smile. She looked down at the notebook. "I love the changes your team is trying."

"Thanks," I said. I wasn't sure what to think of Mrs. Weir. She was always so busy, trying to grade work for her other classes or finish preparing lessons. Sometimes she would check in with our team or go talk to Team A, but half the time she let us do our own thing. She had said one day during class that she was there to be a guide, but in robotics it was up to us to learn through trial and error. It wasn't anything like my other classes.

Mrs. Weir nodded at me and turned toward the door. Not Mrs. Macquarie's door but Principal Gilbert's. Her smile fell as she walked toward the door and disappeared inside.

I bit my lip as the door clicked closed. Why would she be talking to Principal Gilbert? All her kids were good kids. Except for me. But I hadn't caused any trouble recently. I was doing well. Mrs. Macquarie said so!

I glanced around the office. Oma told me this morning how proud she was of me again. If I got in trouble, if they told Oma . . . I shuddered. I had to know what was being said in the principal's office.

I stood up and stretched my arms toward the ceiling. Mrs. Powell looked over, and I flashed her an innocent smile.

Don't mind me. Just stretching to my freakishly tall height.

Mrs. Powell went back to work, and I took two big steps to the side. I sat back down. Only now I sat two chairs closer to Principal Gilbert's office door. I could hear his voice and Mrs. Weir's inside.

"I'm sorry," Principal Gilbert said. The door muffled his voice, and I leaned in to listen better. "You know that your class numbers have been too low all year. Nobody wants to do robotics. We already have massive class sizes, and with Wilfred Charter closing, we're getting an influx of students. I don't want to cancel on you midsemester, but we need to consolidate something."

When Mrs. Weir spoke, she sounded on the verge of tears. "Please, William. Robotics means so much to these kids. I'll do extra after-school duty. I'll work on recruiting more students to robotics. I'll run that reading club you can't find a teacher for. But please don't cancel robotics."

"Marcy, I can't justify keeping a class that only has eleven students. Your engineering classes are far more popular. It would be best if we give you another engineering class instead. Besides, with everything you have been going through, don't you want one fewer subject to plan for? You could have more time to spend with your daughter. To work things out with your family."

I froze in my chair as I listened to their voices bounce back and forth. They weren't talking about me. They were talking about robotics. Principal Gilbert wanted to cancel robotics.

Why does it matter? You don't even care about robotics. The thought echoed in my mind. I whispered the words to myself, and they tasted bitter in my mouth.

The team flashed before my eyes, Varsha laughing while DJ chased her around the room with the robot. Alex and Santino bent over the computer, whispering to each other while Alex worked on the code. And Evelyn.

Evelyn's entire life revolved around robotics. Anyone could see that. She loved robotics. What would she be without it?

What are you going to do about it, sweetie? For a heartbeat, I imagined my mom sitting beside me in the chair. I imagined her hand reaching out to brush against mine as she gave me an encouraging smile. *Sometimes you have to fight for things. Is this your fight?*

The voice was so strong in my mind that I looked over at the chair. It sat empty, the cloth cushions worn and old shapes scratched into the wooden armrests.

The fantasy faded, leaving an ache in my heart. Dad had always been the one to take me places, to show me cool things and tell me about cacti and have fun with me.

Mom didn't spend time with me as much because of her job, but when she did, she was the one who pushed me to be a better person. Who tried to get me to fight for things when I felt they were wrong.

Canceling robotics was wrong. It would devastate the team.

I couldn't let them do it.

Before I changed my mind or chickened out, I stood up and pushed open the door of Principal Gilbert's office.

"You can't do it. You can't cancel robotics!" I barged into the office and stared around with wide eyes.

Principal Gilbert and Mrs. Weir turned to face me.

Principal Gilbert reacted first. He raised one of those bushy eyebrows and stared at me with that judging look. "Allison Wells," he said. "You have no say in these matters. This is a discussion between adults. Please leave my office."

For a moment, the world was painted red. The beast of anger roared into my head, and this time, there was no Alex to cause a distraction, no teammates to calm me. I clenched my fists and opened my mouth, ready to let him have it.

I stopped. If I yelled at him . . . if I screamed out my rage in his office, what good would it do? He'd still cancel robotics, and then I'd be in trouble too. I would disappoint Oma. I'd end up going all the way over to Sunrise, even after having done so well the last couple of weeks.

I gulped and took a deep breath. Then another. Then a third, just like Mrs. Macquarie had taught me.

I squeezed my eyes closed and counted quickly to ten. The anger still burned hot and powerful, painting my bones with fury, making it hard to think. I forced my way through it and tried to find the right words.

"Please," I choked out. "Robotics is important. Look at me. I haven't gotten in trouble since the fight with Evelyn. And now Evelyn and I are friends, because of robotics."

Principal Gilbert looked skeptical, and I glanced wildly at Mrs. Weir. Her eyes widened. She quickly nodded.

"It's true," she said. "Allie's been working very hard with Evelyn and her team."

"Principal Gilbert," I pressed. What could I say to convince him? What would make him care? "Robotics might be small right now, but we are doing fantastic. We'll do amazing at the tournament coming up, and maybe more kids will join."

I was scrambling. I didn't actually know if any more kids would join. How many kids really cared about robotics? Yet there had to be some out there that might join once the team was no longer a giant joke.

My heart raced as I waited for Principal Gilbert to respond. I bit my lip and forced myself not to clench my fists again, not to show anger in my very way of standing.

Principal Gilbert hesitated for a minute.

Mrs. Weir jumped in. "William, I'm taking both the teams to a robotics tournament in two and a half weeks. Why don't you come watch the tournament before you decide? Come see what robotics is all about."

Principal Gilbert hesitated, staring down at his desk and at all the papers scattered across it like splotches of white against the dreary browns. He took a deep breath. Then he nodded.

"All right." He sat back down in his chair and clicked on something on his computer. "I'm adding the tournament to my calendar. I'll wait until then to decide what to do about the robotics class."

The tension in my chest loosened, and even though that red still painted the corners of my vision, I could breathe again. We had a chance. We could still keep robotics. We had to.

Principal Gilbert couldn't take it away. He couldn't steal my last chance to be good for Oma, to be around people who didn't make me explode anymore.

I kept the thought in my head as I found Mrs. Macquarie and collected my hall pass. Then Mrs. Weir ushered me out of the office and back to robotics, since it was almost the end of fourth period, anyway.

Principal Gilbert couldn't cancel robotics. I wouldn't let him do that to me. No . . . I wouldn't let him do that to Evelyn and the others. We had to succeed.

We had to win at the upcoming tournament.

CHAPTER SEVENTEEN
EVELYN

When we came into class that afternoon, we were greeted with terrible news.

Mrs. Weir called us all over to her desk, both Team A and my team, saying she needed to speak with us. Then she took a deep breath and said, "I'm afraid I have bad news. Our class has such low enrollment and . . . and Principal Gilbert may need to cancel it to make room for bigger classes."

We all stared at her, eleven stunned students who couldn't accept what she said. It had to be a joke. A cruel prank. Something! Yet Mrs. Weir looked so sad, and Allie stood beside her, looking angrier than I had seen her since our time in ISS.

"He can't cancel robotics," I said, staring at Mrs. Weir. "He can't!"

"I was there," said Allie. "He wants to get rid of our class."

No. I must have heard her wrong. Or maybe she heard things wrong.

But Mrs. Weir stood behind her desk, looking glum and nodding. Allie wasn't lying.

"I'm telling the truth," said Allie with a shrug. "If we don't do well at the tournament, he'll cancel robotics. One of us has to win."

The kids on Team A shuffled their feet and stared at the ground. They almost never got higher than sixth or seventh place. That was better than our team, though. We got disqualified from our only tournament.

Mrs. Weir adjusted her glasses and looked around at us. "There's nothing we can do now, except do well at the tournament and show him that your class is worth keeping."

She sighed and shook her head.

"Mrs. Weir?" I asked. "Why is Principal Gilbert doing this?" My words caught on the knot in my throat.

She fidgeted with the pockets of her lab coat, hesitating. The shadows under her eyes stood out and as she spoke, her voice shook. "There are a lot of factors that go into deciding classes, and ours is just so small. Some other teachers have almost forty kids in their classes. He has to shift something around and . . . well, robotics is what he's looking at."

She blinked rapidly, fiddling with the hem of her lab coat. "I'm sorry, my dear engineers. If I had recruited more earlier in the year, perhaps this wouldn't be happening. But I was working three extra shifts at my other job every week and—" She took a deep, shuddering breath. "And you don't need those troubles to worry about. Get back to work on your robots. They are so close to ready, and both of your teams are doing a fantastic job."

"But, Mrs. Weir," I whispered. "What if we lose?"

"You have brilliant designs and have come so far this year. I'm sure we have nothing to worry about," she said. She offered a weak smile, then grabbed a few papers off her desk. "Talking to Principal Gilbert ate up my planning time. I need to make these copies, or I won't have them for class tomorrow. Please, go ahead and work on the bots. When I get back, I can check your progress. I trust you all to behave while I'm gone."

Mrs. Weir swept out of the classroom, leaving us with our misery. I stared at the classroom door as it closed behind her, my heart sinking.

The five kids in Team A wandered back to their own table. I barely noticed. My panic was surging back, and no number of deep breaths would help me this time.

We couldn't let Principal Gilbert cancel robotics. If he did that, there'd be no chance of going to State and eventually Worlds. There'd be no way to impress the Tech Tigers. No scholarships and college. No engineering career. No making my moms proud and being able to take care of them so they didn't have to get that frustrated look when Fridays rolled around.

Worse still, I'd lose my chance to see Naiely again. I'd be stuck with phone calls and emails, until eventually our friendship would wither away and disappear, like in the movies when friends grew apart.

My head felt buzzy. My headphones were too tight against my ears. I squeezed my eyes shut, trying to block out the world. Then I opened them.

Buzzy head or not, we had to get to work.

The rest of the team walked back to the robotics table. I ran to join them, my mind already thinking ahead to gears and motors.

Everyone else looked as upset as I felt. Varsha repeatedly smoothed down her shirt, and her eyes shone with tears. DJ held the robot controller, gripping it so tightly, his fingers turned red. Santino was staring down at the table, and Allie was looking to the ceiling, unable to meet anyone's eyes. Alex held his phone, but the screen was blank.

We were a mess of nerves and misery. A mess that might not get past this next tournament if we couldn't pull it together.

My breathing hitched. My vision blurred, and the buzzing got worse, a million bees of stress and anxiety sending me spiraling down, down, down. How could we work on the robot like this? What chance did we have? I was ready to collapse into despair when a crumpled piece of paper smacked my face.

I spun and stared at Santino. He was tearing another sheet of paper out of the notebook and crumpling it up.

"Hey. What gives?" I frowned at Santino.

He shrugged. "So I used to live in Arteaga, where it snows sometimes. We moved away when I was really little, but I still remember that whenever I got upset, snowball fights made me feel better." He threw the crumpled paper at DJ, and it bounced off the controller DJ held.

Allie snorted. She leaned over and grabbed the crumpled piece of paper Santino had thrown at me.

"This isn't a snowball."

"I know. I mean, we live in a desert, so we never get snow here. I thought maybe . . . Why don't we pretend?" Santino blushed.

It was the silliest thing I had ever heard, but at least it had startled me out of my spiral. I took a deep breath, then another, rocking on my feet to let the motion calm me.

Time to focus. We had to get back to working on the robot. We had to make sure everything looked perfect, absolutely perfect, so we would win the tournament. With only two and a half weeks left, there wasn't time to mess around.

Allie squeezed the piece of paper. She tossed it up and down and caught it in her hand. Then she pelted Alex with it. He stared at her with wide eyes as she giggled.

"Hey," said Allie. "This is kind of fun."

I crossed my arms. "Okay, enough. We've got work to do."

Allie stared at me and raised an eyebrow. She reached for her sketchbook, and I knew what she would show me. She would hold up that picture of our dysfunctional team. But she didn't understand. This was different. The stakes had been raised. Robotics was on the line. We didn't have time for goofing around!

Allie flipped open the sketchbook.

I wished Naiely were here. She would help me get everyone back to work. She would understand how important this is. She would . . .

She would probably be throwing paper snowballs already. Naiely liked to have fun, even while we worked. She was the one who got everyone to be happy, while I was the one who kept us focused. When she had been here that first month of school, she always joined DJ and Varsha in pranks. Afterward, she would turn around and convince them to work, and we'd get a lot done.

If Naiely were here, she'd elbow me in the side and tell me to throw one. Have fun for a few minutes. Let everyone come to terms with the bad news before getting back to work.

I let out a breath.

I reached for Santino's notebook and pulled out a piece of lined paper. Everyone watched as I crumpled it up. The paper crinkled in my hands, pressing against my skin. I took another breath. Counted to four. Let it out.

Then I threw the "snowball" at Allie.

It hit her right between her eyes.

I wasn't sure who threw the next snowball or who found the spare paper that we started crumpling up, but the next thing I knew, we were running wildly through the classroom. Paper snowballs flew everywhere as we ducked and dodged and hid behind desks.

A paper snowball pelted past me and bounced off Mrs. Weir's computer as I ran across the room. I took shelter behind the 3D printers, crumpling up another piece of paper. Santino ran past my hiding spot, and I chucked the snowball at him before bolting away.

A snowball hit the ground near where I had been, thrown from above. I looked up and gasped. Allie had somehow climbed up into the rafters. She sat above us all, cackling with laughter while she threw snowball after snowball, until she ran out of paper.

Varsha and Alex darted underneath her as soon as she ran out of snowballs to throw. DJ followed after, holding up an entire ream of brand-new printer paper. Allie's eyes widened as they started crumpling up snowballs and pelting her with them. Soon Allie was begging for mercy.

Then Team A entered the fray, and within minutes it somehow turned from everyone against one another to Team A versus Team B.

"Okay, maybe this was a good idea," I said with a laugh a few minutes later, as my team sat side by side behind one of the robotics tables. DJ crumpled up more snowballs, while Allie and Varsha chucked them across the room. Team A hid behind a line of chairs, a few yards away. We had them outnumbered, though, so they stayed back instead of trying to ambush us.

I felt so . . . light. I was laughing so much that I couldn't think, could only laugh and rock back and forth; my head spun, but in a good way. I was scared about the tournament, but at least it wasn't overwhelming anymore.

Santino's idea was amazing. Paper-snowball fights should be mandatory in every class.

"Alex and I will try to get around behind them," said Santino, with a grin. "You all provide cover." He grabbed a handful of "snowballs" and lunged out from the table. Alex ran the other way, and the boys looped behind Team A's hiding spot.

I giggled and grabbed for another snowball.

Five minutes later, we ran out of paper. We had used all the scrap paper we had and even burned through an entire ream of Mrs. Weir's hidden printer paper.

Allie was the one that ended our fun, calling quits on it when DJ started eyeing her sketchbook.

"No way," she laughed. "You touch that, and you die."

Team A wandered back to their table, laughing and kicking around paper snowballs. The room was littered with them, so much paper scattered about that we had probably killed an entire tree.

I was still giggling as I headed toward our robotics table, paper crunching under my feet. Three snowballs were stuck in the robot, and I quickly pulled them out before starting to inspect it.

"You know, I don't think I've had that much fun in . . . siempre," said DJ as he walked over. He sat down heavily in a chair and leaned forward to help steady the robot arm as I tightened a loose screw. "I am going to hurt tomorrow from all that moving around!"

"Yeah!" Varsha laughed. "I haven't had fun like that since Naiely left."

I looked up in surprise. My team never talked about Naiely, not since she left right after the first month of school.

"Hey," asked Alex. He also joined us at the table. "Do you still talk to her?"

I gulped and nodded. "She doesn't have her own phone yet, but we email a lot."

"How's she doing?"

"She's doing good. Her team made it to California's state championship." I pulled my hair over my shoulder and tugged on the thick red strands as I talked, my giggles gone. Talking aloud about Naiely felt odd. I thought about her all the time, but I hadn't realized the others cared.

"Hey, if they make it to Worlds, we can form an alliance!" said DJ.

"Alliance?" asked Allie. I remembered that Allie was new. She didn't understand everything about robotics.

"At tournaments, you get paired with another team to work with," I explained. "It's called an alliance. You get partnered with random teams at the start of the tournament and play a bunch of matches for points. Then at the end, teams who earned the most points get to choose their alliance. You and your partner team compete together against another alliance in the semifinals. If your alliance wins, that means both you and your partner team become the tournament champions."

Allie nodded. "Huh."

"Hey, we should ask Naiely what her team's bot is like. And then we can add stuff to our robot so it would work well with it," said Alex. He reached up to run a hand along his dark curls, then blushed. "Provided we win the next tournament and robotics doesn't get canceled, that is."

"We need to finish perfecting our bot before we add anything, though," said Varsha. She made a face. "The claw can't pick up more than two cubes."

"It needs more grip." I glanced at the robot as I spoke. Every time it didn't work right, it hurt. And now, knowing that robotics depended on one of our teams winning, it stung even more. But every time we tested it and something failed, we made it a little better. If we hurried, there was time to be ready for the tournament.

Two and a half weeks. It beat in my heart and hung in my breath. Two and a half weeks.

"What if we add cloth to the metal pieces? Like a cushion to help give it grip?" asked Santino.

"I can poke at the programming and see if I can make the motors hold their position longer," suggested Alex.

"Oh, and we can shift the gear ratio. We used a big-to-small gear so the claw would open and close faster, but if we swap it to a small-to-big combo, that'll make the robot hand stronger," said Varsha.

"I'll draw an updated diagram," said Allie. "Oh, and you all need to see the latest picture I added to the notebook."

"Is that me?" asked DJ, leaning toward the robotics notebook. "You drew me so adorable!"

I looked around at my team. We had started class scared, stressed, and ready to cry. But now everyone was smiling and excited, thinking of ideas. This was what we had been missing. This was what I had driven away by being too pushy. We were a team again.

"Let's do it," I said. "Santino, find the grip cloth. Some arrived with the last robotics order. Alex, look at the programming. Varsha, start on the gear swap. DJ, since you can't drive while Varsha's working, help Varsha. Allie, can you also add in some pictures of the grip cloth and an explanation of what it's for?"

They all nodded. Then Allie frowned. "What about you?" she asked.

"I'm going to start an email to Naiely and then clean up the snowballs. Once I get it started, it would be cool if you all come add to it. I think she'd love hearing from everyone on the team. She misses you too, I think."

By the time Mrs. Weir came back to class, we were all scattered around the room, hard at work on our jobs. And when she asked what in the world had happened and why there was paper everywhere, everyone burst out giggling.

CHAPTER EIGHTEEN
ALLIE

One week until the tournament.

Not that I was counting or anything. I didn't care. Really.

My hands trembled as I worked on my drawing. I sat on my bed with my sketchbook propped against my knees, trying not to dwell on the week ahead. It wasn't working. By this time next Saturday, I would be on a bus with the rest of the team, heading to the tournament.

I drew a picture of our robot, turning the clunky-looking thing into something cool. Along with the robot drawing, I added bubble letters saying *Barton Team B* and some bullet points about what our robot was capable of. It made a pretty good business card for the team.

Alex found the idea online. He claimed the best teams made business cards to pass out when trying to convince other teams to pick them as an ally. A good alliance team would help you win the tournament.

Not that I cared.

After the tournament, when we had more time, I'd redo the business card. There wasn't time before this tournament, but if we made it to State, I could also design the team a logo and use fabric paint to draw it into all our shirts. Or maybe I could find somebody to make us new shirts, with the updated logo. I was pretty sure some of Varsha's non-robotics friends were into fashion and stuff. Back in ISS that day, I had told Evelyn that I just wanted to draw the notebook diagrams and be left alone. But maybe I could do a little bit more. Sometimes.

I added more shading to the picture and smiled. It looked perfect.

"What do you think?" I asked. On my bedside table was a picture in a frame. The picture of Mom, Dad, and me. Oma gave it to me when I asked, and after the last few weeks, it seemed like it had always belonged there. I angled my drawing toward Mom and Dad, then closed my eyes and imagined what they might say.

Would they be proud? I hoped so. I was failing math and had a D in science, but I was doing well in robotics. My progress report yesterday said I had an A. It was the only one I had ever gotten. Plus the grades on my math homework were getting better. A little.

I opened my eyes and bit my lip. There was no answer from my parents, not even in my imagination. The silence rang in my ears, and I became aware again of that hole, that empty space that always felt wrong.

"I miss you," I whispered to the picture, my eyes blurring with tears. "I wish you were here and could come watch the tournament. I wish . . . I wish you were still alive."

I took a deep breath and looked back at my drawing. Was that the right thing to say? Or was that wrong? Because no matter how much I wished it, they wouldn't come back.

"Guess what?" I said to the picture instead. "It turns out art can help with robotics. Art is important, even if it isn't as obvious as the smart-people stuff."

Nothing answered me but the ache of my own heart.

I dropped my pencil onto the bed and sniffled. It was early on Saturday. There was a whole weekend stretching out ahead. A long weekend with only me and my broken memories.

Funny. I hated the school days because my teachers wouldn't leave me alone. But on weekends, when I was left all alone? I hated that too. There was nothing to distract me during the long hours. Nothing to stop me from falling back into those painful thoughts.

I flopped back on my bed and sighed, staring at the wall. I had covered my walls with pictures—my own drawings beside posters from my favorite anime. Once upon a time, I used to lose myself in those shows for hours. Ever since that day, though, it was hard to care about my old favorite shows. Hard to care about anything, really.

For a while I lay there, my thoughts bouncing around in my head, back and forth like a Ping-Pong ball.

My phone rang.

I groaned and rolled over. Nobody ever called me, except for scams. Yet it was a distraction, and I needed that right now. I answered, expecting a robot voice to tell me about how they wanted to buy my house or how I've been evading taxes and the IRS is after me if I don't pay, even though I'm only thirteen.

"Go away," I grumbled into the phone.

"No, you!"

I sat up. That was not a robot voice. That was . . . "Alex? How'd you get my phone number?"

"You gave it to Santino last week when working on the robot, remember?"

"Right." I rolled over on the bed and stared at the ceiling, hoping he didn't hear the tremble in my voice. "What do you want?"

"Okay, so Santino and I were hanging out, and Santino got a new drone. We're going to the park to try it. DJ is coming too, and Varsha even said she'd ditch her other friends and come check it out. Want to join? Oh! And do you have Evelyn's number? It can be a Team B adventure!"

I blinked at the ceiling for a moment, trying to sort through the rapid-fire questions from Alex. Team B adventure, huh? That could be fun.

Only . . .

I rolled onto my side, staring at the picture of Mom and Dad. I didn't want to go anywhere today, not when it was only two days away from . . . *that*. I wanted to lie here, to do nothing and be nothing.

"Sorry," I muttered. "Not today. I'll text you Ev's number, though."

"Aw. Are you sure?"

"Yeah." I ended the call and texted Evelyn's number to Alex. Then I dropped the phone beside me and sighed. Perhaps I should go. But the idea of putting on a smile, of being around people, of having to get out of bed and get dressed and do stuff suddenly seemed overwhelming and exhausting.

Oma stepped into my room, her walker clunking against the floor. I blinked. I had been so distracted; I didn't hear her approach.

"Who was that?" she asked.

I sat up and shrugged. "Alex from robotics. He and the others are hanging out in the park."

Oma's face broke into a brilliant smile, crinkling the corners of her eyes. "Well, look at that," she said, her smile riding on her voice. "You're making friends at school. Is Alex cute?"

I blushed. "I mean, the team is cool, but I don't have friends. And I don't like Alex. I don't like anyone, and I don't plan to, ever." I looked down at the comforter on my bed.

"That's okay. Plenty of people don't care for romance. But the friends thing, I can't believe. Are you telling me that they're inviting you out for no reason?" Oma shuffled over to the bed and sat beside me.

"I guess they like me a little."

"And do you like spending time with them?"

"Sure? DJ and Varsha are hilarious, Alex is nice, and Santino seems cool. And Evelyn is okay."

"So they *are* your friends." Oma smirked and crossed her arms. I frowned at Oma, and she laughed—a light, kind sound. She reached out to put a hand on my arm. "Are you going?"

"Naw," I said, staring at the spots and wrinkles on the back of her hand. "I . . . it doesn't feel right. I was thinking of Mom and Dad, and it's almost *that* day, anyway, and I shouldn't be running around having fun. Maybe next time."

"Oh, Allie," said Oma. I looked up at her face, and her eyes sparkled. "You're allowed to have fun. It won't be a betrayal of their memory."

"Are you sure? I mean, it's almost . . ." My voice caught in my throat. I hoped I was starting to be okay with it, but the words stuck, and I couldn't make them come out. My heart twisted, reminding me of that hole that had been ripped into me almost one year ago.

"You know, I visited a therapist the other day, while you were at school," said Oma. She looked up to the ceiling. "I've been feeling the same way. Last week, I caught myself laughing at something, and then I felt guilty. I decided to talk to somebody about it."

"Like I talked to Mrs. Macquarie?" I hesitated, not sure what to say. "Though we mostly talked about my temper and not about any of the sad stuff."

Oma nodded. "I spoke to my therapist about many of my emotions. Never in all my many, many, many, many,

many years did I think I'd need a therapist, but sometimes talking to somebody is exactly what we need." I made a face at Oma, and she chuckled. "Okay, perhaps not that many years. When your opa passed away, I kept my grief to myself. But your father . . . I struggle with losing him, and with losing your mother. Doctor See, the therapist I visited, explained it to me well. We humans aren't meant to handle everything on our own. Sometimes we need somebody to talk to, so we don't bottle everything up until it explodes."

I stared at my hands, Oma's words hitting far too close to my heart. That's what it was, wasn't it? I had all these feelings and emotions, and I tried to hide them, but something would happen, and they would surge up to the surface. Crashing into a wave of anger and frustration that I couldn't stop. I hated that about myself. I hated how I always exploded and got in trouble. But I didn't know how to stop it. How to change.

"One thing she told me," Oma said, drawing me back to her, "is that it's okay to grieve and be sad. It's also okay to find happiness. Allie, you know your mom and dad. Would they really want you to stay sad forever?"

I shook my head. Dad was always happy, all smiles and cheer. He pulled pranks all the time, like in the story with Oma and the wooden spoon. And Mom, while serious, would always let that small smile show when it mattered. They would get upset if they saw Oma and me now, saw how broken we were.

"Your therapist seems smart," I said. I looked at the bed, picking at a loose thread on the comforter.

"She is," said Oma. "I plan to keep talking to her. And, Allie, I think it would help you to talk to a therapist as well."

I bit my lip, yanking on the loose thread. "I'm supposed to meet Mrs. Macquarie again next week."

"I know, but I'd like you to talk to somebody outside the school too. Perhaps one who specializes in grief, like Doctor See."

I hesitated. I was already talking to so many adults. Did I really want to talk to more? But Oma stared at me with that look, her eyes kind and a smile on her lips. Maybe it was worth a try, for Oma, anyway.

"All right." I shrugged.

"Good. Doctor See has a partner who often works with teens. I'll call and get something scheduled." Oma smiled and looked around, her eyes traveling over my posters and the dusty shelf full of my old manga. "We both have a lot of healing to do."

"Yeah," I said. It was hard. I wanted to heal. I wanted to be the Allie I used to be. But she felt far away now. A small part of me whispered that if I acted happy again, I'd forget my parents. I had barely thought about them the other day, during the snowball fight. It felt wrong afterward. I never, ever wanted to do that.

Yet, Oma's words made sense, like they always did.

"You know your parents would want you to live your life. To have fun, even so close to the anniversary of the accident," said Oma. Her eyes shone with tears as she mentioned it, but she forced a smile.

"I guess . . . I don't . . ." How could I explain it? I wanted to hang out with the team. But I didn't want to forget my parents. To get so cheerful that I stopped remembering them.

Oma understood without me needing to say a word. She wiped a tear from my eye, her fingers brushing against my cheek.

"Having fun doesn't make your grief less real. Spending time with friends doesn't mean you don't care. It's okay, Allie. You should call those friends back and go see them. If anything, it would honor your parents more. It would please them to see you happy."

I hesitated, then lunged forward and hugged Oma. "Thanks."

It would be nice, for a day, to be around Alex and everyone. *They* didn't know about my parents. They treated me like everything was normal, with none of the pitying looks or false kindness. None of the "I'm so sorries" that turned into "You can't let this be an excuse" when I didn't behave the way they wanted.

"I'll call Alex back," I said, pulling away from Oma.

"Be back before dinner, okay?" Oma rose from the bed, reaching for her walker. I nodded. I wasn't sure about everything she had said. The therapist thing? It made me nervous. But Oma was right. Dad loved having fun. He'd be heartbroken to see me this way. With that thought in mind, staying home and dwelling in my sadness felt terrible. Seeing my friends though . . .

I forced a smile onto my face, even though I wasn't 100 percent sure if this was okay. If I'd be okay. "Thanks, Oma," I said.

I grabbed my phone and called Alex back.

CHAPTER NINETEEN
EVELYN

Five days until the tournament.

The weekend had been fun, and for a little while, I forgot the impending deadline. On Saturday, I joined the team when Santino tried out his drone. The next day, Varsha messaged us over our new group chat and invited everyone to her house to watch BattleBots on YouTube. She had the biggest house I'd ever seen, and we spent the day on a plush couch eating popcorn from an *actual* popcorn machine. It was two days of pure fun with the team that had nothing to do with the tournament.

It was kind of nice.

Was this what I had been missing out on? I had been so focused on getting to Worlds, so focused on being perfect and seeing Naiely again, that I forgot how to relax and enjoy being around my team. I forgot why I loved robotics.

But lately, I remembered.

Lately, I had friends.

Now, though, it was Monday morning, and there were only five days left. The deadline beat in my heart, clicking into place again and again. Five days. Five days. Only five days.

It sounded in my footsteps when I hurried into school that morning. I worried about the bot. DJ noticed that the robot rolled slowly once it carried five cubes. In fact, it rolled slowly enough that it had trouble turning. The robot had great traction but not enough speed.

We needed to adjust the gear ratio for the wheels again. Or change up the programming.

My mind was locked on the robot, and I almost didn't see Allie sitting in the cactus garden. I reached the blue classroom door before I noticed her.

I stopped and looked. She sat way back, on one of the little benches in the shadow of a mesquite tree. She stared at the saguaro with a funny expression on her face. Normally the entire team met in the classroom in the mornings. We'd work on the robot and sometimes take a break to finish any last-minute homework. So why was Allie hanging out outside, all alone today?

I glanced at the door. There wasn't much time to fix the bot.

I glanced at Allie. As I watched, she reached up to wipe at her eyes. I froze. Was *Allie Wells* crying?

I pursed my lips. I tugged on a strand of my hair. Allie never cried. She was tough as nails. If she was crying, something was really wrong. There wasn't time for this, though! I needed to tell the rest of the team the idea about the gears and—

Allie's becoming a friend. A good friend would care about her.

In the last few weeks, my inner thoughts started sounding a lot like Naiely when she gave me advice. I winced. My inner Not-Naiely was right. Allie had become a friend, and friends helped each other. The robot could wait a minute or two.

I took a deep breath.

Then I rolled my shoulders back and pried myself away from the door, hurrying across the cactus garden. Allie looked up when she heard my footsteps.

"I'm not working this morning," she said. "I have . . . stuff to do." Her eyes looked red.

"That's okay," I blurted out. "I mean, mornings are optional, anyway." I sat down on the edge of the bench and pulled off my headphones, letting them rest around my neck. Allie said nothing, just stared out into the cactus garden with her fists clenched.

The silence stretched on.

Awkward.

Unbearable.

I tugged on a strand of my hair and kicked at the air below my feet. When I sat, my feet didn't quite touch the ground.

"Sooooo." I scrambled for anything to say. This wasn't my strong suit. I wasn't a people person. But Allie was clearly upset, and I had to say something before that clock started ticking in my head again and I fled back to the classroom. "The cactuses are pretty."

"Cacti, actually," said Allie. She sniffled. "If there's more than one you call them 'cacti.'"

I nodded. I knew that. I just forgot with how nervous I was. "The saguaro looks like he's waving to that bush-like one."

Allie let out a weak giggle. "The bush-like one is a Joshua tree. Though it's technically not a tree. It's a succulent."

I turned to stare at Allie. "How do you know all this?"

She shrugged.

Silence descended again, broken only by the sound of other students entering the campus. In our little corner by the cactus garden, it was still peaceful.

"Are you okay?" I asked finally. "Did something happen?"

Allie hesitated. She stared at the ground beneath her feet, kicking around the rocks with a foot. When she spoke, she didn't look at me.

"My parents died on this day a year ago. Oma said I can stay home today, but the tournament is in a week, and I thought I'd be fine. I don't think I can be fine, though." Her voice cracked, and a tear traced down her cheek. She wiped at it and glared at me. "Don't tell anyone you saw me cry."

"I won't! I promise." I bit my lip, searching for the right words. What were you supposed to say in a situation like this? Comforting things, right? Like, "I'm sorry" or "That's so sad." Those words didn't feel right. Instead, I asked, "What were your parents like?"

I flinched even as I spoke. That had to be the wrong thing to say. Why was I bad at this?

Allie blinked and sniffled. She turned to look at the cactus. "Dad was nice. And smart. He knew all about plants, but cacti were his favorite. Mom was super serious and busy a lot, but when she was around, she also was fierce and amazing. Nobody got away with being cruel to others in front of Mom."

"Did your dad teach you about cacti?"

Allie nodded. "Yep. He also got me into art. We used to play a game where we would take turns drawing a picture together. Only Dad was *terrible* at art. Like, so terrible." She giggled a little, then bit her lip and stared at the ground.

"On a scale of one to Alex's stick figures, how bad are we talking?"

"*Worse* than Alex's stick figures."

I pretended to clutch at my heart. "Wow. That's bad."

Allie smiled lightly. "He used to say I sucked all the art skills out of him and Mom, since I can draw so well and they couldn't. Mom would always roll her eyes when he said that and point out that he drew terribly even before I was born."

"I don't think skills can be sucked out of people like that," I said. Allie let out a choked laugh, and I shrugged. "What? It's true. But your parents sound like they were amazing." Allie seemed happy talking about them, even as her eyes brimmed with tears.

"Yeah," she said. "They were the best parents ever."

We fell silent again then, but it wasn't the awkward silence of before. We sat and listened to the sound of the school waking up, the opening and closing of doors and the distant squeaking breaks of the arriving school buses.

A part of me wanted to get up and go, to hurry into the classroom and work before the bell rang. I clamped down on it. Allie needed me. Besides, the team could handle building without me for a morning. Varsha or Santino probably already thought of the gear-ratio problem.

"Hey, thank you," said Allie after a bit. Her crying had stopped, and when she looked up, her eyes weren't as red. "Nobody has asked me that before. Everyone tells me they are sorry, that they understand. Then they look down at me with pity all the time and then get mad when I mess things up."

I shrugged. "Isn't saying you're sorry the normal thing to do when comforting somebody?"

Allie frowned. "Maybe. But I hate it. It's why I don't tell anyone here about Mom and Dad. I don't want anyone to pity me."

"Our team wouldn't pity you," I said. They loved Allie. They listened to her more than to me, and I understood why. For all the times that she got mad and exploded, she was actually really smart. She had good ideas and understood everyone so well. I'd never admit it, but I was a little jealous. She could lead a team the way I wished I could.

"I guess. But I don't want to find out I'm wrong." She sighed and shook her head.

"I get it," I said.

"Really?" asked Allie.

I fiddled with the edge of my headphones and took a deep breath. "I'm autistic. And I know the team wouldn't make fun of me or anything if they knew, but I don't like telling people, anyway. Just in case. So I understand why you don't say anything."

It felt so strange to say it aloud. Naiely was my only friend who had ever known. I wasn't ashamed or anything. Mum and Mama always told me there was nothing to be ashamed about. But other people could be mean, and I didn't want anyone to treat me worse or like a baby, just because they didn't understand autistic kids like me.

"Oh," said Allie. "Is that why you wear your headphones all the time?"

I nodded. "I don't like a lot of noise."

Allie nodded. "Well, if you don't look at me with pity, I promise not to make fun of you."

"Deal." I giggled.

Allie sniffled, then glanced at me out of the corner of her eye. "What are you doing out here, anyway? Shouldn't you be working on the robot?"

"You seemed like you needed company," I said. I didn't mention how my feet itched to rush to the robotics room, or how my mind kept thinking of those gears. Allie was more important than the bot. Instead I wound my hair around my fingers and forced myself to *stay*.

Allie smiled. I had never seen her really smile, not like this. "Wow," she said. "That means a lot from you."

"You're my friend." I hesitated, a frightening thought slipping into my mind. "At least, I think we're friends? Unless you don't want to be."

"Naw," said Allie. She punched me lightly on the shoulder. "I don't know *how,* but yeah. We're friends. And thank you."

I smiled. Then I looked back toward the robotics room. "Nobody would blame you if you wanted to go home."

"Even if I miss a day of robotics?"

I forced myself to shrug. "Taking care of yourself is more important sometimes." It was something Mama said to me once, back when we realized I had anxiety. I forgot it most of the time.

Allie sniffled and wiped at her eyes.

"Yeah," she said. "I guess it is. I don't really want to be alone, though. But . . . I also left Oma all alone, and I feel bad about that."

"Why not do something with your oma?" I asked. My fingers tapped on the bench. Five days. Five days. I forced myself to still. *This* was important. "My mama works at a restaurant downtown. She might be able to get you a discount."

"You know, Oma would probably like that."

By the time I had called Mama and texted her Allie's grandma's number, the morning was almost over. There were only fifteen minutes before the bell would ring, and *five days* pounded in my head. I wasn't upset, though, even as I watched Allie hurry away for the day. Helping Allie had been worth the delay.

After all, Allie was my friend.

CHAPTER TWENTY
ALLIE

One day until the tournament, and Jeremy Jacobs was causing trouble again.

It happened when Evelyn and I were walking toward the robotics room on Friday morning. We met up outside the school, close to the front gates. I was walking over from Oma's house, right as Evelyn's mom pulled up to the parent drop-off.

"Allie!" shouted Evelyn, clambering out of the old car. "Wait for me."

I didn't turn around, but I slowed my steps. It was nice to have Evelyn around. Now that I understood her more, and she had chilled a little, she was cool to talk to. Even now as she ran up to me, she acted like everything was normal. She didn't look at me with pity or sadness in her eyes, not like everyone else when they learned about my parents. It was . . . refreshing.

Maybe Oma was right. Maybe it helped to talk to people sometimes. Talking to Mrs. Macquarie, talking to Evelyn, it all made me feel a little lighter. Maybe the therapist Oma wanted me to see wouldn't be too bad, either.

Evelyn caught up to me, and I forced a grin onto my face.

"You ready for tomorrow?" I asked. I knew she wasn't. She spent all last night messaging the team group chat in a fit of panic about the tournament almost being here. We spent until midnight calming her down.

"No. No, no, no, not even close." Evelyn shook her head so hard that her wild red waves flew around and her headphones were jostled loose. I snickered.

"You'll be fine," I said. "The robot works great."

"I have never been this nervous." Evelyn drew a chunk of her hair over her shoulder and wound her fingers through it. "This is worse than even the time when I asked out Megan Lucio in sixth grade."

I stopped to stare at Evelyn. "You asked out Megan?"

I didn't really know Megan Lucio, but I had her in my English class. She was super bubbly, confident, outgoing . . . and not at all into technology.

Evelyn's blush washed her face with the brilliant, right-to-the-roots red of her hair.

"It was a dare from Naiely. But also, I had a massive crush on Megan because she's pretty, you know? I didn't realize what a jerk she was. She turned me down, called me weird, and laughed at my clothing, and then she told everyone at school about it. It was horrible. But then Naiely told everyone that if they laughed at me, she wouldn't be friends with them, and everyone listens to Naiely."

"I'm just surprised you asked someone out," I said with a shrug. It felt strange to be talking about this. Two girls walking through the school, talking about crushes. Was this what regular kids did? What friends did?

"Why is that surprising?" asked Evelyn.

I hesitated, trying to think of a way to phrase it that wouldn't hurt or offend Evelyn. "I guess you seem so focused on robotics. I've never seen you really show interest in anyone."

"I've been distracted with the tournament and all." Evelyn blushed again. She looked down and kicked at a rock. It skittered along the ground, past my feet. "I guess I've gotten a little obsessive lately."

We walked in silence for a minute, passing under the gate into the school and through the courtyard by the 800 Building. We moved around the library and took a quick stop by the drinking fountain outside the library courtyard. Miss Hawk was walking in the distance, and I took a second to wave to her. She smiled and waved back, before continuing on toward the front office.

"What about you?" Evelyn asked suddenly. "Have you ever asked anyone out?"

I blushed, trying to think how to explain it. How could I say that I didn't like romance or crushes or holding hands? I didn't hate it. I just . . . didn't care about it. "I don't really like anyone, honestly. Everyone talks about having crushes and first kisses and the butterflies-in-your-stomach thing, and I never get that. Is that strange?"

"Is it strange for me to like more than one gender?"

"What? No!" I stopped dead in my tracks and spun to look at Evelyn.

She crossed her arms and smiled. "Then there's nothing weird about you not having crushes. Honestly, it sounds like you're ace. Or maybe aro."

"What's that?"

"Asexual or aromantic. You know. Not into hand-holding, or kissing, or crushes at all."

I stared at Evelyn for a long moment. There was a word for it? Did that mean other people were the same way? I always figured it was something wrong with me. Something broken, like everything else in my life. But if there was a word for it, if it was normal for other people too, then maybe I was wrong.

Talking to Evelyn was easy. It made so much sense the way she looked at things, with that matter-of-fact view. She said it like it was a fact, as true as the robot gears being green and humans breathing oxygen. Every time I shared something with her, she surprised me. Like with my parents earlier this week. I couldn't believe that I had ever hated her.

"Thanks, Ev." I lightly punched her shoulder. "You're the best robotics nerd friend I could ever have."

Evelyn's smile grew brighter. Then it flickered, and that panic raced back into her eyes.

"Let's hurry," she said, taking a shuddering breath. "I want to check over the robot again."

"For the hundredth time?"

She giggled, and we turned the corner toward the cactus garden. There we came to an abrupt stop. Jeremy stood in front of us, his arms crossed and a sneer on his face.

"It doesn't matter how many times you check your robot," he said, his voice grating against my ears. "You're still losers and will lose."

I thought I had been getting calmer, learning how to put a lid on the burning rage. But as Jeremy spoke, it all came rearing back. I clenched my fists and took a step toward Jeremy.

Evelyn grabbed my arm. Her hands were cool to the touch, her fingers insistent as she pulled me back.

"Don't," she said. I glanced at her from the corner of my eye. She looked mad too, a controlled fury. "It's not worth it. We need you at the tournament. Don't throw that away by getting into a fight now."

Jeremy laughed. "Look at you two, all buddy-buddy. Don't worry, Evel-loser. She can't fight me, anyway. I know the secret now. I overheard Principal Gilbert in his office. She's one fight away from going to Sunrise."

He burst out laughing, practically doubling over in hysterics at his own words. Evelyn's fingers dug into my arm, the only thing that kept me from punching that smug face.

"Please," snapped Evelyn. "You're not that far away from going to Sunrise yourself. You're a bully who gets joy from tormenting other people. That's a sad life."

Jeremy's laughter abruptly cut off. He glared at us. "You're a weirdo and a loser. You're going to lose. I'll have fun on Monday watching you walk back into the school in defeat."

Before we could retort, he turned and ran off, darting along the 400 Building and to where his friends waited near the cafeteria.

I bit the inside of my cheek, clenching my hands into fists and trying my hardest to not chase after him. My beast roared in my ears and raged behind my ribs. I stared around the courtyard, desperate for distraction more than just Evelyn. My eyes landed on the saguaro.

What would Dad say if I blew everything? I was doing better. He'd be disappointed if I got into a fight. Oma would be disappointed too. Evelyn was right; if I got into a fight and got kicked out now, the entire team would hurt. Robotics would have one less kid, and the program would get canceled. So many people were counting on me, and I couldn't let them all down like that.

My anger slowly washed away. I took three long, deep breaths and shook my head.

"Sorry," said Evelyn as my calm settled back in. "Jeremy doesn't like me much. He always says stuff like that."

"You aren't a weirdo," I said, clenching and unclenching my fists.

Evelyn shrugged.

"What? You aren't!"

Evelyn shrugged again, but this time she smiled. "I know that. I don't always fit in, but I'm not weird. Jeremy's just a jerk." She fidgeted with her headset, pulling it down around her neck. "You're not going to fight him, right?"

"I'm fine now." I sighed. "Come on. Let's go join the others. We've got work to do."

CHAPTER TWENTY-ONE
EVELYN

Less than seventeen hours until the tournament.

It was fifth period, and all I could think was that in seventeen hours, we would sit on the bus, riding to the school hosting the tournament.

I took a deep, shuddering breath. Then another.

"Relax, Ev," said Allie. "We'll be fine."

"You know what? Allie's right." Varsha leaned over the table, reaching for one of the spare robotics shirts. "We've got this. We have to."

She was packing the robot into a plastic tub, making sure nothing got bent. We had taken some extra robotics shirts to put around it so it wouldn't get banged up on the way, and Varsha carefully slid them into place. Her hands shook as she loaded them in. For all her words, Varsha was nervous too.

Allie smiled from where she sat. Her feet were up on the robotics table, and she propped the design notebook in her lap. She was adding more little drawings to it while the rest of us packed up the robotics stuff.

"How can you be calm?" I asked. "If we lose the tournament, we lose robotics." My palms broke into a sweat at the thought, and I rocked on the balls of my feet, trying to let the motion sooth me. This felt too real now, too close. We needed more time!

DJ walked over with a small toolbox in his left hand and dropped it on the robotics table. "I'm with Evelyn," he said. He shook his head. "This is . . . what's the word? ¡Espantoso! No wait, terrifying!"

Allie sighed. "Look, is our robot good?"

"Yes," I said, wiping my hands on my jeans.

"And is your driving the best thing ever?" She aimed this question at DJ.

He gulped and nodded. "You know it is."

Allie nodded. "See? We will be fine."

Varsha stuck the lid on the plastic tub and closed it. "I agree with Allie. We've got a great notebook, a wonderful Team Lead, a rock-star programmer, and the cutest driver in the world. We'll be okay."

She flashed a brilliant smile at us all, then tossed her hair over her shoulder and turned around to head to the supply room.

"Yeah, I guess," said DJ scratching at his hair. "We do have a— Wait, what was that about the cutest driver?" He hurried after Varsha, leaving me and Allie alone.

My eyes drifted back to the table, covered in spare parts

and tools and the plastic bin. The time was ticking in my head. Less than a day until the tournament.

Allie erased something in her picture and flipped the pencil over. She glanced up at me and gave a quick smile. "I promise it'll be fine," she said. "We've got this."

I gulped and nodded. I closed my eyes and focused on breathing.

Deep breath in.

Everything depended on winning this tournament. Seeing Naiely at Worlds, saving the robotics team, making my moms proud. I wished I knew how to relax like Allie and Varsha, but I didn't. Still, worrying would change nothing. The robot was packed up, and the tournament was tomorrow.

Deep breath out.

Mrs. Weir's phone rang. She picked it up and spoke into it for a second before looking around the room.

"All right, my wonderful engineers," she called out. We all fell silent and listened. "We got the go-ahead. Let's move all our tournament stuff to the office. Tomorrow, when the bus arrives, they will load it up for us. Make sure you take everything you need, including extra parts. Once school ends today, you won't be able to come back into the classroom until Monday."

I gulped.

Varsha hurried out of the supply closet, holding a handful of extra motors and gears. She dropped them into the spare-parts box and picked it up. The rest of the team joined in. We grabbed as much as we could: the big tool-box, the small box of replacement parts, the bolt cutters, Alex's extra programming laptop, the box of goggles and lab coats, extra batteries and the battery charger, and our controller.

Our robot sat in the bin on the table, obscured by the thick plastic. Through the plastic, you couldn't see any-thing except a dark shadow, showing that our robot was there. Packed away and ready. I glanced at it, then looked around the team. Everyone had their hands full, leaving nobody to carry the robot.

"We'll need to make two trips," I said with a shrug. The others nodded, and we followed Mrs. Weir and Team A out the classroom door, leaving our robot behind. We hurried through the school to the office.

"Hey, Ev," said Varsha as we walked. She slowed down to walk beside me.

"Yeah?"

"I'm sorry for all the times I said you were annoying. I was just so frustrated, and I let myself get mean." She stared at the spare-parts bin, her hair falling over her shoulder and across her pretty blue kurti. "It wasn't cool of me, though."

I shrugged, trying to think of the best words to say. "I wasn't being very nice, either. I'm sorry I never let you or the others work with the robot. I was just so scared you'd mess it up, but you and the others are really good at all this stuff. I was wrong."

Varsha smiled. "It's cool. You let us help now."

"I couldn't do it without you," I said, pushing open the door to the office.

Once inside, Mrs. Powell, the office secretary, showed us where to put our stuff in the staff break room. A few teachers were hanging around the room, including Miss Hawk.

"Oh my. Is it already time for the big tournament?" she asked.

I turned to face her and forced a smile. "Yep! We're meeting back here in the morning tomorrow and heading over."

"Well, good luck!" Miss Hawk gave me another of her amazing smiles, the sort that lit up her entire face. "You and Allie worked so hard while in ISS. You'll do fantastically. I'll have to stop by and cheer you on. Oh, Mrs. Weir, can you get me the tournament details?"

Mrs. Weir had followed us into the room. She hurried over to Miss Hawk, and a minute later they were talking about start times and parking.

I took a deep breath and stared back at the boxes. Tomorrow morning, this would all be shoved into the bus's stowage, and we would ride above it all the way to the tournament. I hoped we hadn't forgotten anything.

Varsha and DJ set to work organizing our stuff into a nice, neat pile so nothing would get left behind. Mrs. Weir stayed behind to talk to Miss Hawk while the rest of us quickly hurried out to get the robot and the last of the supplies.

We rounded the corner to the cactus garden when Alex stopped.

"Was that Jeremy?" he asked. "I swear I saw Jeremy leaving the robotics room."

Allie scowled. "I bet he was looking for you guys to torment you again." Her hands clenched into fists. "I'll go find him and ask what he was doing."

"No!" I shouted, at the same time as Alex cried out, "Don't do that!"

Santino stepped forward. "How about Evelyn and I go follow him to see what he was up to?" He took Alex's arm and smiled. "Honestly, you two need to stay away from him."

I hesitated. I didn't exactly like Jeremy, either, what with how he always called me a weirdo and a loser. The idea of confronting him made my palms break out in a sweat. But Allie would explode around him, and if Alex went after Jeremy, Jeremy would pick on him more. Jeremy targeted Alex more than anyone else.

I gulped and nodded. "Let's go."

Santino and I hurried away from the rest of the team. We rounded the corner of the cactus garden and spotted Jeremy disappearing through the gates of the 400 Courtyard. We looked at each other and frowned. That led to the eighth-grade field, outside the school. Why was he going there?

We followed. As we drew near the gate that led out into the eighth-grade field, we heard Jeremy talking. It sounded like he was on the phone.

"Mom, this is a bad time to call. I'm busy."

I pressed my back into the cool bricks of the building and peeked around the corner. Jeremy held his phone to his ear, and his face was red. The voice that came from the other side of the phone sounded so loud and shrill, I almost understood what it was saying. Almost, but not quite. I pulled my headphones down around my neck and strained to hear.

"I'm sorry I forgot to clean it, Mom. I'll do it when I get home. Chill."

The voice got louder, the shouts shriller. And Jeremy, big bully Jeremy who always acted tough and mean, seemed to crumple. His shoulders hunched. His face flushed red. He blinked rapidly, like he was fighting back tears.

"Sorry, Mom. I'll do it right this time. I will," he mumbled into the phone. The angry voice kept shouting over him. "Mom, I—please, can I—I need to go back to class. I was doing something and—"

He fell silent again and seemed to shrink in on himself. The sharp voice kept yelling. Jeremy pulled the phone away from his ears. I could hear what the voice shouted now, and I clapped a hand over my mouth to stifle my gasp.

"You're always useless!" screeched a lady's voice, high and painful and clear, even though his phone wasn't on speaker. "You never do anything right. Why are you even answering your phone right now? Aren't you supposed to be in class? What are you doing outside of class, anyway, you—"

I pulled back and turned to stare at Santino. He looked back at me with wide eyes. We were hearing something private. Something Jeremy didn't want anyone to know.

I remembered something then, something Mama often said. There's a reason people act the way they do. There's always a reason.

That didn't excuse things. Jeremy shouldn't be bullying people, even if his mom bullied him. It wasn't right.

I was so lost in my thoughts, I almost didn't notice that his phone call had ended. Santino poked me and glanced toward the gate again. It was quiet around the corner. I pressed myself up against the red bricks and peeked around the open gate.

Jeremy's face stared right at me.

We both leaped back with a yelp, and Jeremy got even redder than before.

He clenched his fists. "Were you spying on me, Evel-loser?" He spat it out, anger and embarrassment in his voice.

"Yeah," I said. "What were you doing near the robotics room?"

"Nothing," said Jeremy quickly. He glared at me. "I was looking for your friends to tell them about how badly you're gonna lose tomorrow because, you know, you're losers." He scowled and crossed his arms. "But then I got a call I had to take. Which was nothing, by the way."

For once, Jeremy didn't seem overwhelming. His words didn't bite the way they usually did. There was pain underneath them, pain he was trying to hide. It wasn't fair, though.

It wasn't right for him to try and hide that pain by hurting other people.

I took a deep breath and mustered up my best team-leader voice. "Leave my team alone. They don't deserve having to deal with you." I turned around and grabbed Santino's arm. "Come on. We're wasting our time here."

Santino nodded and let me lead him back toward the cactus garden.

But as we drew near the corner, Santino paused and looked back at Jeremy. The school's biggest bully stood by the gate out of the school, glaring at us.

"You're such a mean person," said Santino, loud enough for Jeremy to hear. "But I'm sorry that you have to deal with . . . what you do. Attacking other people won't change it, though. You should go talk to the school counselor. Maybe she can help you. And please stop picking on my friends. Alex is an amazing guy, and he doesn't deserve how you've bullied him all this time."

Jeremy stared open-mouthed at Santino. Soft, kind-hearted Santino always had the perfect words to say.

We left Jeremy behind and went to join the others in packing up the last of the stuff. With less than seventeen hours until the tournament, there was no time to waste on bullies.

CHAPTER TWENTY-TWO
ALLIE

We've got this.

That's what I said yesterday, anyway, when Evelyn was panicking. But now, as we stood in the parking lot of Westview High School on Saturday morning right before the tournament, I wanted to eat my words.

I spun my pencil nervously in my hand as I stared at the high school's sprawling building. There was a loud squeak of brakes as another school bus pulled up. A team with matching jackets spilled out of the bus and ran into the school. A little way away, another team grouped together, talking excitedly. They all wore matching shirts and looked really tall. High-school kids, probably. We would compete not just against other middle schools but also against high schools.

If I cared about robotics, this all would be very nerve-racking. Not that I cared or anything. I was doing this for my deal with Evelyn. That's all.

The other team let out a loud cheer and ran toward the gym.

I gulped.

When I glanced to the side, everyone looked as nervous as I was. No one looked more nervous than Evelyn, though. She clutched her hair as if it were a lifeline, and all the color had drained from her face.

I gulped again. Then I rolled my shoulders back and tried to put on my best tough impression.

"What are we standing around for? Let's go," I said. We grabbed our stuff from the bus and started toward the school. Team A had already headed inside with Mrs. Weir. We followed their route through the front doors and into a massive hallway.

The hallway stretched out, a mix of light browns and deep blues. It had massive pillars near the door and looked really fancy. Was this what high school was? I breathed in the scent of floor cleaner and walked onward, through a hallway with colors like the ocean, leading the others into that vast hall and to the bright noise beyond.

We stepped through the double doors into the high-school gym. I blinked at the bright fluorescent lights, my eyes wide as I took in the strange new world.

In the center of the gym was a massive arena, full of cubes like the ones we had practiced with. Behind it was an enormous projector screen and a camera rig hanging over the arena.

"Oh wow," said DJ. "They're livestreaming this one. Looks like I picked a good time for my new style." Today the side of DJ's hair had a robot shaved into it, one that looked remarkably like our robot. He was also wearing a new leg splint, this one shinier than before and with red straps that matched our Barton Team B robotics shirts.

Our whole team was wearing the robotics shirts, though mine was half hidden under my hoodie. Varsha had even taken the time to draw gears on her shorts and wore a matching red scrunchie around her usual ponytail.

Around the arena were about thirty tables, all spread apart. Signs taped to each table told us the different team names: Cordell Wolves. Tech Tigers. Maricopa High. Barton Team A. Cortex Crew. Silver Junior High. And there, in the back corner behind several other teams, Barton Team B.

I clenched my fist around the design notebook.

We had this. We would be fine. I wasn't nervous. I wouldn't get nervous over something silly like robotics.

The robot was perfect, everything was wonderful, and it would be fine.

I hoped the notebook would be good enough. I hoped my art was good enough. What if the judges didn't like the little drawings I had added in? What if they hated anime style? What if the whole team got disqualified because they hated the notebook *that* much?

I shuddered and ran my hand over the notebook's cover.

We wove between the other tables toward our own. Most of the teams had already arrived. They were pulling the robots out of their bins, laying out parts, and quickly shouting commands at one another.

Our own table was tucked away in the gym corner, in a small bubble of calm, far from the arena and bleachers where the audience would sit.

"Oh, this is nice," said Evelyn. "It's quieter back here."

I nodded and set down my stuff. "What now?"

"Oh. Um . . . ," said Evelyn. "Let's get the robot out and make sure it survived transport. Then Allie can take the notebook to the judge's table, and we can go to the robot inspection station and check in." She smiled around at us and nodded to Varsha.

Varsha dropped the plastic bin onto our table. She yanked off the lid and reached for the robot. Then she froze. The lid fell from her hands and clattered against the polished gym floor.

"Oh no," whispered Varsha.

We all crowded in to see. The robot was in the plastic bin, with old shirts packed around it. The metal parts and wheels all looked good. But the wires that led from the robot brain to all the motors . . . they were cut in half.

Evelyn let out a small choking sound.

I stared at the bot in shock. What had happened? It was fine when Varsha had packed it up yesterday. I had been sitting right there, drawing a picture of her checking it over. It had been in perfect shape. She had closed it into the tub, and we started transporting supplies to the office. When would somebody have—

My hands curled into fists. "Jeremy Jacobs."

Evelyn whimpered. Alex gasped. Santino shook his head, and DJ's face turned purple. Varsha scowled.

"I knew I saw him leaving the robotics room," said Alex.

"He must've cut the wires." I frowned. We had left the robot all alone in the classroom. He might have seen us leave. He might have been coming over to torment us, like he had told Evelyn and Santino. But when he saw the tub with the robot in it, all alone . . . it was the perfect opportunity. And then we came back and hauled the tub off to the office, without even checking to make sure everything was okay.

Evelyn took a deep breath. Then she took another. Her hands were trembling. Her eyes brimmed with tears.

"He ruined it." She sniffled, rocking back on her feet. "What can we do? We can't compete if our robot is broken!"

It didn't matter that I had finished the notebook. It didn't matter that I had helped Evelyn get the team back together. Jeremy broke the robot. We had no chance now. While once I might not have cared, today it felt like a stab through my calm.

That beast of anger came shredding back and piercing through my soul.

The team worked hard for this. This was their dream, the ultimate goal for Evelyn and the others. They fought hard to be here. And because he was a jerk, Jeremy had ruined it.

I looked around the gym, clenching my fists and trying to fight back that rage. I wanted to lash out. To shove the robot off the table, or to throw my notebook across the gym, or to do anything that would let me get all the emotions out of my head.

I took a deep breath. I couldn't do that. I was trying to be better than that.

I thought about what Mrs. Macquarie had taught me. Three deep breaths. Count to ten. Don't react right away.

My eyes drifted across the gym and widened. Oma walked through the double doors, and beside her was a red-headed lady I recognized as Mrs. Cole. We had met Evelyn's mom when we went to the restaurant the other day. Now they chatted happily away as they walked inside. Another lady, with long golden hair and flowing skirts, held Mrs. Cole's hand. Evelyn's other mom, probably.

Oma was still using her walker, but she seemed relaxed. Happy. She looked across the gym and saw me. She smiled and waved, then turned to the bleachers and let Evelyn's moms help her up the bleacher stairs.

My heart wrenched.

Oma had come all this way to watch the tournament. Oma had been proud of me lately, proud of how I was part of robotics now. I hadn't disappointed Oma since the fight with Evelyn. I couldn't let her down now.

We had to fix this.

I spun around and stared at Evelyn. She had a faraway expression as she rocked on her feet and stared at the robot.

"Evelyn, snap out of it." I clapped in front of her face, and she blinked. "We can do this. What do we need to fix it?"

Evelyn took a deep, shuddering breath. She shook her head and tugged on her hair.

"We could—no. Maybe . . . no, wait . . ." She took one more deep breath. Then a third. When she spoke again, she sounded calmer. "If Naiely were here, she'd tell us to go talk to the other teams."

"Oh," said DJ. "Maybe somebody brought extra wires."

"We have two extras in the toolbox," said Varsha. She hauled the lid off the toolbox and dug around in it, sending gears and screws and Allen wrenches flying. She held up two wires triumphantly. "Let's replace the wires in the wheel motors. As long as the robot can roll, we can compete. We might have to push cubes into the goal zones instead of lifting them up and stacking them, but that's better than nothing."

Alex reached for his computer. "I'll make a backup program, so the robot can work off two motors. But if we can find more wires, we might not even need it."

I nodded. This sounded like a plan. This could work.

"Okay," said Evelyn. Some color had returned to her face. She took another deep breath. "Okay. We know what to do. We can fix this. Alex, you stay here and work on the programming. DJ, stay with him in case he needs anything. The rest of us, let's split up and go talk to other teams."

Everyone scattered. I grabbed my notebook and a pencil and rushed toward the nearest group.

The team I approached was another middle school, wearing bright blue shirts with paw prints on them and a logo that said Cortex Crew. They looked like they were having as much of a problem as we were.

"It's still too wide," cried one boy on the team. The other three fought with one of the wheels, trying to push it closer to the robot.

"We need a smaller driveshaft," said another. He grunted as the wheel slid back half a centimeter. "I told you we should've checked this before the tournament."

On the table lay a pile of screws and bolts and gears, and in the middle of it, an extra wire.

I walked up to the first boy. He was standing back with his arms crossed and seemed to be the team leader.

"Hey," I asked. "Can I borrow that extra wire?"

The boy sent me an exasperated expression.

"No," he said. "We might need it. Go away. We're dealing with a problem here."

I scowled. He reminded me of Evelyn when I first met her, quick to judge and impatient. If I were to draw him, it would be with an irritation mark across his head and a glare in his eyes.

"This isn't working," cried another boy. He looked up with desperation washing across his face. "We should've brought a saw. Then we could cut this extra piece off, and it wouldn't be too wide anymore. Ugh! We can't get disqualified for this!"

An idea hit me. I remembered Friday afternoon when we were taking everything to the office. DJ carried the bolt cutters along with some extra batteries. He had slung them over his shoulder and walked in a silly march that had us all in tears with laughter.

I was sure that DJ had brought them into the gym today.

"We have bolt cutters you can borrow," I said.

The Cortex Crew froze. The boys all turned to look at me.

"Really?" asked their leader. The annoyed look dropped off his face. "You're sure we can borrow them?"

I nodded. I pointed across the room to where Alex and DJ worked in their dark red shirts.

"See those two boys over there? Ask the one with the robot in his hair. He'll grab it for you."

"Thank you!" The team leader ran off across the gym floor, bound for our table.

"Seriously though, thanks," said one of the other boys. They stopped messing with the robot and stepped away from it.

One grimaced and scratched sheepishly at his hair. "We forgot to measure our robot before the tournament, and it's one inch too wide. But that's because this driveshaft is sticking out too far. If we can cut the end off, the robot will pass inspection, and we'll be able to compete."

I smiled and nodded, pretending like I had a clue what he was saying.

"Can we do anything to thank you?" That question came from another of the boys.

I smirked and crossed my arms, standing proudly at my full height. "Let's talk about that spare wire you guys have . . ."

I returned to my table a few minutes later, triumphantly clinging to one spare wire. I tossed it to DJ, and he quickly got to work swapping it out for one of the broken ones. A minute later, Evelyn ran over.

"The Tech Tigers have two extra wires," she cried. "But one of their gears broke, and the rest of their twenty-four-tooth gears are warped. I think they ordered from the same bad batch we did a while ago. Also, I'm talking to the Tech Tigers and—oh my God!"

She bounced up and down on the balls of her feet and stared at us with wide eyes.

She didn't have to say anything more. DJ and I dove into the mess of our supply box, grabbing as many good twenty-four-tooth gears as we had to spare. We tossed them to Evelyn, and she ran back toward the Tech Tigers.

By the time she came back to the table with the two wires, Santino and Varsha had returned too.

"I talked to the Wolves. They didn't have any wires, but they forgot to bring the right-size Allen wrench so I'm gonna loan them our extra one," said Santino before hurrying off again.

"Team A had one extra wire. Mrs. Weir was helping them with a wheel problem but said she'll be over in a minute if we still need to find more," said Varsha. She held it up. Then she grinned as she noticed what Evelyn and I had brought back. "I think we have enough now. We did it!"

We had solved the problem. In the time it took for our families to find their spots in the bleachers, we had found four extra wires. We saved the robot.

I sighed and grabbed the design notebook. While the team quickly fixed the bot and got it ready for inspection, I added one last picture. It was us, all standing around the robot. Underneath, I labeled it, "High-key, the Best Team Ever."

Then it was time to check in for the tournament.

CHAPTER TWENTY-THREE
EVELYN

I let out a massive sigh as Varsha plugged in the last wire. Broken wires lay sprawled across the table, a reminder of the near disaster.

I would never forgive Jeremy for this. When we got back, I would report him to Principal Gilbert so fast.

There was no time to be afraid anymore. No time to panic. Allie ran off to turn in our design notebook. Alex made last-minute fixes to the code. DJ was watching other teams drive. By the time the tournament started, he'd know who we wanted to partner with when the alliance selection came around after lunch. Before lunch, we'd be given random teams as our alliance partners for each match. If we made it into the semifinals, though? Then we'd get to choose.

I knew who I wanted as an alliance, but I didn't dare let myself dream. Even so, I couldn't help glancing over at the Tech Tigers's table. They worked well together, swapping out the broken gears and preparing their robot. I, Evelyn, had helped them. I talked to them! I brought them the new gears they needed in exchange for the wires we needed. Maybe that would count for something.

I took a deep breath in.

Our robot was ready.

Deep breath out.

We were ready.

I shoved a strand of hair under my headphones and behind my ear, and I took one last deep breath. Then I picked up the robot and looked at Varsha. "Ready for inspection?"

"Only if you are, Team Lead." Varsha smiled big and bright, and together we walked toward the inspection table.

The next few minutes became a blur. The judges measured our robot. Mrs. Weir stopped by to watch, then headed off to check on Team A again. After a few long moments, the judges told us it was the perfect size and approved it. Then Varsha grabbed the robot from me and took it to where DJ waited by the arena so he could practice with it before the match started.

They'd make a cute couple. With their pranks and silliness, Varsha and DJ were meant for each other.

I headed back toward the table alone, where I sat down and let out a lengthy sigh, enjoying the calm of our corner. Allie was already there, drawing in her sketchbook. She gave me a quick smile before turning back to her picture.

The notebook was turned in, the robot was done, and there was nothing left for me to do right now. We had reached the "hurry up and wait" part of the tournament.

Somebody tapped my shoulder. I turned around. Mum and Mama stood behind me, both wearing shirts that said "Go, Barton Team B!" They smiled at me, and Mama's dimples showed at full force.

I lunged at them and tried to hug both my moms at once.

Mum giggled. Her bracelets jangled as she wrapped an arm around me and the other around Mama. It was a big and perfect Cole family hug.

"I know we're supposed to stay in the stands, but we had to come tell you good luck," said Mum. Her voice sounded musical and sweet.

"We're proud of you," added Mama. "Whatever happens, you worked hard, and we love you."

"We're not going to get disqualified again," I said, hugging my moms tighter. "I won't disappoint you this time."

"Evelyn?" Mama gasped and pulled back to look at me. "You didn't think you disappointed us at your last tournament, did you?"

I blushed and looked down at the wooden floors.

"I mean, I got disqualified. You wasted all that gas money to go, and I know we don't have a lot right now, and . . ." My words stuck in my throat, a million worries riding on my moms' strained conversations at night and the things it might mean. "I just want to do good. I want to win the tournaments, and get to Worlds, and get on a good high-school team, and get to college, so I can have a good job and take care of *you* someday!"

I took a deep breath and peered up at Mama.

She stared at me, her hand over her mouth. "Oh, Evelyn, have you been worried about that this whole time?"

I swallowed hard and nodded.

"Sweetie, money might be tight, but we're not in trouble," said Mum. She put a gentle hand on my shoulder. "We just have to plan things out and budget carefully. And eventually, I'll have a job again, or my jewelry business will start doing better, and that will be that."

"It's our job to care for you," said Mama. "You don't need to shoulder that burden. I promise." Mama put a finger under my chin, lifting my head.

"Darling," she continued, "We were sad for you at the last tournament, not disappointed. If anything, I was mad at the judges for disqualifying you."

My moms stepped back and exchanged a look. Mama nodded, and Mum fished around in her purse. She pulled out a small gift bag and handed it to me.

"I made this for you," she said. "To bring you luck. I hope it helps you see that we weren't disappointed."

"I picked out the beads she used," added Mama. She reached for Mum's hand, and they both smiled as I opened up the gift bag. Inside lay a small silver bracelet. I pulled it out and gasped.

It was a charm bracelet, like the ones Mum loved to wear. But while Mum's charms were from places she and Mama always talked about visiting one day, this one had little robot charms on it.

"It's so pretty!" I cried. I tried putting it on but couldn't get the latch open.

Mama took my arm. "Here," she said. "Let me help."

She looped the bracelet around my wrist and secured the latch. "I hope this shows you we are proud of you. You are our smart, genius engineer, no matter what happens today."

"You don't have to worry about taking care of us," said Mum. "You can just have fun with your robotics. And, oh my. Speaking of that, your robot looks impressive!" She turned to look at the arena where DJ drove the bot around.

I smiled and held up my arm, admiring the way the light shone on the silver bracelet. It was loose enough that it didn't bother my wrists much, and it was so pretty! The color reminded me of the metal of the robot, perfect and strong. It warmed me almost as much as their words.

"Thank you," I said. "I love you both!"

Mama tucked a strand of her red hair behind her ears. "We love you too, sweetheart. Now, go stand by the table. Your mum needs a picture. Oh, is that Allie, I see? Allie, join in, please!"

Allie rolled her eyes but scooted closer to the robot. I leaned in also, and Mum held up her phone to snap a picture.

Out of the corner of my eye, I noticed one of the tournament volunteers walking toward our table, wearing a concerned frown. Parents weren't supposed to be near the pit tables. It got too crowded if all the parents were hanging out with us. They allowed only students and coaches in this area.

I pushed Mama lightly.

"Mum and Mama, I'll find you in between the matches. But go away before we get in trouble. I love you!"

Mama made a face. Mum laughed. She lifted her phone and took one last picture, then smiled and dragged Mama away.

"Your moms are cool," said Allie. She still sat at the table, sketching a picture.

"Yeah. They're the best," I said. I glanced at Allie, hesitant. Then I added, "I think they like you."

"They barely know me." Allie laughed.

"Yeah, but you're my best friend. They have to like you."

I took a seat at the table again, and Allie sat beside me. Around us was the sound of all the teams running to and from inspection, or hauling their robots to the arena. Excited chatter filled the air, crackling like electricity through my veins and loud enough to be almost overwhelming despite my headphones. I couldn't sit still, couldn't stop my feet from tapping on the floor and my hands from trembling.

It was almost time.

"Do you mean it?" asked Allie suddenly.

"Mean what?"

"What you said about me being your best friend?"

I blushed and nodded. "Naiely is my *best* best friend, but you're a best friend too now."

Allie smiled and punched me lightly on the shoulder. "You're not too bad yourself."

I grinned. "Maybe you can come over sometime and hang out."

I blushed as I spoke and glanced at the ground. Usually people didn't come over to my house. For one thing, I didn't used to have any friends, other than Naiely. For another, it was *embarrassing*. Most of the kids at school lived in nice houses, and we were in a tiny apartment. I never wanted anyone to see how small my room was or how old the TV was. I didn't want them to see the stack of bills Mum hid in the kitchen cabinet, or how our fridge was sometimes more empty than full. But Allie didn't seem like somebody who would care. Allie wouldn't make fun of me for it. She was my friend.

"That would be fun," said Allie. She turned back to her sketchbook. "You can come hang out with me at my oma's house too, if you want."

"I'd like that!"

I smiled at Allie. Then I sighed and looked around the gym. This might be the only calm moment we had in the next eight hours. As soon as every team finished with inspection, the real fun would start. We would get our match list and learn who we were competing with and competing against. From then until lunch, every minute would be full of matches and competitions. And after lunch, if we did well enough, we'd get to choose a partner team and compete in the semifinals.

I took a deep breath, reminding myself to enjoy the moment. Last tournament, my team had already ditched me by now, and my robot fell apart. It was different this time. My team liked me. They were my friends. We had overcome an enormous challenge together. The only thing that would make this day better would be having Naiely here.

But that wouldn't happen. She was off in California, and her parents had no time to drive her all the way back to Arizona just because her friend missed her. I shook my head. I should focus on enjoying the time with my friends that *were* here. Besides, I'd see Naiely soon enough. At Worlds.

My phone buzzed. I pulled it out and made a face at the cracked screen.

"Spam call?" asked Allie. She hunched over her sketchbook, already working on a picture of the tournament arena.

I shrugged and reached to hang up.

I froze.

I didn't recognize the phone number, but I knew that area code. The call was coming from California. My hands shook as I answered the phone. I hardly dared to hope.

"Hello?"

"Ev! Ev, Ev, Ev, Ev, Ev! It hasn't started yet, right?" Naiely's voice sounded clear through the phone. I gasped.

"We passed inspection and are waiting for the matches to start," I said, trying to stay calm. I looked at Allie with wide eyes and mouthed: *Naiely!* Allie grinned and gave me a thumbs-up.

"Oh good! I got a phone. Can you believe it?" Her excitement rang through her voice. "I wanted my first call to be with you, so I can wish you luck."

"Thanks, Nai." My nervousness faded as I talked to Naiely. It was amazing to hear her! This wasn't as good as her being here, but it was the next best thing. "I'm happy you called!"

"You'll talk to me all day long when you get to Worlds! Good luck today. Don't forget to take deep breaths and stay calm. I found the livestream, and I'll be watching and cheering you all on. Oh! I think Varsha is on the screen!"

I looked over at the practice arena where DJ sat in a chair while Varsha restacked the cubes he knocked over. An idea hit me. I leaped up from the table and ran to the arena. I leaned in and looked up at the camera, smiling and waving wildly.

"Oh!" shrieked Naiely. "I see you! I see you!"

I laughed and waved again, then looked over at DJ and Varsha. They stared at me with wide eyes, probably wondering if I was losing it.

"Naiely is watching the livestream," I explained. Naiely laughed from the other side of the phone, even as DJ and Varsha popped their heads in the arena and waved at the camera.

Santino ran over, holding a piece of paper in his hands.

"We have the match list," he shouted. He thrust the list toward us. "We are going first! First! I'm so nervous."

I gasped. "Naiely, I've got to go," I said. "But I'll call you when we're done. I promise."

Naiely laughed, bright and happy. "You better. I need to test out my new phone as much as possible."

The line went silent. Naiely had ended the call. I made a face at the camera one last time, knowing she watched.

Then I joined my team as we took the robot back to our table. Mrs. Weir waited there, highlighters in hand.

"Make sure to mark your matches when you have a chance," she said, dropping them onto our table.

I forced a smile, even as DJ nodded and Varsha grinned.

"We've got this!" said Varsha.

"Of course you do. I am so proud of how your team has pulled together." Mrs. Weir smiled, then glanced over her shoulder. "If you'll excuse me, my brilliant engineers, Team A has been having a crisis with a broken motor. But good luck! I'll be watching your match!" She turned and bustled away, weaving past the arena that was now being set up for the first match and across the gym to Team A.

I stared at the match list and shuddered. My nerves were bouncing around again, locking in place in my mind. I couldn't focus. Couldn't breathe. Our alliance team was already lining up at the arena, and our opponents were there as well.

For a moment, panic seized me. I considered grabbing the robot and driving it myself to make sure nothing went wrong.

No.

That was the thought of controlling Evelyn. My team knew what they were doing. DJ was a better driver than I ever could be. I had to trust him.

Santino and I picked up the robot and carried it over toward the arena. We set it down and ran to join Varsha, Allie, and Alex at the edge, where they sat and watched.

The arena was an enormous square, with different-colored foam mats on the ground and a line down the center showing where each team's side was. There were three goal zones on each side and enormous plastic cubes stacked all throughout the arena. The more cubes you stacked in your goal zones, the more points you got, but the other teams could knock cubes out too. You had to stack up cubes while also defending your zones.

They divided our robots into two teams. Us and our randomly assigned alliance partner—the Cortex Crew—on the blue side, while the enemy bots were red. DJ walked up to the blue side of the arena, then sat in a chair they provided for him, holding his controller. He pulled his goggles over his eyes and grinned.

With all four teams there, it was time to start the match.

"You've got this, DJ!" shouted Allie.

"You can do it," I cried. I believed it. DJ was the best driver we ever had.

The countdown started. Ten. Nine. Eight. Seven. Six.

Five.

Four.

Three.

Two.

One.

A horn blared through the air, and just like that the robots were rolling. DJ drove perfectly, racing the robot into the center of the arena and grabbing a stack of five cubes with our robot's spatula hands. Then he drove toward one of the goal zones on our side of the line. With a flick of his controller, he set all five cubes down perfectly in the goal zones.

We all screamed and cheered.

DJ was driving again. At first, I wasn't sure what he was doing, because he drove past four perfectly good cube stacks. Then I realized it.

Our alliance partner tried to pick up a cube with their claw bot, but every time the robot's claw closed around the cube, the enemy would "accidentally" bump into them, making the robot drop it. The Cortex Crew's driver looked ready to cry. DJ's eyes narrowed as he drove right at the enemy bot.

I froze. Purposely attacking other bots went against the rules and could get us disqualified. What was DJ doing?

But DJ didn't collide with the red team's robot. Instead, he spun our bot around, sliding it perfectly into place between the enemy bot and our alliance's.

"Now," he called to the other alliance driver. "¡Vamos!"

The kid smiled and quickly closed his robot's claw around a cube. He lifted it up and drove toward our side of the arena with DJ staying behind to guard him.

I let out a breath.

As DJ followed our partner, he deftly grabbed a stack of four more cubes. After our alliance partner stuck his cube in the goal zone, DJ manipulated the robot and put his four cubes on top of the one.

Time was ticking. The enemy team placed five cubes in their own goal zone. We had more cubes than them, but now the other enemy robot drove wildly toward one of our stacks, ready to knock it over.

"DJ! Run interference," I screamed. DJ looked across the arena and saw the danger. His hand flew over the controls, and he drove our bot toward the enemy.

There was no way. He wouldn't make it in time. There were only twenty seconds left on the clock. If they knocked over our stack, we would have fewer points than they did when time ran out. We were about to lose!

But somehow, DJ did it. His robot sped in front of the enemy's, right as it was about to ram into our leftmost goal zone. Instead of colliding with the tower of cubes, the other robot had to veer out of the way. The enemy team groaned.

DJ spun his bot around to grab one more cube from the arena. He lifted the robot's arm, opened the spatula hands, and dropped that cube on the stack he had saved.

The horn sounded. The robots stopped moving. Time was up.

Even though the judges still counted up points, it was clear to anyone looking that we had the most cubes in the goal zones. We had won our first match!

CHAPTER TWENTY-FOUR
ALLIE

By the fifth match, my voice hurt from cheering and screaming. But I couldn't stop. No matter how much I tried to tell myself that I didn't care about robotics, the excitement was infectious.

DJ drove the robot again for the fifth match, the last one we had before lunch. The timer counted down. The robots raced around the field. DJ was an amazing driver, zipping the robot this way and that with perfect precision.

The timer buzzed, and we all screamed out in excitement. All three of our goal zones were packed full of the plastic cubes. We had won again.

The judges finished counting the points and gave the all clear for teams to take their robots off the field. We got up and ran to help DJ with the robot, stopping to shake hands with the losing team before we left the arena. It was good sportsmanship and all. But as soon as we had shaken the last hand, we ran back toward our table, carrying the robot with us.

"Okay, I think I saw the wheel wobbling that last match," said Evelyn. "Santino, can you get on that?"

Santino nodded and set to work on the robot.

"Oh, and Alex, I noticed the robot is listing to the left a bit." Evelyn tapped on the left motor. "The motor might be wearing out, but we don't have time to replace it. Can you increase the rpm in the code to correct it?"

"On it," said Alex. He pulled out his laptop and set to work.

As Evelyn gave out orders, I glanced around the gym, searching for the next thing to draw. My eyes drifted past the enormous screen with the team rankings scrolling on it. I froze and gasped.

"Ev, look!"

With this latest win, we reached rank eight. Evelyn let out a sound like a gasp and a cry all at once. Her hands fluttered to her mouth.

"We did it!" Evelyn sounded breathless as she turned to grin at me and the rest of the team. "We're in the top eight! We'll be in the semifinals after lunch!"

"It's a dream come true," cried Varsha.

"This is . . . ¡Guau!," said DJ.

"We might win the tournament if we keep this up!" said Santino as he tightened a screw by the bot's front wheel.

Their joy wound through me, and I found myself grinning from ear to ear. I looked over my shoulder to the stands where Oma sat halfway up. Did she know? Had she seen the rankings yet?

"Varsha," Evelyn said. She rocked on her feet and looked

around. "If we're in the top eight, we need a good alliance. You're the most confident among us. Take the business cards and go introduce our team to the other top-eight teams. If we can get a good alliance . . ." She didn't finish her sentence. We were all thinking it.

If one of the best teams would ally with us, we'd be unstoppable.

"Ohhhhh . . . ," said Varsha. "I'll start with the Tech Tigers." She bounced up and down, then hesitated and looked at Evelyn. "But maybe you should come with me to talk to them?"

Evelyn had a strange look on her face as Varsha mentioned the Tigers, but the minute Varsha asked her to come along, her expression turned into excitement. Right. The *Tech Tigers*, that team she had been talking about. The one she dreamed of joining. The one our entire team seemed to be in love with.

Well, good for them.

"I'm going to go see my oma," I said. I'd been waiting all day to talk to her.

The others nodded. I walked away from the team, heading toward the bleachers. Oma chatted with Evelyn's moms, halfway up in the bleachers, where they had the best view. She seemed to like them. That was nice. Sometimes I worried about how lonely Oma was.

Maybe Oma needed friends too.

When I reached the stands, Oma's eyes brightened.

"Oh, Allie," she said. She opened her arms for a hug, and I leaped up the stairs to her. Her arms wrapped around me, like a blanket of comfort and warmth. "This is all very exciting! You are doing amazing."

I grinned and pulled back. I tucked a strand of my hair behind my ears and shrugged. "I mean, my job was the robotics notebook. I'm not really doing anything for the team *now*."

Oma crossed her arms. "Nonsense. I've watched you cheering on your team and supporting them. I saw you helping them grab supplies and solve problems. Just because you're not the driver doesn't mean you're not helping." Her smile grew wider, and she shook her head. "Oh, Allie, I am proud of all the hard work you've done. You know your parents would be proud too."

They *would* be proud of me. I was sure of that now. But it was nice to hear Oma say it aloud. I lunged forward and wrapped Oma in another hug.

"Thank you, Oma. I have to go help the team now, but thank you."

"You go be with your friends. I'm taking Mrs. and Mrs. Cole here to lunch in a few minutes. Don't you worry about me." Oma smiled brightly and nodded to where Evelyn's moms were gathering up their purses. Then she beamed back at me. "Oh, I am so proud of you."

"Thanks, Oma," I said. "I'll come say hi again when you get back from lunch."

I let Oma go and ran back down the bleacher stairs. As I reached the bottom step, I noticed somebody else familiar sitting near the edge of the bleachers. For a second, I froze.

Then I rolled my shoulders back and walked over to Principal Gilbert.

"Hi, Principal Gilbert." I clutched at my shirt, twisting the red fabric through my fingers. It was weird to spot him outside the office, strange to talk to him. But I had to know . . . What did he think? Was he impressed? Was he considering letting us keep robotics?

"Allison, good afternoon," he said.

My hands clenched into fists. I forced myself to stay calm. Today was a good day. I would not let Principal Gilbert ruin that. I also couldn't let this go. Not anymore.

"Principal Gilbert, I prefer to be called Allie. Nobody calls me Allison. My parents didn't even call me that. You always want me to be respectful and make better choices, but how respectful is it to call somebody the wrong name all the time? Hearing my full name makes me really upset."

It was the most I had ever said to him at once, and it caught his attention. Principal Gilbert's eyes widened. He folded his hands in his lap and looked studiously around the gym.

"My apologies. I will make a note of that . . . Allie."

Well. That was unexpected.

Principal Gilbert cleared his throat. "Anyway. Good job."

That was it? Just "good job"? We were working our butts off at this tournament and that's all he had to say?

"Good job on what?" I crossed my arms and waited.

"The tournament," he said. "Your team is impressive. Top eight, hmm? I don't think a Barton team has ever done that well."

I nodded. We were doing amazing. Even Team A had only gotten to rank sixteen.

"We're doing well," I said. "We're learning teamwork, and robotics, and have been learning how to work with other teams too. We're sharing our supplies and helping people, all while learning an important skill. I'd say robotics is pretty critical, wouldn't you?"

"I suppose it is. And these tournaments are far more exciting than I realized." Principal Gilbert cleared his throat and looked around the gym. "Oh, excuse me, Allie. I see your teacher over there . . ." He got up and hurried away, off to where Mrs. Weir was walking across the gym.

I watched him walk away. I hoped he understood, that he saw how important this was. If we won, if we brought the Tournament Champions trophy home to Barton Junior High, he couldn't cancel the robotics team, right?

Only when Principal Gilbert reached Mrs. Weir did I turn and head back toward my team.

When I got to the table, everyone was talking at once.

"We need to hurry and—"

"I can't believe—"

"Did you see their Team Lead? They're so cool and—"

"So exciting and—"

I blinked and stared around the table, then dropped my sketchbook loudly onto the fake wooden tabletop. It hit with a *thwack*. The others fell silent and turned to look at me.

"What's going on?" I asked.

Evelyn grinned. "The Tech Tigers want to be our alliance partner for the semifinals!" She let out a small shriek and jumped up and down.

"Oh, and DJ's dad is bringing us all pizza and fresh-baked pan dulce," added Varsha. "But mostly we're freaking out about the Tech Tigers."

The Tech Tigers. I looked across the gym to the scoreboard. They were in rank one right now, the best team at the tournament. With a team like them on our side, we were sure to win.

CHAPTER TWENTY-FIVE
EVELYN

I was living in a dream come true.

Our team had made it to the semifinals. We were close to winning the tournament. And better yet, the Tech Tigers wanted to ally with us. The *Tech Tigers!*

I barely believed it.

As our team ate lunch and giggled with excitement, I sent a text to Naiely, letting her know. Within seconds, my phone buzzed with her response:

OMG!!!!!!!!! YOU ARE DEF GETTING TO WORLDS!!!!

I giggled as I read it. It was true, though. With the Tech Tigers on our side, how could we possibly lose?

Even so, my heartbeat felt wild. My palms were sweaty, and I had to keep reminding myself to take deep breaths. Everything relied on us winning. *Everything.* Still, Naiely believed in us, and that brought me some calm.

I grabbed my phone and opened the camera app. I held it out.

"Hey, everyone, smile. I'm sending this to Naiely."

The rest of the team leaned in and smiled. I snapped the picture, then sent it to Naiely with a message: *We all miss you!*

She replied a second later with a long string of hearts.

It was amazing to talk to Naiely so easily now, with texting. This was 1,000 percent better than emails.

Soon enough, the lunch break ended. It was time for the first of the semifinal matches. We joined the Tech Tigers at the arena. I stuck the robot at the edge of the playing field, then sat with the rest of the team, pulling my headphones on in preparation for how loud I knew the audience would get soon. DJ grabbed his controller and sat in the driver's space on the red-team side. The Tech Tiger driver came to stand next to him, holding up a hand for a high five before they began.

"Hey," said a muffled voice next to me.

A high schooler sat on the gym floor beside me. They were tall and pretty, the sort of pretty that made my heart stutter a little. They had short black hair, brown eyes, and a heart-shaped face. I had already met them earlier, when they introduced themselves to the team as Ayleen and told us they went by "they/them" pronouns.

The words "Tech Tigers Team Lead" were written in big white letters on the back of their yellow-and-black jacket. Ayleen didn't look that old. They had to be only a year or two older than me, which made their rank as Team Lead even more impressive.

Be still, my heart.

They smiled at me now and mimed taking off head-phones. I blushed, realizing they wanted to talk to me.

"I can hear you," I mumbled, running a hand along my headphones. "These don't block all sound, just some. It's so loud in here, you know? But I can still hear you. I just . . . I um . . ."

I froze, not sure how much I should explain or if I was overexplaining. People didn't always understand. I needed my headphones, the same way I needed shirts with loose collars and sleeves that weren't too tight. Sounds and sen-sations could be a *lot* to deal with. I didn't know how to explain it, though, and I didn't want to say so much that Ayleen thought I was strange, not when they were so cool!

"Ev always wears her headphones," said Alex, leaning forward. He sat behind me, holding Santino's hand. "If we ever see her without them, we know it's not really her but an impostor."

"They're her thing," added Varsha. She smiled at me, and I relaxed a little. "And they're cool."

Allie, sitting beside me, nodded.

"Oooh," said Ayleen. They glanced around the gym, then grinned. "That's smart. It *is* really loud in here."

I nodded, still blushing but feeling a lot better. My team never really mentioned my headphones, not since the begin-ning of the year when Varsha had asked why I always had them. Naiely had been there to help me explain that time. But hearing them help me, hearing them accept me . . . it made me feel so good.

"It is so loud," I said. I shrugged, then smiled. "Hey, thanks for being our alliance team."

"No problem," they said. Ayleen ran a hand through their short, cropped hair. "We rarely ally with middle-school teams, but you all are good."

My heart felt like it might burst. Could it get better than this?

"Thanks," I said, glancing behind me. The others were pretending to talk to one another now, but from Santino's giant grin, Alex's raised eyebrows, and Varsha's smug look, I knew they had heard too. "Our team is pretty awesome."

"So," Ayleen said, keeping one eye on the match as the enemy team put their robots in position on the blue side of the arena. "When this is over, can you email me a list of all the eighth-graders on your team? I want to know who to watch out for next year. A lot of our seniors are graduating, and we need fresh blood." They grinned, a mischievous look that made my heart pound even faster.

I opened my mouth and closed it. Then did it again. Words. What were the words I needed? My mind sputtered and stalled. Allie jabbed me in the side with her elbow.

I nodded quickly. "I— Yes. I can get that for you." I think my voice rose an octave. Beside me, I heard Allie cough in a way that sounded suspiciously like laughter.

Ayleen smiled that beautiful smile. I wondered if they were dating anyone. I wondered if they'd want to date a girl like me.

Ayleen held out a small business card. "Here's my phone number and my email. Send me the list when you have a chance. And if you can tell me what each team member is skilled at, that would be awesome."

I reached out a trembling hand and took Ayleen's business card. A business card! I mean, sure, all the teams made them to hand out to other teams, but Ayleen had their own personal business card. It had embossed edges with a picture of a robot in one corner and a sugar skull in the other. In fancy letters were the words:

Ayleen Suárez

Tech Tigers Team Lead and Future Engineer

Wow.

Allie jabbed me in the side with her elbow again. "Look, it's time," she said.

The enemy teams had the robots on their side of the arena, ready to go. The countdown had started.

Five.

Four.

Three.

Two.

One.

The horn sounded, and the match began.

The Tech Tigers were an amazing ally. Their robot moved so fast, it left ours in the dust. They rolled to the other side of the arena, and Ayleen shouted out, "All right, remember the plan!"

We had worked on the plan for the first half of lunch. It was a good plan. The Tech Tigers's robot could stack seven cubes at once. But they didn't have an arm like ours. Our robot could reach even higher than theirs but only held five cubes at once and wasn't as fast. They would stack their cubes first, and we'd put more on top after.

The Tech Tigers's robot whizzed around the arena, sucking up the cubes and quickly laying them into a perfect stack of seven in each of the three goal zones.

"DJ, our turn!" I shouted to DJ.

The Tigers drove the robot away from us, toward the enemy bots to play interference. Then, while they kept impeding the enemy, DJ's robot swooped in and grabbed a stack of five cubes. He deftly drove the robot over to one of our goal zones. The robot arm lifted, the spatula hands opened, and DJ placed all five cubes on top of the ones the Tech Tigers had already stacked.

The audience cheered and clapped, and even though it was painfully loud, it was also exciting. We made a stack of twelve cubes in the goal zone. That was unheard of! DJ laughed and turned his robot for another stack of five.

One of the enemy bots swooped around the Tigers's robot and made a beeline for our fresh stack, ready to knock it over.

"Fred, we've got company!" shouted Ayleen to the driver. Fred whipped the Tech Tigers's robot around and barreled past the enemy bot to get in its way. Meanwhile, DJ picked up five more cubes and was carefully stacking them.

The audience cheered again as he completed the next stack, making another group of twelve cubes in our second goal zone. The other enemy robot was focusing on stack-ing up their own cubes, but their stacks were only four high.

Our opponents started whispering to one another, seeming to realize that there was no way for them to beat our stacks. The driver scowled and clutched at the remote, and a moment later, the second opponent bot was driving wildly toward ours.

DJ had turned our robot to grab more cubes. He didn't see the danger. I shouted his name, but it was too late. The enemy robot collided with ours. There was a crash of metal on metal.

"Hey!" I cried, "Attacking bots is against the rules!"

The referee let out a blast of his whistle. "Two-point penalty to blue team! Cordell Wolves, remove your bot from the arena."

The blue-team driver scowled and drove his bot to the edge of the arena. Now there were only three robots competing, ours and the Tigers's, and the other blue-team robot. But the damage was done. DJ tried to drive our robot forward, and it spun in a circle. The crash knocked the right-side wheel out of the motor, and all the robot could do now was spin in useless circles.

I groaned.

"Fred! Play defensive! Protect our cubes," shouted Ayleen. They grinned at me. "It's okay, we still have way more cubes than they do."

For the last thirty seconds of the match, the Tech Tigers

kept the robot playing interference, blocking the remaining robot whenever it tried to get near our stack of cubes. Then the horn blew.

The match was over.

We waited with bated breath as the referees counted up the cubes. The winner flashed on the screen. Red team had won. We had won!

"Yes!" I shrieked. The excitement buzzed through me from my fingers to my toes, rocking me back and forth.

Allie punched me in the shoulder, smiling wider than I had ever seen her. Varsha leaped up and ran to give DJ a hug. Then they quickly stepped apart and blushed. Santino and Alex high-fived.

We were continuing on to the last round.

We quickly shook hands with the opponent team. Allie glared at the team that had crashed their robot into ours, even as we followed the rules of good sportsmanship. I understood. They had played dirty.

Then we grabbed the robot and hurried to our table. Half of the Tech Tigers followed.

"Do you need any help?" asked Ayleen.

I shook my head. "I think it's only the wheel that broke?"

DJ nodded. "The left wheels were working fine. It's the right, center wheel that stopped working."

Santino and Varsha already were bent over the robot, yanking at the wheel.

Varsha looked up at me. "Looks like the driveshaft got knocked out of place and bent. Should be easy to replace."

Allie quickly dove into the spare-parts box, scrounging around for a new driveshaft. While Santino and Varsha worked to pry out the old wheel, I grabbed an Allen wrench and started tightening all screws. A few were loosened when the robot crash happened.

"If you need anything, let us know," said Ayleen. "But wow, y'all have got this together." They laughed and looked at one of their teammates that had come with them. "We have got to recruit them next year."

As Ayleen and their teammate walked away, I couldn't help giggling. They said it like it would be hard to recruit us. Ayleen had no idea. Any of us would die for a chance to be on that team.

"Aaaaand, wheel is fixed," said Santino. He looked up and smiled. "Am I good, or am I good?"

"You're the best," Alex laughed. Santino blushed and smiled.

The robot looked good again, and when DJ turned it on to test it, it drove perfectly. Across the gym, the horn sounded for the next match to start. Whichever alliance won would compete against us in the final match of the tournament. We had a few minutes while they competed. A chance to breathe. I was ready to go talk to the Tech Tigers again when Mrs. Weir swept over.

"Congratulations, my rock-star engineers," she said. "That was a wonderful win."

"Thanks!" I beamed. "Though it was all DJ. Best driver ever."

DJ laughed. "Naw. Alex's code is what really did the trick. This thing drives so smoothly, and it's easy to control one handed." He laughed and waved his right hand in the air, clenched into a fist.

Alex grinned and stared down at his phone. "Yeah, well, my programming would be pointless if it weren't for Ev, Santino, and Varsha actually building the robot."

"Please," said Varsha. "We wouldn't know what to build if Allie didn't do such good sketches in the design notebook."

We all looked around at one another, then burst into giggles. Mrs. Weir waited for us to calm down, a smile on her face.

"Well," she said when our giggles subsided. "Regardless of who is responsible for your success, I am so proud. I wasn't sure you could do it. Your team seemed to be struggling for a while, and truth be told, it took me far too long to realize you needed help. I was distracted by everything going on outside school." A strange look passed through her eyes, and her shoulders seemed to sag.

"Mrs. Weir?" I asked. "Are you okay?"

She smiled again, but this time it was sadder. "I am. Right now I have a lot going on at home. But you young engineers and your determination bring me so much joy. I'm so thankful I get to teach your class and watch how you all pulled together again, even after things got so tough. You are truly one of the best groups I have ever taught."

Allie grinned and crossed her arms. "Please, it's barely second quarter. A little early to say that, isn't it? You know, I could start another fight for old times' sake."

Mrs. Weir nudged down her glasses and gave Allie a chilling *teacher* look. "You do that, and you'll spend the rest of the year organizing the spare robotics supplies."

We all shuddered at the threat. The supply closet was crammed with boxes of spare parts, many of which hadn't been sorted out in years. Still, Mrs. Weir smiled, showing she was joking. Probably.

"Fine. No fighting. I guess I'll just have to keep working on the notebook instead," said Allie with a roll of her eyes.

Mrs. Weir laughed. "You've done a wonderful job with that notebook."

Just then the horn sounded. The last match had ended, and it was our turn next. We all turned to look at the arena.

I took a deep breath. "It's time."

As soon as the winning team from the last match repaired their robot, the final match would start. It was time to see who would win the tournament.

CHAPTER TWENTY-SIX
ALLIE

I didn't care about robotics.

That's what I'd told myself for the last month. Even when it became fun, even when I made friends, I told myself I didn't actually care. After all, robotics was for smart kids, and I didn't want to be in that class in the first place.

Who was I kidding?

I, Allie Wells, enjoyed robotics.

Okay, I didn't like the building part much, and fetching supplies was a little annoying. But I'd done an excellent job on the design notebook. Now, as I watched the team prepare for the last match and drew a few quick sketches trying to capture their expressions, I was enjoying myself.

I hadn't even thought of my parents all that much today.

No, that wasn't right. I thought about them a lot. When we watched the last match, I imagined Dad cheering us on, and Mom shaking her head when the other team broke the rules. When we fixed the robot, I imagined Mom and Dad sneaking down to the pit tables to hug me, like Evelyn's moms had earlier. I thought about how excited they would be. I imagined Mom beside me when I talked to Principal Gilbert, tall and confident and proud of me for speaking up.

I always thought about my parents. Today, though, it didn't hurt so much. Today I knew they would be proud of me, and that made me happy.

I missed them, and it still hurt. I had that big hole inside me, all those feelings I didn't quite know what to do with. But the hole was a little smaller now, and with everything going on, those feelings didn't seem so overwhelming. I was sure I'd still blow up sometimes. I wasn't a good kid now, just because I had joined robotics. But I was doing better. I had my beast under control most of the time. I understood myself more. I had friends. People to help me calm down and who accepted me. I had the words for who I was:

An artist.

Oma's pride.

Aro or ace. Maybe even both.

Evelyn's friend.

A robotics nerd.

So yeah, maybe I liked robotics a little.

My team waited for the new match to start. We sat on the edge of the arena as DJ got into place on the red-team side. In the stands behind us sat our families, our teacher, our principal, and even Miss Hawk and Mrs. Macquarie, who had wandered in together shortly after lunch. So many people watching us, rooting for us. Depending on us.

Varsha bit her lip and sat with her fingers crossed. Santino leaned against Alex, and Alex filmed the match from his phone. Evelyn alternated between looking like she would be ill and trying not to make googly eyes at Ayleen, the Tech Tigers Team Lead.

I finished catching Evelyn's expression in my sketchbook and added some shading to the curves of her face. I'd draw DJ next. Try to get that intense expression he wore when he drove the robot.

The countdown started. The horn blew, and the robots took off, like a whirlwind of metal and light. I watched as I sketched, my pencil flying across the page as the robots flew across the arena.

DJ was good. Like last time, the Tech Tigers stacked cubes in the goal zones first, while DJ played interference and made sure the enemy team couldn't send their robots across to our side. Not that it was a problem. They focused on stacking their own cubes into their three goal zones and ignored ours.

Soon all the goal zones were stacked high with cubes. As I sketched out the furrows between DJ's eyes, he started increasing our stacks. There were so many cubes, it was hard to tell who was winning.

Then Ayleen and Evelyn shouted, "Watch out!" at the same time. One of the enemy bots drove toward our leftmost goal zone, while the other stayed back to protect their own.

My hand stilled on the page. I gripped the pencil tightly, my knuckles turning white.

Thirty seconds left in the match.

The enemy bot almost reached our left goal zone. The Tech Tigers drove their robot in between, blocking it so it couldn't get at the cubes.

Twenty seconds left.

The enemy bot swerved to the right, barreling toward the middle goal zone instead. DJ had stacked up three more cubes, making a towering pile in our right-hand zone. His eyes widened as he realized the danger. He backed the bot up, trying to turn it around and get to the middle before the enemy.

Ten seconds.

DJ wasn't fast enough. The enemy bot crashed into our middle goal zone, sending the cubes tumbling to the ground.

Five seconds.

Our opponents turned their robot toward the right-hand goal zone. The robot raced forward, but this time DJ navigated our robot to be in the way, and they crashed into it instead.

The buzzer rang, and the robots grew still.

There were tons of cubes in the goal zones. I couldn't tell who won. I saw Evelyn's mouth moving as she silently counted. DJ's hand clenched into a fist. Alex and Santino held each other's hands, and Varsha, sitting behind me, barely breathed.

The judges walked around the arena, counting up the cubes. They typed something into their tablets.

Even the stands had gone quiet. Oma, Evelyn's moms, Mrs. Weir, Mrs. Macquarie, and Miss Hawk, even Principal Gilbert. They all learned forward, eyes wide and eager.

The big screen lit up.

Barton Team B and Tech Tigers – 33 cubes

Saguaro High School and Vertigo Team C – 35 cubes

The other team had two points more than we did. Two cubes more.

We lost.

The audience broke into cheers, and the other team started jumping around. The sound washed around me, odd and out of place with the disappointment I felt.

We lost. It was over.

Evelyn looked ready to cry.

Varsha was crying, small sniffles that she tried to hide.

We lost.

"Come on," I heard myself say. "We need to shake hands."

We got up and walked to the other team, shaking their hands even as the world seemed to collapse around us. They laughed and cried and hugged one another, and it felt unfair. That was supposed to be us. *We* were supposed to win.

We trudged back to the table in quiet defeat. Evelyn set the robot down and collapsed onto a chair, twisting her hair through her fingers.

I blinked rapidly, fighting back the tears that threatened to overwhelm me.

We lost.

"This sucks," muttered Alex. He closed his laptop and shoved it into his backpack.

"I'm sorry . . . ," said DJ. "I should have seen it. I just . . . I was so focused on stacking more cubes, and I didn't realize that they would ram our stack and . . ."

He fell silent.

For a few minutes, we sat at the table, a bubble of silence and sadness in the corner of the gym. Then Santino sniffled.

"Heads up," he muttered.

We looked across the gym, following his gaze. Mrs. Weir and Principal Gilbert walked our way. My heart sank. We lost, and Team A never even made it into the semifinals, which meant only one thing:

No more robotics. The class would get canceled, and I'd end up back in art or PE or somewhere terrible. Somewhere I'd keep getting angry until eventually I got expelled and went to Sunrise.

"What do I tell Naiely?" whispered Evelyn. "I won't get to see her at Worlds."

"She definitely knows if she was watching the livestream," said Varsha. She dropped her head into her hands. "I don't want to lose robotics. I don't want to lose you all."

"I'm sorry," whispered DJ again. "I'm so sorry."

"Robotics was the only class that would let me do programming," grumbled Alex. He reached for his phone, then clenched his hand into a fist instead, leaving it untouched.

Santino sniffled, leaning against Alex's shoulder. "Hi, Mrs. Weir. Principal Gilbert," he said sadly as the two reached our table.

Principal Gilbert stood over us. He ran a hand across his head and let out a long breath, glancing over at the screen with its scores. This was it. It was over.

Then he said, "Wonderful job. I cannot believe how exciting that was. You all did amazing!" A smile broke out on his face.

We gawked at Principal Gilbert.

"Are you sure you watched the right team?" asked Alex. "We lost."

"Yes, that was unfortunate. But second place? We've never had a team do this well!" Principal Gilbert smiled wider, beaming around the table.

"My young engineers *are* very impressive," added Mrs. Weir.

Even though I always told myself I didn't care what teachers said, my heart swelled with a little pride at her words. We *were* impressive.

"This tournament pits middle schoolers against high schoolers," added Mrs. Weir. "The middle-school teams rarely keep up with the high-school teams, but look at how our kids did! Consider how well they'll do next time."

I stared at Mrs. Weir and Principal Gilbert. For a moment we were all silent. Everyone had the same question, but nobody dared to ask it.

I clenched my fists around my sketchbook. "Does this mean you aren't canceling robotics?"

Varsha sat up. Alex and Santino crossed their fingers. DJ leaned forward. And Evelyn . . . Evelyn sat so still she was like a marble statue, ready to shine or crumble depending on what was said.

"No. I'm not canceling robotics. I'd like to see what you young folks are capable of," Principal Gilbert said. "Mrs. Weir and I have spoken about it. We will keep robotics going this year and see if we can work up some interest in the class. Perhaps we can get a few more students to swap electives and join robotics next semester. In fact, I'd like to have you and Team A show off your robots at our upcoming assembly. Then we'll see what enrollment looks like before deciding anything for next school year."

"And," said Mrs. Weir breathlessly, looking at Principal Gilbert, "Principal Gilbert is allocating some funds so we can all attend one more tournament in early December. You'll have one last try before State rolls around in second semester."

Evelyn gasped. "We'll have another chance to make it to State?"

Principal Gilbert nodded. "I'm impressed." When he spoke, he looked at me. "You've done well."

I smirked. Of course we had, and I didn't need Principal Gilbert to tell me that. I didn't need his approval or support. I had my friends for that. I was working hard on the stuff Mrs. Macquarie had taught me, so when I met with her again, I could tell her about all the times that I'd controlled my temper. I had an appointment scheduled with the therapist Oma wanted me to see too. I was going to keep trying harder, really trying. For my friends. For Oma. For my parents.

I had a lot of work ahead, but I could live with that.

"Hey," I said. "Thanks. Though . . . can I talk to you? You need to know what Jeremy Jacobs did. We *almost* didn't get to compete because of him."

Even as I spoke, filling in a shocked Principal Gilbert, my mind was already racing ahead. One more chance. One more tournament.

I shouldn't be so excited. After all, I had been trying to tell myself I hated robotics.

But really . . . as long as I had such a great team around, I loved robotics after all.

CHAPTER TWENTY-SEVEN
EVELYN

It was time for awards.

It felt bittersweet, in a way. We had lost the tournament. We weren't going to State yet. Worlds was so far away.

Yet, we had another chance. Principal Gilbert wasn't canceling robotics. We could make it. I already had five texts from Naiely, full of ideas for helping the robot. Her latest one had me fighting back tears all over again.

Dad says we can visit AZ for Winter Break! I can come hang out for two weeks. Can I be an honorary Barton Team B member and help you all build? You are getting together over Winter Break to build more, right? I want to join!!!!!

When I showed it to Allie, she raised an eyebrow. "*Are we getting together over Winter Break to work on the robot?*"

Winter Break was still over a month away. We would get two weeks off from school, two weeks to relax. But if we made it to State at the next tournament, then we'd probably want to work on the bot over those two weeks, when not celebrating holidays and all.

"If Mrs. Weir lets one of us take the robot home, I'd love that," I said. Given how excited she was for us to improve the robot, I'd be shocked if she told us we couldn't.

"I vote we meet at your place," said Varsha. "I bet you already have all sorts of tools and robot parts there."

I shrugged. "My place is kind of small." Though I did have a lot of robotics parts in my room, scavenged from yard sales and Goodwill.

"That's fine. We can also meet at my house," said DJ. He leaned over my shoulder and looked at my phone. "Oh, tell Naiely she better bring doughnuts as an apology for ditching us."

"I can't believe you all are thinking about Winter Break already," Santino laughed. "It's so far away!"

I laughed too and typed my reply to Naiely.

We all made our way to the bleachers as we talked. A lot of the parents had left and some teams too. We stuck around, though, even though we probably wouldn't win any awards. It was good sportsmanship and all.

Ayleen and the Tech Tigers sat down next to us.

"Sorry about the match," Ayleen said.

I shrugged and adjusted my headphones. It was a lot easier to talk now that more people had left, and there weren't so many conversations in the air. "I'm sorry too. We let you down."

"Naw." They waved their hand in the air and made a face. "It's no big deal. We won the tournament last month, which means we get to go to State, anyway. We came to this one to get more practice."

"Oh," I said, blinking at them. No wonder the Tech Tigers teamed up with our middle-school team. They already won once. It didn't matter if they lost the rest of their tournaments, since they were going to State no matter what. "Well, congrats."

"Hey, y'all will get there. You were so close." Ayleen smiled at me. "We can give you some pointers and help you with your robot before your next tournament, if you want. Call me tomorrow, and we can coordinate times to meet, cool?"

My heart stuttered again. A chance to talk with Ayleen more? That would be amazing. I blushed, from the bottoms of my toes to the tip of my bright red hair.

"Yeah. That would be great."

Somebody tapped on the microphone. The chatter in the stands stopped, and we all watched as a judge stepped forward.

"Testing. Testing," he murmured into the microphone. "All right, it is time for awards!"

Everyone cheered, and even though I felt a little sad, I made myself applaud.

"Thank you for attending the Fifth Annual Westview High School Robotics Tournament. To start off, we have our tournament champions. Congrats to . . ."

The crowd cheered again, loud enough to drown his voice out and ring painfully even through my headphones. The Team Leads for the two winning teams hopped off the stands and rushed forward, smiling and laughing as they accepted their award.

Jealousy burned bitterly in my throat. That should have been us up there. It could have been us.

I took a deep breath and forced myself to applaud. Next time. We would make it next time. We had one more tournament coming up. One more chance. We made it further than ever before. My team was amazing. Nothing would stop us next time. I let out the breath.

The winning teams sat down, and the awards continued on. The Judge's Award came next. Then the Design Award. Those didn't send you to State, but they gave you a cool trophy. I held my breath as the judge announced each award, hoping maybe we would at least win one of those.

Barton Team B never got called.

It was hard to keep applauding, to hide the disappointment. Finally, it was the last award. The judge paced back and forth before the stands as he spoke.

"This final award is a special one. It's the Excellence Award. We give this to a team that showed perseverance and good teamwork. A team that worked hard and showed dedication to robotics."

I didn't even dare to hope. The Excellence Award always went to the best teams, teams like the Tech Tigers. It never went to little middle schools like us.

"This award brings with it not only a trophy but also a State qualification. The team that receives this award will get to compete in the State championship."

My breath caught, and I stared at the metal stands below my feet. How nice would that be? How lovely. It was fine, though. We would have our second chance at the next tournament. We'd make our robot perfect and then get to State.

"The team that won the award this time truly inspired us. They worked well together and solved problems quickly and efficiently, even when things went terribly wrong. They helped the other teams and loaned them supplies, and they showed consistent good sportsmanship throughout the tournament. But most impressive was their design notebook. This notebook was the best one we judges have seen in *years*."

A small, frightening bit of hope twisted at me. Allie grabbed my arm, her eyes wide.

"This notebook didn't just have technical drawings and labels, but some of the most interesting descriptions we have ever seen. And the pictures . . . There were fantastic pictures, not only of the robot but of the team in various stages of work. After seeing this notebook, we knew that this team deserved the Excellence Award."

I bit my lip and clenched my hands in my lap, not daring to even breathe. Allie's fingers dug into my arm, and I heard her breath catch.

"The Excellence Award goes to . . . Barton Team B! Please send up your Team Lead!"

The roar from the stands was almost drowned out by the roaring in my head. It was so loud I had to squish my headphones to my ears to quiet the world down, but I barely cared. We won! We won the Excellence Award. We were going to State!

My phone buzzed, and I knew it was Naiely texting me a million messages as she watched the livestream. I heard my moms farther back in the stands, screaming my name in excitement. Ayleen yelled congrats and hit my back. My dreams and goals flashed before my eyes, closer than ever.

I stood up and took a step forward, almost in a daze. Then I stopped. I turned around and grabbed Allie's arm, then motioned for Varsha to come too.

"Come on," I shouted over the cheers of the crowd. "You made the notebook! You two did most of the work on it. Come up with me!"

Allie's freckled face flushed, and she smiled. Varsha laughed and grabbed Allie's other arm. Together, we ran over to the judge to accept the trophy.

He handed it over. "Wonderful job," he said. "Truly wonderful. Congratulations."

We turned around, and together Allie, Varsha, and I held up the trophy. I saw my moms in the stands, laughing and hugging. Mum pulled out her phone and started taking pictures. Allie's grandma stood beside them, a wide smile lighting up her eyes as she applauded.

My view was blocked as DJ hurried over. The rest of the team followed, with Santino and Alex piling on, forming a massive group hug.

"We did it!" somebody was screaming, and after a second, I realized it was me. "You all did it! You are amazing! We're going to State!"

"I will make the notebook even *better* before then!" shrieked Allie.

We laughed and hugged and hugged until Mum ran down onto the gym floor and started calling for us to face her so she could take a team picture.

No. Not just a team picture.

A family picture.

This was my family standing with me, as true as Mum and Mama were. With them, it didn't matter if I was nervous or awkward or sometimes got too obsessed about things. It didn't matter if I got stressed and anxious. They liked me, and they helped me be better. Together, we could do anything. We were going to State, and Worlds would follow.

We would be amazing.

I knew, because we already were.

ACKNOWLEDGMENTS

Just like the team's robot wasn't built by one person, this story wouldn't be possible without so many people's support.

I'd like to start by thanking my agent, Emily Forney. Emily saw the potential in my little book and helped it truly gain its wings. Thank you, Emily, for believing in my story and constantly championing it. You are as amazing as the little swoosh curl in Henry Cavill's hair in *Enola Holmes*.

Also a huge thank-you to my editor, Jonah Heller. Thank you, Jonah, for helping me make this story better than I ever imagined. You saw straight to the heart of it, through my constant overuse of stomach emotions, and pushed me to make it stronger than ever before. Your comments made me laugh and think, and you have been a joy to work with.

Thank you to my amazing art director, Adela Pons, and to Maria Fazio for designing the cover. Also, thank you, Kris Mukai, for illustrating the cover and bringing my robotics kids to life!

Thank you to the amazing beta readers who read some very early and very rough versions of this story: Darian Bemis, Gabe Moses, Taylor Tracy, Christina Li, Shondra Walker, and Holly Underhill. This story wouldn't have taken shape without your thoughts and feedback.

Huge thank-you to Bethany Mangle, my awesome friend who cheered me on, let me ask her literally a billion publishing questions, and makes the best funny dog-mimicking voice.

Also a big thanks to Rosiee Thor, who I can always count on to talk video games with and who answers my other billion publishing questions.

I have to give a massive shout-out also to my friend Caitlin Colvin, who beta read this story as well as many, many, many of my other stories in the past. Caitlin, you are an amazing friend and writer! Who would have thought that a conversation about dragon books would turn into hanging out at a comic con, and eventually lead us to where we are now? Thank you for all your guidance shaping my story. I can't wait to see what life has in store for your writing too!

To Melissa See, my critique partner and agent sibling. From random calls as we panic about publishing, to bouncing and brainstorming off each other, to making sure I did DJ the justice he deserved in the story, to sending each other random pictures of our pets, our friendship has become something truly great. You are an amazing friend and writer. Love you, Melissa!

Also big thanks to Ashley Jean, who cheered me on through early versions of this story, read it so many times, and all around helped me shape it into something great.

Also for all the chats about Disneyland love and our hopes and dreams for the publishing future.

Thank you to all the other friends who were there for me on this journey: Sara Kapadia for the talk of writing and dogs. Cara Liebowitz for the help with my questions and great *Among Us* distractions. Val, James Z., Spencer, Morgan, Brian, Lyndsay, James C., and all the board game crew. Sierra, Robert, Amanda, and all the friends who encouraged me with my early writing.

To Andrew Joseph White, a huge thank-you. For chats about books and neurodivergence and all the important things. For the art you drew of our characters, at which point I *knew* we had to be friends, and for cheering on Evelyn.

Thank you to my colleague Scott Weiler for helping me ensure I got the technical details right. Also to Pratik Khatri for reading it through and giving me your thoughts. A huge thank-you as well to the Space Exploration Educator Crew. There are too many of you to name, but seeing you in February is the highlight of my year. Without the Crew I might never have fallen so in love with robotics and engineering.

A shout-out too to the Ahwatukee Writers group, which I met every Wednesday and who helped me really pick apart and improve my writing, chapter by chapter. To Victoria, Ed, Andy, and Robert, thank you all for the feedback you gave during those sessions.

Speaking of critique groups, also thank you to my old Friday critique group! Neil, Caitlin, Alexander, and Zach, you are all amazing writers who gave such great feedback.

Big thanks to Mom and Dad, who supported me, drove me to many bookstore visits, and always encouraged my love of reading and storytelling. Also thanks to my brother, Kevin. I don't know if you remember the days when we used to write stories in notebooks and tell each other about them, but those are some of my earliest and fondest memories of writing.

Thank you to Grandpa and Grandma, who always had room for me to come visit. Whether hanging out in Grandpa's woodworking shop or hearing stories from Grandma, where you are is always home. Same with Ohma, whose kindness and warmth inspired me greatly when writing Allie's oma. Christmas Eve spent visiting you is the best time of every year.

And thank you to my husband, Mike. You've been there for me through so much, and you are always cheering me on and pushing me to keep going. I would not be an author right now if it wasn't for your unceasing support. You are amazing, funny, and perfect. I love you so much. Also, I find it hilarious when you sing to the dogs and birds, even if I pretend to be annoyed because I'm trying to focus on writing! You are my world.

To all the authors of LGBTQ+ books that came before me: I never dreamed that someday I'd get to write the LGBTQ+ rep I so longed for, but your books made that possible. You kicked down doors long before I came on the scene and paved a path for my own story to exist.

And to all the authors writing authentic autism rep, thank you. Your books helped me find a sense of self-acceptance that I once could barely imagine. I'm grateful for characters like Vivy Cohen and Tally Olivia Adams, like

Denise and Nova. These characters showed me I wasn't alone in the world, and I am so thankful to their authors for bringing them to life. You showed me I can be proud of who I am and gave me the courage to write my own autistic characters too.

To my robotics teams, past and present: This book is a love letter to the determination and hard work you show every year, to the way you strive to solve problems and keep going even when things get tough. Teaching you robotics is always a blast.

To Mrs. Wiedeman, the teacher who first showed me I could dream of being a writer. I don't remember much about my fourth-grade year, but I do remember your endless encouragement and support. When I was about to move on to middle school a few years later, you encouraged me to enter a young writer's contest, and that little gesture got me thinking for the first time that I really could be an author one day.

To Dale Shewalter, the teacher who taught me to dream big and never give up on writing. He was the best fifth- and sixth-grade teacher a girl could have, and he taught me to love learning, exploring, and hiking. He founded the Arizona Trail and had so many amazing stories to tell. Mr. Shewalter passed away in 2010, and I will always regret that I never went back and told him how much his teaching meant to me before that. He was a wonderful teacher, a wonderful human, and an example many people still look up to every day. Rest in peace, Mr. Shewalter.

And lastly, to you, the reader: Thank you for giving my book a chance and joining my robotics kids on their journey. I am so happy to share this story with you.

ABOUT THE AUTHOR

Michelle Mohrweis is a middle school robotics and engineering teacher in Arizona. They live with their husband, two dogs, two parakeets, and one very grumpy parrot. When not writing, they can be found chasing their dogs around the house with remote control robots and launching paper rockets down the middle of their street.

Visit them on the web at *MichelleMohrweis.com* and follow them on Twitter @Mohrweis_Writes.